Evyn would dutifully take the pen and copy till the tablet was covered with small letters. Often Lewys would shake his head and say, "Do this over." With a knife heated over a candle, he'd smooth the wax surface, erasing all of Evyn's scrawled letters, and Evyn would begin the task of recopying. When the trees on the hillside turned red and gold, Evyn began to put the letters together. Working with Lewys, he copied strings of words onto the wax tablet. Each time he completed a line, Evyn slid it to Lewys's side of the table. Lewys might look up from his own work and either nod approvingly or shake his head over some line that remained illegible.

Over the course of weeks, Evyn slowly realized that the curves, lines, and dots had begun to lose their mystery. There is *the*, Evyn thought, glancing over a sheet of parchment. There are the words *In this year*...

Finally, when the trees waved their bare arms and a thin frost covered the meadows, Evyn saw something that seemed miraculous to him. There, in the open book before him, lay the words *In this year (1053) Earl Godwin passed away; he was taken ill while he was staying with the King at Winchester.* Evyn touched the parchment gently with his fingertips. *I know this*, he thought, realizing that he had mastered a precious, almost magical skill. *I know this. Earl Godwin was Harold's father. I can read.*

ALSO AVAILABLE IN LAUREL-LEAF BOOKS:

JOHNNY TREMAIN, *Esther Forbes*
THE SLAVE DANCER, *Paula Fox*
THE WITCH OF BLACKBIRD POND, *Elizabeth George Speare*
ISLAND OF THE BLUE DOLPHINS, *Scott O'Dell*
ZIA, *Scott O'Dell*
THE BLACK PEARL, *Scott O'Dell*
BOTH SIDES OF TIME, *Caroline B. Cooney*
OUT OF TIME, *Caroline B. Cooney*
NIGHTJOHN, *Gary Paulsen*
THE CROSSING, *Gary Paulsen*

THE KING'S SHADOW

Elizabeth Alder

Published by
Bantam Doubleday Dell Books for Young Readers
a division of
Bantam Doubleday Dell Publishing Group, Inc.
1540 Broadway
New York, New York 10036

Grateful acknowledgment is made to Anne Serraillier for permission to excerpt from *Beowulf the Warrior* by Ian Serraillier, published in 1954 by Oxford University Press, and to Everyman's Library, David Campbell Publishers Ltd. for permission to excerpt from *The Anglo-Saxon Chronicle*, translated and edited by G. N. Garmonsway, published in 1953 by Everyman's Library. Excerpts from *The Song of Roland* are taken from the translation by Isabel Butler, published in 1904 by Houghton Mifflin Company.

ISBN: 0-440-22011-4

RL: 6.0

Reprinted by arrangement with Farrar Straus Giroux

Printed in the United States of America

August 1997

10 9 8 7 6 5 4 3 2

OPM

For Francis

AUTHOR'S NOTE

More than a thousand years ago, when most of Europe remained in the Dark Ages, the monks of England began the task of recording their country's history. Each monastery kept its own Chronicle of Events. Later, many of these individual chronicles were gathered together. Although it is actually several different documents, this collection is called *The Anglo-Saxon Chronicle.*

Because of the monks' hard work, we know today what happened during that time in English history. The Battle of Hastings in 1066 was an important turning point, since it marked the end of the Anglo-Saxon period and the beginning of Norman times.

In *The King's Shadow,* I have tried to remain as close as possible to historical fact. However, history is an art, not a science, and when historians differed about specific events I sometimes chose the interpretation best suited to the story. For example, it is recorded that in the year 1064 Harold Godwinson spent several weeks in Normandy at the court of Duke William. Some historians say he sailed there deliberately on a diplomatic mission, while others claim he was surprised by a storm at sea and shipwrecked on the hostile Norman coast. The latter interpretation seemed more intriguing to me and made for better storytelling. That he was in Normandy, that he joined Duke William as the Conqueror crushed an insurrection in Brittany, and that he saved a drowning Norman infantryman are all supported by evidence. So, too, with the events of 1066: I have tried to re-create those last days of Anglo-Saxon England as accurately as possible, basing most of my work on the research of F. M. Stenton and Dorothy Whitelock, noted scholars in the field of Anglo-Saxon history. I am grateful to Denis Butler, as well, whose imagination brought this era to life for me. I am indebted to them and many other historians. Their work was invaluable to me. Any errors that remain are purely my own.

I am most indebted to Marianne Slattery and Alison Picard for their generous advice and unflagging encouragement. To Laura Tillotson, a thousand thank-yous are due.

My thanks go also to Esther Buchser of Harford Day School and Fr. Davish of Loyola College for their respective assistance with French and Old English translations.

Although Evyn is not mentioned by name in any of the chronicles, there is every reason to suppose that King Harold would have a squire to serve him, and with the exception of Lewys, Hakon, and Brother Alfred, all the major characters are based on real people whose passion, loyalty, selflessness, greed, mercilessness, and determination changed the fate of a nation.

THE KING'S SHADOW

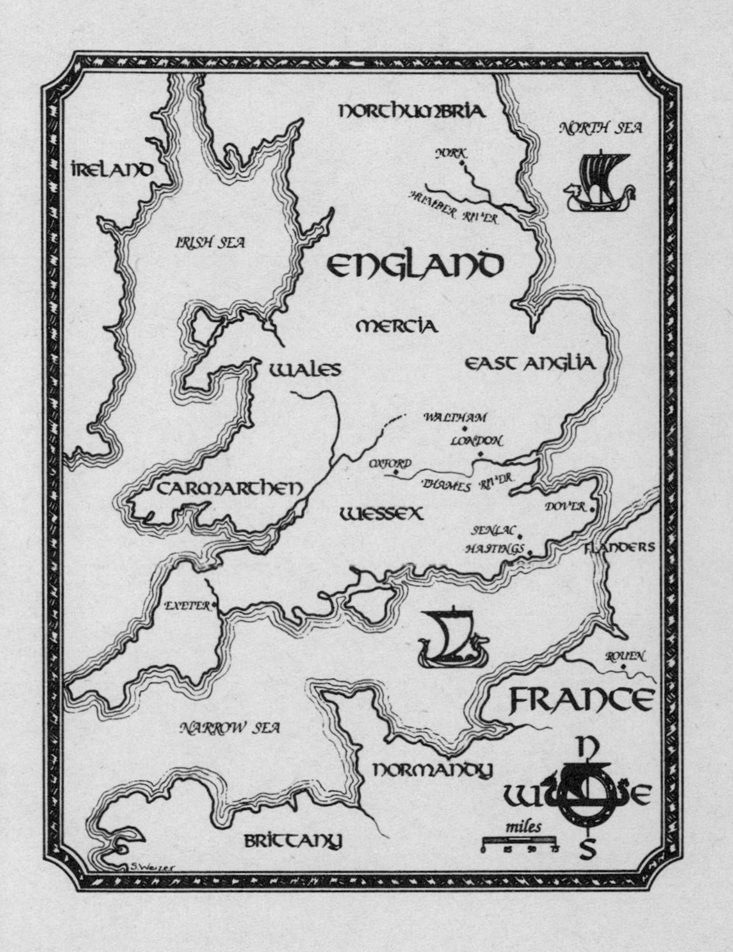
NORTHUMBRIA
NORTH SEA
IRELAND
YORK
HUMBER RIVER
IRISH SEA
ENGLAND
MERCIA
EAST ANGLIA
WALES
WALTHAM
LONDON
OXFORD
THAMES RIVER
CARMARTHEN
WESSEX
DOVER
SENLAC
HASTINGS
FLANDERS
EXETER
ROUEN
FRANCE
NARROW SEA
NORMANDY
N
W
E
S
miles
BRITTANY
S.Weizer

1063

In this year my reckless young uncle returned . . .
bringing Death as his companion.

Thunder rumbled in the distance like the growl of angry wolves.

Evyn scrambled up the rocky hillside. Above him the dark clouds hung low and swollen over the rounded hills of Carmarthen. When he reached the top, he saw that it was already raining on the westernmost ridge of hills. Far below him three hooded shepherds urged their flock back to the stockaded settlement.

If he hurried, he would have time to recite the chant once more before he need get under shelter. He had been so busy with the sheep that he'd not had the chance to practice for nearly a week. Now it was Eostre Sunday already, the day he had been waiting for so long.

Evyn filled his lungs with the cool hill air and began:

"High are the hills and dark the valleys, brown are the rocks and dread the defiles . . . When Roland sees the peers, and Oliver whom he so loved, lying dead, pity takes him and he begins to weep . . . So great is his grief he cannot stand."

The boy's voice, a mellow tenor, flowed like the water of a deep river, but the chant suddenly stopped.

"Glory be!" Evyn swore. "What is the next line?"

He could never remember it. He would make a fool of himself in front of the entire settlement if he forgot tonight. It was not every day that a serf was called upon to recite at his lord's Eostre festival. Evyn had memorized *The Song of Roland* one verse at a time from the wandering *storiawrs*. If he could read, it would be easier. But, of course, Evyn could not read—none but the monks could read—and even if he could, there were no books to be had in sleepy Carmarthen. Beautiful Carmarthen, dull little outpost on the western edge of the kingdom of the Angles and Saxons.

Evyn plucked absentmindedly at the new spring grass as he repeated the verse, hoping to commit the words to memory. How he longed to tell the story of Roland, who, as leader of Charlemagne's rear guard, had chosen to stand and fight and die to protect the King from his enemies.

"High are the hills . . ."

The lad was blessed with a *storiawr*'s voice. He counted himself lucky for that good fortune. Although his voice had changed in the last year, it retained its rich, even ring, and the added depth was like a coating of honey.

"High are the hills and dark the valleys . . ."

His people, the Cymry, whom outsiders called Welsh, or sometimes British, treasured their storytellers. Indeed, *storiawrs* were respected throughout all of the northern lands. Evyn knew his voice might earn him some slim chance of escape from the narrow life of a land-bound serf. By law he was a free man, but in practice he was tied to the land like his father and his father's father before him. But a *storiawr* was able to roam wherever he pleased, for every landowner was obliged to offer hospitality in return for a tale. Tonight was Evyn's chance. If he told the story well, it might change his destiny. He could lift himself and his father up from their cold, spare life.

A damp breeze struck Evyn in the face. As he shook the black hair out of his eyes, he noticed a traveler cresting the hill an arrow's shot away from him. The stranger trudged toward Rhywallon's stockaded *dyn,* built where the slope leveled at Evyn's back. Evyn squinted for a better look: travelers were so rare here.

The stranger was a grown man yet still young. Like Evyn's, his hair shone blue-black and hung long and straight over his neck. He was built neither tall nor broad but wiry, like many of the British hill people. On his back he carried a worn traveling satchel. His gait was steady like that of one who has been on a long journey; but as he spied the walls of Rhywallon's *dyn,* he broke into an easy trot. His movement flushed a raven, black as starless night, from the roadside ditch. The startled scavenger flapped across the man's path, cawing angrily. The man stopped stiff in his tracks. Among the hill people, it was a bad omen to be raven-shadowed.

The messenger of death, Evyn thought, watching the bird disappear into the gray mist.

The traveler seemed distraught for a moment, but then he made the sign of the cross and continued on his way.

Evyn studied the stranger in silence as the man passed unaware along the road below the boy's hilltop ledge. *His face is so familiar:* a spot of color high on each cheek brightening a pale complexion, so like his father and so like Evyn himself. The boy allowed the stranger to pass without calling out. Usually Evyn stopped every traveler to ask about the news he might carry. That was how he had learned a little English from tinkers and merchants, but this was different. He was not eager to befriend a raven-shadowed man.

No doubt he is a wandering tradesman hoping for a bit of work at Rhywallon's bidding, Evyn thought. However, the man left the trail that led toward Rhywallon's Hall. He turned to the hut Evyn shared with his father. When the man ducked inside without the proper courtesy of calling out beforehand, the boy's alarm grew. His father was expecting no one.

Evyn raced down the hill, all thought of *The Song of Roland* gone from his head. As the wind rushed past his face, he felt the first few stray drops of rain. Glancing up, he saw that the distant hills were hidden now by the dark clouds. He scuttled, crablike, down the steepest part of the hill and flew over the ground, hardly aware of his surroundings: the village girls bringing in the sheep and lambs from the common field, his neighbor's flock of geese squawking angrily as he dashed through their midst. He reached his hut and darted inside. How surprised he was to see his father and the stranger locked in a hearty embrace!

"You will stay with us, of course," Evyn's father was saying.

The stranger stared dubiously around the tiny one-room hut. It was barely three strides from wall to wall, the wind whistled through the chinks where the daub had chipped away, and only a few poor tunics hung on pegs by the door.

"Have you room for me?" he asked.

"Too much room," Evyn's father said, the smile melting from his face. "Joan and the little ones all died from a fever that swept through the village last winter."

Evyn glanced at the empty spot where his mother had

slept with his baby sisters, and the old heaviness returned to his heart. The past months had been a sad time.

"Evyn, you are back," his father said, glad to speak of something else. "Come, give a greeting to your Uncle Morgan."

Uncle? Evyn felt the fool, and the color in his cheeks heightened. So the mysterious stranger was blood kin. He should have guessed it—the man was so like his father.

"Uncle, I welcome you."

"I thank you, Nephew." Uncle Morgan sized Evyn up and down like a crafty horse trader. "You stood less than your father's belt the last time I saw you. And now," he said with a grin, "you must have seen thirteen winters, is that not right?"

"Look at you," Evyn's father broke in. "You have changed much as well. You left as a skinny and restless youth—what was it . . . eight, nine years ago? And look at you now, a grown man with arms as muscled as any blacksmith's."

Evyn studied his uncle and was amazed at the similarities between the two men before him. They stood eye to eye for height, neither one too broad or too lean. Each had hair dark as pitch and eyes gray as the sea. Their skin was pale except for the blush high on their cheeks. Each wore dark breeches in the British style with brown tunics belted at the waist. So alike on the outside, yet, if the tales were true, so different in their hearts. For Evyn's father was a calm and patient man, slow to anger, and steady as the hills, while Evyn could see that his uncle was all fluid movement and excitement. The stories Father had told of his wild and dangerous younger brother had been of a reckless youth and finally of a desperate parting.

The two men embraced again. If there had been anger in

the past, it was gone now. "I am in need of a place, Brother," Uncle Morgan said apologetically. "I would earn my bread . . . I am a good man with horses."

Evyn's father laughed. "More likely you will work like a horse. Things haven't changed much here in Carmarthen since you left. The earth grows stones and the rain falls in buckets. Though there is one more mouth to feed, two extra hands will be most welcome."

"You have come in time for the Eostre festival," Evyn added. "There is to be music and song tonight in the lord's Hall."

"Evyn is too modest," his father said. "He leaves out the best part. Lord Rhywallon has requested that Evyn recite. He says Evyn has a voice to match those of the best *storiawrs.*"

Uncle Morgan's dark eyebrows shot up in admiration and pride. "He honors our family, eh . . . this young storyteller. What will Evyn Golden-Tongue recite? A French romance or a tale from King Arthur's days, perhaps?"

"Here less than an hour and jesting already," Father chided.

"No, no," Uncle Morgan protested. "I do not jest. Evyn, take me to your festival. It is good to rejoice with Christ at Eostre time." Then he added, "I am obliged to see Rhywallon and beg his leave to work his land once again. It would be wise to ask him after he's had some ale to warm his heart. And, if the truth be out," he said with a sigh, "I am longing for a celebration myself."

Evyn looked to his father.

"Go along, Evyn," his father said. "I want to finish working this bridle; I will join you later this evening." He ruffled Evyn's hair affectionately. "I will not be long, for I, too, wish to hear you tell the story," he said with pride.

Morgan clapped his arm around Evyn's shoulder as they left the little hut and strode up the slope to the Hall. Father stood in the open door. "See that he stays far from trouble, Evyn," he shouted after them, and then he laughed. Evyn smiled and waved a last time before he turned.

He and his uncle followed the lane to Rhywallon's *dyn*. A stockade wall of logs with shaved tops enclosed the settlement. Inside stood a large steep-roofed barn, workshops for the blacksmith and carpenter, the slaves' hut and several smaller huts, all of wattle-and-daub with thatched roofs, and finally Rhywallon's great wooden two-story Hall with its spacious upper loft for the women. Evyn's lord was a landowner of some means. Though not as powerful or wealthy as his ill-tempered neighbor Gryffin, Rhywallon was still well off, with hundreds of sheep and scores of cattle. He owned more than thirty Irish-born slaves, and nearly that many serfs were under oath to work his land and shops.

Although it was twilight, the gate remained open. A freckled slave boy stood watch while the music of a harp drifted through the yard. "I wonder what joy the evening holds for us," Uncle Morgan said as they stepped through the wide doors of Rhywallon's Hall. It was as though they had crossed the threshold into a magical land of surpassing beauty and enchantment, leaving behind the sweat and hunger and backbreaking toil of everyday life. Smoke from the fire pit in the center of the Hall drifted through the cavernous room in a warm, dreamy haze. The oil lamps, hung high on their posts, cast soft, wavering shadows. Banners of crimson, azure, and gold woven with fantastic dragons and hawks hung from the roof beams.

Evyn greeted the people around him. Everyone in the settlement had looked forward to this gathering for many months. It was an occasion of great joy, and Evyn found himself surrounded by smiling faces, friendly chatter, and silvery laughter. The harper, a blind man, sat in a place of honor at Rhywallon's side at the High Table, holding the instrument in his lap and plucking a melody.

The aroma of boiled venison mingled with that of warm, freshly baked bread. Platters of cheese and last year's apples adorned the tables. Slaves bustled around Evyn bearing pitchers of honey-flavored mead.

"Ah!" Uncle Morgan said, choosing a little honey cake from the nearest table, "Rhywallon always knew how to celebrate the high feasts."

Eostre, the spring festival named after the Saxon goddess of the dawn and of fertility, was from the old pagan days. It was a sign that the hunger of the long winter months was drawing to an end. Since the Christian monks had come, it was regarded as the celebration of Christ's resurrection from the dead. Sometimes the ancient customs and names refused to fade away. Rather than begin feuds, the Christian priests felt it wise to join the old with the new. So Eostre it had remained. But not everyone was Christian; even now there were tribesmen farther up in the hills who clung to the ancient ways of the Druids, and down in the seaports lived many with Viking blood who still swore by Thor. But Rhywallon was a Christian and had seen to it that all his serfs and slaves were likewise baptized. Here, in Rhywallon's *dyn*, they honored only Christ.

So after planting himself comfortably on a bench at one of the long trestle tables, Uncle Morgan raised the mead-filled drinking bowl set before him and made his first toast to "our Risen Lord."

A jubilant shout of agreement rose to the rafters. Drinking horns were thrust out to be refilled, and soon the talk throughout the Hall returned to a noisy murmur like the buzzing of a beehive.

Evyn found a few of the other boys and talked of the spring planting, guessing when Rhywallon would call for the sowing to begin, and who had the best hopes for the fattest pigs by summer's end. Some suggested getting up a game of sticks and balls tomorrow, after the day's work had been done.

As a red-haired slave girl made her rounds with a heavy pitcher, Evyn saw that Uncle Morgan often hailed her to refill his drinking bowl. Before long his face grew flushed, his speech slurred, and he laughed louder and more readily than the others.

The chatter stopped suddenly, and an awkward quiet filled the Hall. One after another, in the way that news spreads silently through a crowd, heads turned to the open doors of the Great Hall.

There stood three newly arrived guests, the sons of Gryffin. They were well known to all as arrogant scoundrels, protected from the law by their powerful father. They were as dangerous and unpredictable as the wild boar they wore as their family crest. Several of Rhywallon's men had good reason to remember them as the ones who gave out broken noses or teeth or slashed forearms. Though they were feared and hated throughout the valley, no lord dared refuse them hospitality, for that would be an insult to their mighty family; and Gryffin's gold was sufficient for him to keep his own permanent garrison of men-at-arms.

"Drink up, friends," one brother said, grabbing the pitcher of mead from the passing slave girl. When the villagers stared at him suspiciously, he repeated, "Drink up. We merely come to share our Eostre joy with you." He laughed and staggered to a bench. Evyn could see that this was not the first drinking party he had attended this day.

When his uncle lurched forward with an angry look, Evyn rushed to him. Taking his arm, he said, "Uncle, sit here by the High Table." Evyn knew something had to be done to distract his uncle and avoid trouble. Though his father still had not come, he would have to begin reciting.

Uncle Morgan sat back down on the bench and leaned against a heavy post, while Evyn spoke in the harper's ear.

The meter of the melody changed to a rhythmic strumming as Evyn stood by the harper's side, his hair shining in the firelight. Anxiety played on his nerves; it was always difficult to begin. But after he uttered the first lines, the pounding in his chest slowed, and the words, which at first were rushed and spoken too high, took their natural pace and tone as he eased into his tale.

Evyn told the sad story of Roland, the beloved nephew of Charlemagne. This was a story of courage and honor and death, worth telling well.

"Charles the King, our great Emperor, has been for seven long years in Spain; he has conquered all the high land down to the sea; not a castle holds out against him, not a wall or city is left unshattered, save Saragossa, which stands high on a mountain. King Marsila holds it, who loves not God . . ."

Evyn scanned the Hall. There was a different kind of hush now; fear of Gryffin's sons receded and pleasure slowly returned. The old men sat along the tables, their chins cupped in their palms, listening to each word, even though they'd heard the story many times. The women, gathered in clusters, all turned to the High Table where Evyn stood. In one corner the boys ceased their noisy game of bones. The harper, his eyes dark, sat by Evyn's side, wreathed in the glow of the firelight.

"High are the hills and dark the valleys, brown are the rocks and dread the defiles. That same day the main host of the Franks pass with toil and travail, and fifteen leagues away men might hear the noise of their march. But when they draw near to Gascony, their lord's domain, they call to mind their own fiefs, their young maidens and gentle wives, till there is not one that does not weep for pity. More than all the rest is Charles heavy of heart, in that he has left his nephew in the passes of Spain; pity takes him, and he cannot help but weep."

Evyn closed his eyes for a moment as he spoke, and the scene of that sad, far-off day came to him clearly. He paused. The crackling of the fire sounded before him. At the other end of the Hall, across the fire, it seemed to Evyn that his listeners wavered ghostlike in the heated light. He took a deep breath and continued:

"Then Oliver goes up into a high mountain and sees the host of the heathen . . . And he called to Roland, his comrade, saying: 'From the side of Spain I see a great light coming, thousands of white hauberks and thousands of gleaming helms. They will fall upon our Franks with great wrath.' Wondrous is the shine of helmets studded with gold, of shields and broidered hauberks, of lances and gonfanons . . . and no man may give count thereof, so great is the multitude.

" 'I have seen the paynims,' said Oliver; 'never was so great a multitude seen of living men. Those of the vanguard are upon a hundred thousand, all armed with shields and helmets, and clad in white hauberks; right straight are the shafts of their lances, and bright the points . . .

" 'Great is the host of the heathen,' saith Oliver, 'and few is our fellowship. Roland, fair comrade, I pray thee sound thy horn of ivory that Charles may hear it and return again with all his host.'

" 'That were but folly,' quoth Roland. 'Now God forfend that through me my kinsman be brought to shame. First I will lay on with Durendal, the good sword that is girded here at my side, and thou shalt see the blade all reddened.'

"Roland is brave, and Oliver is wise, and both are good men . . . once armed and a-horseback, rather would they die than flee the battle.

"High are the hills and dark the valleys . . ."

While Rhywallon's people listened, captivated by Evyn's warm voice, the sons of Gryffin sat gloomily at a table whispering among themselves. The youngest suddenly rose on unsteady feet. He held his drinking horn high, interrupting Evyn with a taunt to the whole village.

"A toast to Eostre, the goddess of fertility."

Evyn halted. The harper paused, his fingers motionless over the trembling strings. The villagers turned, shock upon their faces.

This was a deliberate insult to Rhywallon's house. Rhywallon was a Christian and Gryffin's sons knew it. Honor called for revenge, but wisdom called for silence in the name of Christian peace. Perhaps the man was drunk and did not know what he was saying. It would be best to keep quiet.

But Evyn's uncle, who thought with his proud heart and not with his head, and who had foolishly drunk too much, staggered to his feet.

"In this household we salute only the Christ," he said.

Evyn felt the blood pounding in his throat. Sweat broke out on the back of his neck.

Gryffin's youngest son spat in the rushes spread on the floor. "You Christians will be the end of us Britons. We were once brave men in Carmarthen, but these monks are turning us into frightened rabbits."

"What have the old gods done for you?" Uncle Morgan sneered. "You are proud to display every vice."

Darting forward, the youngest son pulled his dagger from its sheath. "I will teach you!" he cried.

"Uncle, save yourself!" Evyn shouted.

Uncle Morgan turned to Evyn with a jerk, the drunken look in his eyes clearing, and then, suddenly, he dashed from the Hall.

All three of Gryffin's sons followed a shadow's length behind him, shouting angrily.

Then came a rush of events so lightning-quick that afterward Evyn could hardly recall what had happened. He raced to the door of the Great Hall, his feet barely touching the rushes. It had grown dark outside now, and the rain fell steadily. Uncle Morgan, cornered by the three men between the blacksmith's stall and the slave hut, turned desperately. Gryffin's sons advanced on him, daggers drawn. Uncle Morgan grabbed the only weapon within reach, one of the blacksmith's irons left to cool in the water trough. He gripped it with both hands as though it were a battle-ax and swung at the brother closest to him. It was the youngest, he who had hurled the insult. The blow landed on the side of his head, and he crumpled to the ground noiselessly, his blue cloak covering his face and shoulders.

It all happened so quickly, just a shadowy blow and a muffled thud in the darkness. As the other two men knelt by their brother, Uncle Morgan dropped the iron and ran through the open gate.

"He's dead," the fair-haired brother said, staring angrily.

Then without another word both men sped through the gate in pursuit.

Evyn followed quickly, fearing for his uncle.

The sons of Gryffin had seen a man of average height, neither too tall nor too broad, with shiny black hair. He'd worn a dark tunic and breeches. So when they came upon that same man outside a hut, they rushed upon him with upraised daggers and stabbed him without warning.

Evyn saw everything from the deserted lane. The chase had been in silence, the daggers had been drawn in silence, and the murder had been committed in silence. Evyn's scream as his father fell dead broke that eerie stillness.

"*No!*"

His scream echoed back and forth between the hills. When it died away, there was only the cold patter of rain filling puddles along the path.

The murderers wheeled around at the noise.

"He was with him! He called him 'Uncle,' " the brother with the fair hair cried, pointing to Evyn. "We'll fix this little rabbit, too."

He plunged ahead of his brother, and before Evyn realized what was happening, the man with the fair hair toppled him to the ground and knelt on his chest. Evyn felt the air whoosh out of his lungs. He struggled to free himself, but his arms were pinned to his sides.

The steady drizzle grew to a downpour, and the rain splashed on Evyn's face like icy needles. While the first brother laughed cruelly, his greasy hair falling over his face, the other took his dagger and came forward, pulling Evyn's chin down. He sliced quickly, and Evyn felt something terribly hot in his mouth. Then it was gone, and his throat filled with choking blood.

The brothers stood back, looking down at him. "No more old stories from this little one."

Their laughter deafened Evyn. It seemed to fill the whole valley. Then he knew what had happened. They had cut out his tongue. He had been punished for being kin to the man who killed their kin. Out of spite, they had maimed him in a manner suitable only for slaves.

In his pain, Evyn felt a beating on the ground—hoof-beats. A horseman galloped toward them, a man of average size, neither too broad nor too lean, dressed in a dark tunic, with shiny black hair and a spot of color high on each cheek.

"You murdered the wrong man," the horseman shouted angrily, reining in Rhywallon's strongest bay stallion. "You have murdered my innocent brother."

Gryffin's sons looked at each other, dumbfounded.

"I killed your brother in self-defense after he provoked a fight," Uncle Morgan said. "But you have murdered my brother for no just cause. I am a free man, and I will take you before the shire reeve to seek justice."

But the yellow-haired brother sneered. He spoke loudly so that all the terrified villagers who had gathered by the gate could hear. "It is a pity that we killed the wrong man. But under the law you owe us the man-price for the loss of our brother, who was of noble blood, and who was therefore worth more than your kin, who was nothing but a serf."

His dark-haired brother, unsure at first, now grinned. "Yes, and do not tell us about the shire reeve. He is beholden to our father for half his land. Do you think he will pass judgment against us?"

"*You owe us!*" the fair-haired brother roared, his lips curling around each word. "The man-price due us for the death of our brother is one pound of silver pennies. We will return tomorrow, with our men, to collect it."

Lightning flashed over the hills as Evyn struggled to his feet. The warm, sticky taste still filled his mouth, and he spat blood on the ground. Thunder followed upon the lightning and Uncle Morgan's horse reared nervously at the crack.

"We will take the lad as hostage for your surety," the fair-haired man yelled, reaching for Evyn.

Uncle Morgan kicked the bay toward them. "No, the lad is the last of my kin," he said in a hard-edged voice. "You shall not have him." He grabbed Evyn by the arm, pulled him up behind him, and kicked the great horse forward.

1063

In this year the Lady Ealdgyth Swan Neck visited her Exeter estate.

A hand grasped Evyn's ankle like an iron claw, jerking him backward, nearly off the bay's haunches. The horse stumbled in the slippery grass and whinnied in fright. Uncle Morgan twisted in the saddle and, with a blow to the pursuer's head, freed Evyn. The bay sprang forward, and the sound of cursing grew faint in the darkness behind them.

"By God's Bread! I swear we'll find you. We'll track you down!"

"We'll have revenge!"

Lightning etched the western sky again, followed quickly by a deafening thunderclap. With his one brief glimpse of the hills, Uncle Morgan jerked the horse's head and spurred him toward the woods of northern Carmarthen.

Evyn drifted in and out of the wakeful world, dazed and unaware. His mouth stung, and blood flowed hot and thick from the raw wound. It choked him as it filled his throat and spilled over his lips. Where were they going? Dizziness engulfed him. It took all his strength to keep his hands locked about his uncle's waist.

His uncle kept the bay at a gallop for nearly a league, then doubled back on his tracks. They rode through a stream for another half league, then up the opposite bank as Uncle Morgan frantically used every trick he knew to throw off the trackers who would surely follow at daybreak. Back into the stream they rode. Cold dark water, up to the horse's belly, swirled around their knees. Later, they rode northeast toward the wild hills. Evyn rested his head on his uncle's back, the rain roaring in his ears like a rushing waterfall.

They followed a dark, overgrown trail. Thickets brushed against them, and soon Evyn's drenched tunic clung to his ribs. Uncle Morgan slowed the horse to a walk, stopping now and then to peer into the darkness ahead. Once he made the horse turn back and retrace his steps till they regained the northeastern trail.

Thus they rode long into the night, or so it seemed to Evyn, who had lost all sense of time. Cautiously riding forward under the moonless sky, they sometimes doubled back, then rode forward again, often losing the trail, then finding it. Once it seemed to Evyn that they rode along a narrow track, no wider than a deer path, hugging the edge of a deep ravine. Evyn closed his eyes, for the sight made his head reel. Finally, when his arms ached so much that he felt sure he could no longer hold on, Uncle Morgan pulled the reins tight. "Whooa."

The hoofbeats, squishing in the wet earth, again slowed from a trot to a walk. The horse halted, and then there was only the sound of rain dripping off the branches overhead.

"Take heart, Evyn," his uncle said. "We are safe for the night."

But as Evyn slipped to the ground his knees buckled, and he fell heavily. The blackness of the forest became the blackness of a dreamless sleep.

When Evyn woke, it seemed much later, perhaps the hour before daybreak. He was not sure. His head pounded, and he felt that he had the devil sickness in his stomach. He shivered, and his teeth chattered beyond his control. He opened his eyes and saw Uncle Morgan on one knee beside him, the damp walls of a cave glistening at his back.

" 'Tis a hard task starting a fire with wet kindling," his uncle said apologetically, nodding toward a small pile of twigs and branches flickering weakly before them. "I knew of this cave when I was a boy," Uncle Morgan explained. "It made a safe haven for me when I wanted to shirk my chores for a day or two. I did not think I would be able to find it again. It opens into a much larger cavern deep within the hill. I'll show you later."

Evyn struggled to keep his eyes open. The pounding in his head grew louder and louder. He grimaced with the pain in his mouth and put his hands over his face. Then he slipped back into the black sleep.

When he woke again, it was to the cool touch of his uncle's hand upon his brow. "You have a fever, lad," Uncle Morgan said, a line of worry creasing his forehead.

A thin shaft of sunlight pierced the cave from its entrance. Was it midmorning? Uncle Morgan had managed to build a small fire. But the warmth, which Evyn would have welcomed a few hours earlier, now seemed oppressive. He wanted to inch away from it but found that his muscles would not obey.

Uncle Morgan wet his hands on the damp wall and gently patted Evyn's face. "Your skin is on fire," he said. "Rest now, if you can."

Evyn stared at his uncle's face. The handsome details of the clever gray eyes and the smiling lips blurred, and he could only make out the pale skin framed by black hair. A searing pain filled Evyn's mouth. He closed his eyes, and within moments a dizzy sleep overtook him again. He felt lost, tumbling in the blackness for a long while. This time he dreamed of rain hitting his face like icy needles and something burning in his mouth.

Much later, Evyn dimly heard a voice. "Nephew, I was fearful over you. It was in my mind that you might die before the sun set again. You have spent a long day and night and then again much of this day in a burning fever. But now your brow has cooled, and your breath comes easily."

Evyn turned his head and focused his eyes with difficulty.

"Nephew, how do you fare?" Uncle Morgan asked in a low voice.

Evyn stirred a bit, too weak still to turn over on his side. He opened his mouth to speak. He wanted to say that he felt a little better, but the noise that came from his throat was garbled. His mouth felt so odd, as if his tongue had become a piece of wood. He was confused and tried speaking once more, but he stopped abruptly as he saw Uncle Morgan's face contort in disgust. Then suddenly Evyn remembered. They had cut out his tongue: he could speak no more. The sons of Gryffin had no right to do this to him. THEY HAD NO RIGHT! The words screamed in Evyn's brain and remained there, chained within the walls of his skull. To be maimed like a slave was a humiliation too great to bear. It was true that his father had not been wealthy or of high rank. But he had been free, protected by the laws which served all free men. His father . . . His father lay dead and unburied, his uncle branded an outlaw, no doubt, and he, Evyn, had been shamefully mutilated. To speak no more. It was beyond his understanding. Oh, why hadn't they killed him, too, as they had killed his father?

Uncle Morgan jumped to his feet and left the cave without looking back. Evyn saw his hair shine in the sunlight briefly, before he disappeared. As he heard the clop-clop of the horse making his way down the trail, Evyn closed his eyes in despair. His uncle was ashamed of him. He was deserting him. He would leave him here to die all alone. Evyn felt empty and exhausted. Then once again he fell into a deep sleep, but this time it was of one who has no reason to wake.

But he did wake several hours later, and Uncle Morgan was there again, squatting by Evyn's side and eating a bit of coarse bread. He faced a newly built fire but turned as Evyn shifted his weight. Taking a small loaf of bread from a pouch at his side, he moistened it with some water.

"Chew this slowly," he said, handing it to Evyn. "It will make you feel better."

Evyn saw his uncle's kindness, but he felt a coolness in his manner. He sat far away from Evyn and avoided his glance. When he spoke he stared into the fire. When he handed him the bread he was careful that Evyn's fingers should not touch his. But his words were warm and sweet, and he talked long into the night. Now and then he would forget and ask Evyn a question. Then there would follow an embarrassed silence till Uncle Morgan covered his mistake with foolish talk.

"I have a friend, Evyn, who lives in the village on the east edge of these woods. He's agreed to go to Rhywallon's *dyn* and see that your father is buried with the rest of the family." Uncle Morgan snapped a twig and fed it to the fire. "As for us, Nephew, perhaps we can turn our misery into something better. Perhaps you knew that I had run away to live with the Saxon English. I worked on a large estate as a stable hand. We will go there to find work. Gryffin's sons will think that we vanished into the hills. We'll be safe there, and we'll be free."

Evyn watched Uncle Morgan as he spoke. He had the charmer's way about him, his eyes sparkling with hope, his voice light with excitement. But Evyn also noticed that when Uncle Morgan uttered the word *free* he seemed uneasy.

After a short silence, Uncle Morgan added, "Perhaps you can work as a stableboy. In your spare time you can master the weapon skills with the boys who are training to be housecarls. A good fighting man can always earn his bread."

Evyn smiled, picturing himself as a housecarl. He had seen a battle-ax only once in his life and had barely been able to lift it with both hands. He held his arm up for Uncle Morgan to see, placing his fingers around his biceps. Uncle Morgan laughed. "No, perhaps not a housecarl. But surely you will find your place somewhere."

Evyn took a bite of the bread, chewing it slowly. It had little taste, as if the cook had had no salt to add. Then he realized that his wound would make eating a joyless chore. Chewing was so clumsy, and Evyn felt painfully aware of how foolish he now appeared. When he swallowed, it was like a rock scraping his throat. But his stomach, empty for so long, was grateful, and he slowly took another bite and then another until the bread was gone.

That night Evyn dreamed of Gryffin's sons. They had returned to kill him. One knelt on his chest as the other raised his dagger. Evyn flailed helplessly under the weight while villagers gathered around him. He screamed for help, but there was no sound, and no one came to his aid. As the knife swung down, Evyn woke suddenly, gasping for breath. The blackness of the cave surrounded him. His chest heaved as though he'd run a long way. The fire had burned down to embers, and he shivered in the night air. Gazing at the mouth of the cave, he searched for movement. Were they out there? He strained his ears to catch the sound of footsteps outside, but heard only his uncle's gentle snore. He stared at Morgan, his brain slowly clearing to wakefulness. He checked the mouth of the cave once more; it was empty. There was no one there . . . now. But Evyn feared they would come. They would kill him. He lay awake the rest of the night, watching and listening, his heart pounding against his ribs. Finally, when dawn broke, he slept.

Three days later he was strong enough to travel. During the afternoon he and Uncle Morgan washed in a clear pool deep in the cave. It was as Morgan had described it. The light of their torch illuminated the large second room of the cavern, showing it to be nearly the size of a barn. Uncle Morgan said, "This evening at sundown we leave for Exeter."

Evyn glanced at his uncle anxiously. No one traveled at night. The forest swarmed with evil spirits eager to enter the souls of those who recklessly ventured abroad after dark. It was said that owls clawed out the eyes of those who saw their nocturnal flights through the forest. Only outlaws and witches crept about by night. His face betrayed his fear.

"Evyn, it is not my choice!" his uncle shouted. "For us it is far more dangerous to be seen in daylight. We must take our chances in the dark."

That evening Uncle Morgan freed Rhywallon's bay. With a hard slap on the charger's flanks, he sent the animal cantering down the trail. "There," he said, "with some luck he will find his way back to Rhywallon's stable. Though some would surely call me a knave, I am no horse thief."

They walked east for five nights, always keeping to the hills and woods. Although Uncle Morgan's friend had given them some bread, they were often hungry, and Evyn longed to stop at one of the *dyns* they passed nestled in the Welsh valleys. By the fifth night, the hills became less steep as they entered the land of the English. Here Uncle Morgan turned southwest. "We will go to Exeter," he said. Evyn had heard of Exeter. It was one of the great cities of Wessex, built on the river Exe not far from where it flowed into the Narrow Sea.

As the sun rose on the morning of their eighth day of travel, Uncle Morgan shook Evyn from a light sleep. "Today we walk in sunlight."

Soon they reached a crossroads. They left the beaten trail they had followed and took a wide, well-traveled road the Romans had laid out centuries before. Days later, as they crested one last hill, the great towers of Exeter rose far in the distance, still a half day's walk away. For the first time since Rhywallon's Eostre festival, Evyn's dark mood lifted. The bright color returned to his pale cheeks. He clapped his uncle playfully on the back and pointed with admiration at the distant city.

Uncle Morgan returned a stiff-lipped smile and walked on. "I reckon it is best to get on with it," he said over his shoulder. Evyn trotted after him.

They kept to the old Roman road leading south toward the city. Long before they drew near Exeter, they reached a sprawling estate. As they walked, Uncle Morgan talked constantly, as though his nerves allowed him no peace. "This land is held by the Lady Ealdgyth. This is where I worked," Uncle Morgan said with a nod to the vast fields under cultivation. "It was given to her by Harold, the Earl of Wessex. Wait till you see her," he said, turning around to look at Evyn. "Though she is no longer young, she is still quite a beauty. The Lady will let us stay here and work. An estate this size is always in need of more hands. It will be a good life," Uncle Morgan said quietly, almost to himself. "It will be a good life for us," he repeated, his voice quavering a little.

They passed the first of the Lady's cultivated fields, where a crew of sowers scattered barley seed. In the next field, bounded by a hedgerow, a plowman, ankle-deep in the soft dirt, guided a pair of yoked oxen. The land to the east of the road had been left wooded, and there beekeepers checked a stand of hives along the treeline. Farther on, a large pond reflected the pink light of morning. Ring-necked geese, protecting their new goslings, hissed and spit from the reed-covered shoreline. On the road before them, shepherds led a huge flock of bleating sheep out to pasture.

Evyn was amazed. He touched his uncle's arm to get his attention and made a circle in the air with his hands, a question in his eyes. "How big is this holding?" his uncle guessed. Evyn nodded. "We have been walking through her land since yesterday."

Impressed, Evyn drew a large circle in the air, extending his arms full length.

"Yes, Evyn, you are right. Her holdings are large indeed, and this is only one of her estates."

Evyn shook his head in wonder. Rhywallon had been counted a wealthy man, but his *dyn* was nothing compared to this. These fields and ponds would feed hundreds, perhaps thousands. The flock of sheep that crowded about them on every side was beyond counting. This was an estate worthy of the consort of England's mightiest earl.

Soon they reached the village walls. The gatekeeper, perched high up on the catwalk, recognized Morgan and shouted to him.

"So, you are back, you scoundrel," he said with a laugh.

Morgan threw back his head and asked the gatekeeper, "Is the Lady here?"

"Yes, she is making the rounds now." He called down to his men, "Let them pass."

Although each estate had its own steward, when the Lady was there she handled much of the business herself. This meant that she, with her steward's advice, planned the sowing, the shearing, the hunting. She set limits on the amount of trees to be felled in her woods. It was the Lady who estimated the amount of wool needed for the coming year, and then instructed her shepherds and weaving women accordingly. She set aside the goods to be used toward the King's yearly tax each autumn and calculated how much could be traded for other goods.

Uncle Morgan led the way through the spacious yard with Evyn a step behind him. The day's work had begun, and few took notice of them. This was not like Rhywallon's *dyn*, where every stranger was a welcome source of news. The blacksmith's boy blew on his master's fire pit to light the fire. The embers glowed red with each puff as he bent low over his task. A cluster of girls set up their looms to begin weaving, glad to work in the sunshine after the long, dark winter months spent behind walls. The stableboys called to one another as they led the heavy-footed horses out to pasture.

The door of the carpenter's shop swung open and a tall, pale woman squinted as she stepped out into the light. She wore a mossy-green kirtle covered by a white Flemish tunic embroidered in gold thread. A jeweled girdle cinched her slim waist, and a ring of keys hung at her side. She was followed by two men. The first wore a thick black mustache which hung over his mouth. As he walked, he wrote upon a ledger. The second man trailed behind carrying a new saddle. The woman turned and spoke to the man with the saddle: "Wulfgar, this is lovely work." She caressed the saddle with her fingertips. It had a high pommel carved with a dragon head, a narrow seat, and a high wide back continuing the motif with a dragon tail. The wood, a light oak, had been rubbed and polished till it shone. "I know the Earl will be pleased," the woman said.

Uncle Morgan turned to Evyn. "Wait here while I speak to the Lady."

He hesitated for a moment, took a deep breath, and then walked forward. Evyn watched him drop to one knee before the Lady. She signaled for him to rise, and Evyn could see by her expression that she recognized his uncle.

Uncle Morgan's voice was an indistinct murmur to Evyn. The Lady looked beyond Morgan to Evyn, her eyebrows frowning with a question. She nodded gravely at something Uncle Morgan said. Then he shifted his weight, and the Lady was hidden behind his shoulder. A moment later the man with the thick black mustache left the Lady's side and disappeared inside the Great Hall. When he returned, he carried a small pouch that jingled as he walked. He gave it to the Lady, and she placed it in Uncle Morgan's hands. He knelt again and kissed the hem of her kirtle and then took his leave. As he reached Evyn, he placed his hand on his shoulder.

"I am sorry, Nephew; there was no other way."

He did not look into Evyn's eyes; instead his gaze fell to the pouch he now clutched in his hand. A look of shame crossed his face. "I must pay that man-price or they will surely kill me. You must serve the Lady well. Go now, she beckons you."

In truth, she had not beckoned Evyn at all but was conferring with her steward and her carpenter, as though the strange boy and his uncle were of little concern to her. But when Evyn looked back to his uncle with a question on his face, he saw only Uncle Morgan's back as he raced through the open gate.

Puzzled, Evyn turned once again to the Lady, and for the first time he really looked at her. Like all matrons, she wore a veil over her hair, but he could tell by her eyebrows that her hair was auburn. Her skin, pale as a seashell, was marked only by laugh lines at her eyes. A dark amber necklace circled her long white throat, the contrast in color emphasizing her fairness. Evyn had to look up into her dark brown eyes, as she was taller than he by nearly a head.

He stiffened as she approached. Why had Uncle Morgan left like that? Where was he going? When would he return? Evyn's face burned and his stomach twisted into a cramp. What did he mean, *there was no other way*?

The Lady spoke, and her voice was like the middle tones on the harp, not at all shrill, but soft and rounded. Evyn cursed himself for not studying more thoroughly the language of the Saxon traders who occasionally stopped by Rhywallon's *dyn*. He could make out little more than half of what this Lady said. But he understood all too well the meaning of her next utterance.

"Your kinsman told me that you cannot speak. It is a pity," she said matter-of-factly. "But he also said that you learn quickly. Go to the slave master over there," she said, nodding toward a large hut by the side of the enclosure. "He will assign you work."

The slave master!

Evyn took a step backward and unconsciously clenched his fists. The steward quickly strode forward and gripped his arm firmly.

"You seem surprised, lad," the Lady said. "Your kinsman did not tell you his plans?" She sighed sympathetically at Evyn's confusion. "He told me he must pay a wergild or forfeit his life." She paused for a moment. "He said you were an orphan and that your life was in danger as well had you remained in your village. Do not despair. You are not the first boy to be sold into slavery by a desperate kinsman." She smiled. "I am not so harsh a mistress." Then, nodding toward the gate, she said, "Your uncle, as you can see, has made haste to return to Carmarthen to repay his debt. He did not say your name. Is it possible that you can write it for me?"

Evyn shook his head. Who among the hill Britons could read or write?

"I feared so," the Lady said. She reached out and touched Evyn's hair.

How dare she! Evyn thought angrily. The only ones to do that had been his mother and father. When he recoiled, she dropped her hand, but she seemed neither offended nor angry. "It is as black as a shadow," she said admiringly. "We will call you Shadow."

Then she nodded to her steward and turned abruptly, her gown swishing as she continued her rounds.

Evyn turned one last time as the steward dragged him stumbling to the slave quarters. The gate through which Uncle Morgan had brought him was now closed and barred.

1063

That same year Harold Godwinson and his brothers met for the solstice feast near Exeter.

Later that day the blacksmith locked a thrall ring around Evyn's neck, marking him as a slave.

A dog's collar, Evyn thought bitterly.

Rage boiled in his heart. Each night in the slave quarters, Evyn lay in the foul-smelling straw, his head teeming with angry thoughts. *My beloved Uncle Morgan*, he thought bitterly, *now, that is a fine joke for a fool. To fill my heart with stories of the good life we would have here and then to betray me . . . to sell me like an extra pig. Dishonorable knave. He is a nithing.* Evyn stirred restlessly as though his soul itched. He rolled over so that his back was to the other slaves crowding the hut. *Why did he not sell himself into slavery? It was through Morgan's violent hand that Father was murdered. Yes, it is as though he struck Father down himself. His foolish tongue caused me to lose mine, and his recklessness provoked the sons of Gryffin into a death hunt for us.* The breath caught in Evyn's throat. *Now he has stolen my freedom, too. He has stolen everything from me. He has turned me into a collared dog. He is a liar!*

The words struggled in his mind to escape, but they remained locked within, silent and powerless. He had always spoken so easily. The right word always came to mind. Now everything had changed. He would never grow accustomed to the clumsy stump of his tongue. It felt so strange, and it was a constant reminder of his silence. This, the silence, is what he found to be the most painful part of his existence now. If he could only voice his anger, give word to his hatred, grab someone's arm and make him listen. He longed to bellow, *"My uncle betrayed me!"*

The moon shone full that week, and from then until the next full moon these thoughts burned in Evyn's heart till he felt he would burst.

He did not notice the growing warmth of the sun or the gentle breezes that foretold the coming of summer. He did not notice the graylag goose honking far overhead on her northbound flight. His mind clouded so that he failed to follow the simplest directions. The slave master called him a fool, and Evyn felt the searing heat of the whip many times. To others, he seemed as if he were caught in a thick fog. He kept his head down and refused to look anyone in the eye. "Perhaps he is simple-minded," they whispered. Word spread quickly throughout the Lady's estate that she had a new slave boy, a strange, silent, black-haired lad from the Welsh hill country far to the west. "Poor thing," they said, laughing, "and not a drop of English blood in his veins."

But slowly the burning in his heart began to diminish like a fire left to die, for it was not in Evyn's nature to weep for himself. He came from a race that had always survived the worst. Yet there was little comfort in what those in the slave hut often said to one another: "Better to be a slave in the House of Godwin than a starving freeman."

The House of Godwin. He had heard the name but knew little of it. How ignorant he had been, shut away in his isolated hill village.

Of course, Godwin himself was long dead. Ten years earlier the powerful and grasping Earl of Wessex had suddenly collapsed in a convulsive fit that killed him. The event had been recorded in the monastery Chronicle in this manner: *This same year* [1053] *Earl Godwin passed away; he was taken ill while he was staying with the King at Winchester.* But Evyn knew nothing of monastery Chronicles.

Although the ink had dried long ago, the English continued to gossip over it. Some said he had been poisoned. Powerful men always have enemies, and Godwin had been very powerful, second only to King Edward. But if it had been murder, Godwin had his revenge, for he was the father of many sons and daughters who snatched up the torch he dropped and carried his light throughout all of England.

His firstborn, Swein, was dead now, too. He had been an unstable and dangerous man, and there were few to grieve when he fell sick and died.

But then there was Harold, and he held all of the promise that the brooding Swein had lacked. Courageous and intelligent, he showed no part of the cruel streak that had dominated both Godwin and his firstborn son. Harold governed Wessex, the land of the West Saxons, the rich and fertile country of southern England. He brought justice to the land and security to the Saxons under his protection. His power came directly from King Edward, who held this most experienced and capable earl in high esteem. It was well-earned respect, too, for in times of war Harold commanded the kingdom's army with dazzling skill. In times of peace he judged fairly when he sat in the moot hall of each village, hearing legal cases and interpreting the law. He oversaw the minting of the realm's coin and collected the harvest tax so that none would starve. The King, known for his piety and little else, relied heavily on Harold's experience and good sense.

The third son, Tostig of the Red Hair, had grown from a handsome and charming boy into a handsome and charming man. Sweet words fell from his lips, and he enjoyed the admiration of many. But he failed to command his passionate nature, and he easily took offense. Tostig ruled Northumbria on the northeast coast of England. This was Viking-settled land, and its people tolerated their Saxon earl with uneasy suspicion.

Gyrth, the next brother, was as big as Harold and Tostig put together, the kind of man one wants by his side on the battlefield. Competent in his own right but content to follow, he looked to Harold for counsel. East Anglia, the land of the East Angles, had been parceled out for him to govern.

Young Leofwine was the last of Godwin's sons. Tall, spindly, and with hair like yellow flax, Leofwine was much loved for his simple ways and feared by no one. He ruled Kent, Surrey, and the friendly shires north of London with an easy hand.

For his youngest child, a winsome girl, Godwin achieved perhaps his greatest success. Before he died, he contrived a royal marriage for her with the reluctant King Edward, long a bachelor. His daughter a queen, his sons earls, Godwin had reason to die a contented man.

So, as the Chronicle truthfully recorded it, the year 1063 found England prospering under the strong and just rule of the Godwin family. It failed to note that Evyn of Carmarthen found himself that same year a slave in the household of the auburn-haired Lady Ealdgyth, the woman Earl Harold of Wessex loved.

Each morning at dawn, the slave master unlocked the door of the slave hut. He stooped to enter through the low door, showing his high, shiny forehead and thin patch of tangled hair. A coiled whip lay tucked in his belt. "Sun up, sun up!" he shouted at the men and boys who shared the musty hut. As they stepped into their breeches and pulled their tunics over their heads, he told each his day's work.

"Sitric, Wolf, and Knude, join the men in the east barley field and do whatever the lead man says."

The three boys left, all laughing at some silly joke, happy to be sharing a task.

Evyn watched them leave. How he longed to be sent with them. But the slave master thought he was too stupid to do anything but the simplest chores.

"You, Shadow!" the slave master shouted, as though Evyn were deaf as well as dumb. Laughter erupted behind him. "Shadow" was what they called dogs or horses. Evyn burned with shame. Uncle Morgan had even stolen his name. "Shadow, clear out the rushes from the Hall." Evyn jumped to his feet quickly, determined to avoid the whip today. His back still stung from yesterday's blows.

While in the Great Hall, Evyn listened as Lady Ealdgyth told a group of new pages about their history. He found his knowledge of the English tongue improving. He'd always known enough to get by with the Saxon traders who came to Rhywallon's *dyn*, but now he was learning the fullness of the language, its breadth and imagery. The boys, who were seven or eight years old, had come from all parts of Wessex to begin their training. For most, it was their first time away from home.

"Like my own sons, who are at the court of King Dermot of Ireland, you have come from some distance to further your education. It is difficult, I know, but you are lucky to be here," she said as she walked back and forth in front of the bench where the boys huddled closely together. "You come here as boys . . . you will leave as men. First you will learn good manners: how to serve at your lord's table, how to treat others, men and women, and those of different ranks. Later you'll learn how to ride and care for a horse, how to wield the battle-ax and the great two-handed sword." The little boys sat up straight and smiled at one another; they all wanted to be warriors. "You'll learn to follow orders from your commanding officer. You will learn," she said, pausing until all the boys looked at her, "what it means to be English." She ceased pacing, looked one lad in the eye, and asked, "Do you know anything of your history?"

The boy froze and shook his head.

The Lady turned her back to them, catching Evyn's eye for a second as he worked. He quickly turned away and pretended to ignore her. "The Saxons came from across the sea more than five hundred years ago," the Lady said to the boys. "They came with other tribes like them, the Angles and the Jutes. Sailing in their great longships, with their women and their children and all their belongings on board, they set course for this new country. When they landed, they fought the great Vortigern at the Battle of Aylesford, and the fields ran with blood. Then the Saxons pushed the British and the Picts to the west and north, to Wales and Scotland. But they could push them no farther, for the British are good fighters, too, and have much to be proud of."

The Lady smiled at Evyn, a compliment to his British ancestors who finally stopped the Saxons after the disheartened Roman settlers failed. Like the Saxons, Evyn's people were fierce warriors. But they were independent by nature and failed to form a united army. They slowly lost their land in the fertile southern and eastern lowlands. Evyn knew most of this already. He knew that old King Edward, called the Confessor, ruled both England and Evyn's beloved Wales, and that he had friendly ties with King Malcolm of Scotland, as well.

"Your people are proud and courageous, and, above all else, they are loyal," the Lady said, turning again to the boys. "Be faithful to your lord, whether it is at the council table or on the battlefield. Someday you may have the honor of fighting by your lord's side. Never run from the battlefield unless your lord sounds the retreat. Shame is the lot of the man who survives his chief in battle. Take courage—be like the lion. And Earl Harold will be proud to call you his man."

Not long after came the time of year the Romans had called June and the Saxons called Litha, in honor of the moon. It was a week before Midsummer's Eve, when Evyn heard much more.

One late morning he was carrying water to the cook, who said, "Make haste, boy. I will have no patience for shirkers during the next fortnight. There is much to be done." Seeing Evyn's confused look, he added, "Do you not know that the Earl of Wessex is hosting his brothers and their retinues for a midsummer celebration here at the Lady's manor?"

When Evyn took water to the stablemen, he overheard the hostler giving directions to his boys. "Take the hunting horses and give them a good workout. They will need to be in top condition."

As he passed the chicken yard, he saw a girl chasing the plumpest birds into another smaller enclosure where the butcher's boys could easily grab them.

Then the blacksmith needed more water to cool the hot iron he was hammering into a dagger. After that, Evyn carried water to the gate for the field hands who came to slake their thirst at noontime. Then he trudged back to the kitchen, where the girls needed water and sand to scour the cooking pots. Everywhere he went, men and women and children worked quickly and a little nervously.

After the midday meal, the slave master told Evyn to carry water to the women's loft of the Great Hall. Once more he hauled the heavy buckets up from the depths of the well. When he reached the Great Hall, he unhooked the buckets and stood the wooden yoke in a corner. He climbed the narrow winding steps to the women's quarters, a bucket of sloshing water in each hand. It was usually a forbidden area to the boys and men, but as a mute slave Evyn was considered to be of so little consequence that it did not matter.

"Dump the water here," a wrinkled old woman ordered him, pointing to a deep cauldron over the hearth fire. When he saw the wooden tubs in the middle of the chamber and realized that the women would be bathing that day, he turned red from his forehead to his throat. The scent of their heavy imported perfumes filled his nostrils. Their clean white chemises hung on pegs along the wall. Giggling came from one corner, where a few girls watched him uneasily completing his task.

Evyn clenched his teeth and turned, eager to leave as quickly as possible, when he bumped into the Lady. Since she was in the women's quarters, she had removed her veil. Her warm auburn hair lay coiled and looped in long braids at the back of her head. Her face, with its flawless delicacy, wore its usual expression of confidence and humor, which Evyn found so unsettling. He had seen her half a dozen times since that first day, and the sight of her always reminded him of the bitterness he felt over his uncle's betrayal.

"Slow down!" she said, and when she saw his discomfiture she smiled. "So, it is our black-haired Briton from the hill country. How do you fare?"

She knows I cannot speak, Evyn thought. *Why is she taunting me?*

Evyn made no sign to her—he neither bowed his head nor bent his knee; no sign of recognition or respect at all. He pretended not to understand.

"Come now, do not play the idiot with me. I know you understand me quite well enough. The rogues got your tongue, not your brain."

She looked him over carefully, from the filthy hair and the ragged tunic, torn where the whip had sliced it, to his bare and dusty feet.

"Turn around," she demanded, "and lift your tunic."

Evyn hesitated.

"Do as I say. I have many chores myself today and have not the time to coax you."

Humiliated, Evyn obeyed, seething with hatred for this powerful woman. He turned, untied the cord at his waist, and lifted the stiff, bloodstained tunic. He could feel her eyes staring at the fresh welts on his back.

"We will kindle no love for the Godwins with this manner of welcome, will we? Finish your chores for the slave master today. Tomorrow you will help the cook. He can use a strong lad like you, as there will be some extra butchering over the next few days. I think it will go easier with you. When the cook loses his temper, he hits with a wooden spoon, not a whip," she said with a wry smile.

The next day Evyn was chasing chickens and breaking their necks as they squawked and clawed his hands. Then the tedious chore of plucking began, and he quickly found himself in the middle of a soft blizzard of downy feathers. From his place outside the kitchen, he saw that the air of expectation continued to grow. The stableboys brushed the sleek horses out in the yard till their glossy coats shone in the warm summer sun. The housekeeper had all the trestle tables brought outside and scrubbed. Clothes were washed and hung out to dry in the breeze. After supper the housekeeper gave Evyn a new tunic and breeches and then sent him off to the tanner for new shoes.

By week's end the whispering began. "Harold comes today!" It started in the Great Hall and thence to the kitchen, repeated by pages serving at table. It drifted out of doors and passed over the stalls where the stableboys braided the horses' manes. The women and girls working the looms shouted it to one another over the whirring of their beaters. By midmorning even the field hands talked of it. "Harold comes today!"

That morning, when Lady Ealdgyth stopped by the kitchen to confer with the cook, she called Evyn over to her. "Tonight you will serve with the pages in the Great Hall. Keep your ears and eyes open and mind your manners. I think you have learned a good deal already, but you are still very ignorant."

Evyn was surprised. Mutilated slaves rarely saw the inside of their masters' Halls in Saxon England. Normally only young boys from noble families served as pages in the

Great Hall. It was the first step in their education. To serve with the pages was an honor he had not expected. Pleased, Evyn let slip the stony expression he always wore in the Lady's presence, and she smiled. She took her leave, but as she passed under the wide lintel of the kitchen doorway, she turned abruptly to him so that her veil fluttered back from her face. "I know you will not disappoint me."

That day the steward screamed till he was hoarse. "Pull out the tables and benches," he called, and they were dragged to the center of the room and set up, the High Table at the far end with side tables extending the length of the Hall. Women slaves shook out white linen cloths and smoothed them over the tables. Pages gathered platters, drinking bowls, and ivory horns from the huge storage chests, while the tallest squires climbed on one another's shoulders to hang banners of all the great families of Wessex, as well as the banners of Harold's brothers. The Earl's own banners, the Golden Dragon of Wessex and his personal banner, the Fighting Man, hung in places of honor. Later, servants lit the torches and oil lamps, and because it was cool, the fire was kindled. Musicians took up their stations, tuning their harps.

Whenever the cook turned his back, Evyn peered through the open kitchen door to the stable yard beyond. Horses and riders arrived throughout the day, the younger men and women on horseback, the older dames and graybeards in litters. By early afternoon the stable was filled, and soon the yard was crowded with the tethered horses of guests. The interior kitchen door opened onto the Great Hall, where Evyn watched the nobility of England mill about in small clusters, talking quietly and with anticipation. The women wore linen dresses and earrings of precious gold. Their girdles twinkled with jet and azure jewels. The men fingered their long, thick mustaches as they waited eagerly for the Earl to arrive.

When the tables had been set to the steward's satisfaction, a page scurried upstairs to the Lady. A moment later, with the sun casting a warm rosy glow through the open doors of the Great Hall, Lady Ealdgyth Swan Neck glided down the stairs, her kidskin slippers scudding softly against the wood. She wore a sea-blue gown of imported silk covered by a white linen mantle. Deep blue Celtic embroidery edged the neckline and cuffs. Her girdle, wrought of gold links and set with rubies, swung gently with each measured step. The circlet holding her gauzy veil in place was also gold set with rubies. Her eyelashes were blackened and blush tinted her pale cheeks, but her fair and delicate neck was unadorned. From the kitchen door, Evyn heard admiring murmurs from both the men and the women.

"Look, there is the Swan."

Or: "Hush, the Lady Swan Neck comes now."

The Lady wore her pale beauty with such unaffected and regal modesty that she had long ago been likened to a swan, and that had become her name. She took her place at the High Table but remained standing, waiting for her lord to enter. Her guests followed her example, taking their places at the side tables according to rank.

A blast from the gatekeeper's horn was echoed by the trumpeters standing at attention high up in the loft. The entrance to the Great Hall darkened and the four sons of Godwin stood there shoulder to shoulder like pillars, framed by the evening light. The setting sun at their backs transformed them into mysterious silhouettes, throwing long shadows deep into the Hall. The light burnished their hair to copper, and a soft haze circled their golden heads like halos.

Evyn drank in the details of these four long-anticipated guests. The man second from the left drew Evyn's attention immediately, and he found it hard to take his eyes from him. He was neither the tallest nor the most richly dressed, yet there was something commanding in the way he held his head. Neither was he the most handsome of the four, although with his bright hair and golden mustache Evyn could see that he might easily be a favorite with the ladies. He was dressed well but not ostentatiously, in a bleached tunic. His shoulders, wide and straight as a board, were covered by a scarlet cloak that fell in folds to his knees. He wore white linen breeches cross-gartered in dark bands, and his riding spurs still circled his ankles. Evyn's eyes kept returning to the man's face, for his features spoke of intelligence and strength. There was something magnetic about his presence, something forceful but without the least hint of arrogance. He scanned the room, overlooking nothing. Though there were lines under his eyes, and he was clearly a man old enough to have grown sons, he did not appear spent, as many a man his age would. On the contrary, he seemed watchful, like one who is not easily fooled. When he spotted the Lady at the High Table, a smile played on his lips.

"That is Harold Godwinson in the scarlet cloak," a page whispered to Evyn. And all Evyn could think was: *Ah . . . so that is the Earl of Wessex.*

Everyone remained silent for a long time, or perhaps it only seemed that way to Evyn, who felt as if he had slipped under a spell. Only the sound of the trumpets lingering over their melody settled upon the guests, who stood in rapt attention.

The page whispered again. "To the left is his brother Tostig—sometimes he is called Tostig Red Hair."

Tostig was tall enough to look Harold in the eye but was more slender in build. His fiery hair fell straight to his shoulders, and he had adopted the northern custom of braiding his forelocks, which suited him. His cloak, of forest green and edged in yellow bands, set off his hair to advantage. His skin was pale and his deep brown eyes were filled with mockery. Evyn watched him deliberately throw his cloak back over his shoulder to reveal thick bands of precious gold circling his arms and wrists. Tostig's glance drifted across the Hall. He grinned at a beautiful woman and lazily arched one eyebrow.

On Harold's other side stood a sturdy, broad-shouldered man, who Evyn guessed must be Gyrth, the warrior brother. Tall and barrel-chested, he had a square jaw suggesting a fearless man who relished carrying his battle-ax to war.

The youngest brother, Leofwine, stood next to Gyrth. His limp flaxen hair fell into his eyes and his long, spindly arms hung at his sides. He rarely took his eyes from his brother Harold.

As the last note of the trumpet died away, a magnificent hound, sleek and long-legged, recognized Tostig as the one who had reared her from a pup. She bounded up to her old master and threw her paws on the Earl of Northumbria's shoulders. The Earl laughed with genuine pleasure and stroked the dog affectionately. His brothers laughed, too, and teased him, setting the mood for the evening.

The spell had been cast and the guests enchanted. Moving from sunlight to torchlight, the four brothers, led by Harold, strode triumphantly through the Hall, stopping to speak to an old aide here or saluting a friend there. They laughed and shared jokes. The torchlight made flickering shadows among the revelers, and the music of harps filled the air. All who were noblest in England celebrated that midsummer evening.

With the other pages, Evyn served the guests, filling their drinking bowls with the strong honey-flavored mead that was enough to send one into a misty reverie after a few deep sips. In the kitchen, platters laden with steaming joints of mutton and pork were hoisted onto the shoulders of two strong men and carried to the Hall. Plates of bread were passed down the length of the tables. Bowls of early berries and fruits appeared, and soon the revelers' fingertips were stained red with the sweet juice.

After the main course, the toasts began.

A man from Kent rose, his drinking horn raised, declaring, "Blessings on the sons of Godwin—they have brought peace and prosperity to Kent."

Then his neighbor rose and in a loud voice said, "To Earl Harold and his brothers, and to their great father, Godwin, who is much missed."

Harold bowed with gratitude and drank to his father's memory.

There were many acclamations among the guests, shouts of support, laughter, and loving embraces. Then the shire reeve from the coastal city of Dover rose. He held his drinking bowl in both hands before him, waiting patiently for the servants and pages to refill empty bowls and goblets. Finally, satisfied that all were ready, he shouted, "May God continue to give Earl Harold strength to protect our southern coast from William the Bastard of Normandy!"

Chatter ceased. Evyn looked up from pouring mead to see the guests about him suddenly grow very serious. He saw Gyrth's jaw tighten. Tostig looked uneasily toward Harold. All those present, from earl to noble to merchant to thrall, were reminded of England's mortal danger. For, although England and Normandy were officially at peace—King Edward himself was half-Norman by blood and full Norman by his upbringing there—Duke William of Normandy was known to covet England and would take it by force if he could. The joy that was present in the Hall a moment ago suddenly vanished.

Harold pushed his chair back and stood, scanning the pained faces of his people. Without a word, he commanded the attention of all those present. Then, for the first time, Evyn heard that golden voice, a voice which could match that of the most gifted *storiawr*. Its volume was full but not harsh, its rise and fall rich and full of subtlety, the tone self-assured and fearless.

"To Duke William: may he reign long," the Earl said, raising his bowl in a toast while the stunned revelers stared at him in disbelief. Then Earl Harold made to sit down, but straightened and added, "in Normandy."

Gyrth, warmed by the mead, broke into laughter and shouted his approval. His outburst was followed by laughter throughout the cavernous Hall. The tension that had gripped everyone a moment before snapped like a broken cord.

Evyn found himself looking once again at the man at the High Table who spoke with such grace and ease. His quick wit had demonstrated through one simple joke the confidence his people had in him. Harold, well aware of the impression he made on them, now had eyes only for the lady at his side. He put his hand over hers and whispered in her ear. She smiled and gazed up into his eyes.

Then the harpists plucked their strings, and the tables were pushed back. Lords danced with their ladies to the delicate music, while Evyn and the other servants and pages removed platters and bowls and brushed the crumbs away. Later, jugglers amazed the guests by tossing three, four, then five balls high up into the rafters. They sat on one another's shoulders and tossed the balls back and forth till they became a blur of movement. The evening fire burned, and the Hall glowed in its warmth.

When the jugglers pocketed their balls and retired, Earl Harold signaled for the storyteller to begin and the guests quieted. Through stories the English learned of their grandfathers and great-grandfathers and all those who went before them. They learned of the kings and queens and bishops of old, those who ruled a land hard-earned through bloody battles and kept through vigilance and courage.

The storyteller walked about the center of the Hall, telling the history that the Saxons loved to hear. He was a tall man whose body came alive with the storytelling. His expressive hands glittered with rings, the gifts of kings and nobles, and his voice carried to the farthest corners of the Hall.

He spoke of how, long ago in the year 937,

> "*. . . king Aethelstan, lord of warriors,*
> *Ring-giver of men, with his brother prince Edmund,*
> *Won undying glory with the edges of swords,*
> *In warfare around Brunanburh.*
> *With their hammered blades, the sons of Edward*
> *Clove the shield-wall and hacked the linden bucklers . . .*
> *The foemen were laid low . . . The field*
> *Grew dark with the blood of men.*"

The storyteller paused here, and the following silence was as dramatic as his voice had been. How Evyn envied him.

"All through the day the West Saxons in troops
Pressed on in pursuit of the hostile peoples,
Fiercely, with swords sharpened on grindstone,
They cut down the fugitives as they fled . . .
Where standards clashed, and spear met spear
And man fought man, upon a field
Where swords were crossed . . .
There . . . the aged Constantine,
The grey-haired warrior, set off in flight.
No cause
Had he to exult in that clash of swords . . .
On that place of slaughter
He left his young son, mangled by wounds,
Received in the fight."

Evyn, listening as he cleared platters of food, suddenly had to shut his eyes tight to keep tears from rolling down his face. That was his place. He should have been the *storiawr*. It was what he had dreamed of for so long, and now it would never be. Now he wore a dog's collar and could not even say his own name. He leaned to pick up one last dish and heard an old man whisper to his neighbor, "It is a sad tale, is it not?"

Evyn clenched his jaw in anger, wondering bitterly why so much had been denied him.

1063

That summer Earl Tostig visited the abbot of Aethelney Monastery before fighting the Welsh.

The next day, as Evyn lowered the bucket at the stone well, the housecarls gathered to wash and exchange gossip. All around him the men yawned and made idle talk.

"We'll see fighting soon, no doubt," one of the younger soldiers said.

"Aye, but it's not likely to last long. Harold's too smart to let the men of Radnor outwit him," an experienced soldier answered.

His friend, knotting his tunic belt, agreed. "No, we need not fear them. I'll tell you who we need to watch—that bastard William of Normandy."

"What makes you think so?" the young soldier asked. "He cannot muster as many fighting men as our Earl Harold."

"But he is rich. He could hire mercenary soldiers from Flanders, Brittany, even France."

"I have heard it told that the sight of his cavalry charging will chill a man's blood," the young soldier said as he tied his soft leather boots at the ankles.

"And your blood is easily chilled, is it not?" came a joker's reply from the edge of the crowd.

Everyone laughed.

"How would he reach us? He has not the ships to move an entire army across the Narrow Sea."

An older warrior with a gray mustache looked up from lacing his breeches. "Perhaps there will be no fighting at all." He folded his arms across his knees thoughtfully. "Old King Edward has no sons to succeed him and no daughters to marry off to an heir. He spent most of his life in Normandy and likes the fussy cider-drinkers. Some say he will name William as his successor, and I wouldn't gamble a month's pay against it."

Several of the soldiers frowned.

"But our Earl Harold is surely the best choice for heir," one said. "It would be good for the English people to have an English king."

"He is not direct in the royal line," someone said.

"But his sister is our queen, and his mother is from the royal house of Denmark."

The older warrior answered, "I don't argue with anything you say, yet I do know William believes England should be his."

Evyn reluctantly left them, for he admired their camaraderie. *But they do not speak to me*, he thought. Hardly a soul had spoken to him in the two months that he had been at the Lady's estate. During the day, they shouldered their way past him, and at night the boys turned their backs to him when they began their games of dice. The women whispered about him. "He's cursed," they said behind their hands. "A witch has taken his voice." He brooded over these slights and did not see the spilled water on the stone threshold to the kitchen. He slipped, dropped the bucket, and fell on his outstretched arm. His head hit the stone.

When Evyn woke, he found himself stretched out on a wooden table with the surgeon holding his limp arm between the wrist and elbow. They were in a small chamber he had not been in before.

"Can you push against my hand?" the surgeon asked, seeing Evyn open his eyes.

As Evyn pressed against the surgeon's open palm, a stabbing pain raced up his arm.

"As I thought, the bone is broken," the surgeon said matter-of-factly.

A cool feminine voice answered from behind Evyn, "What are we to do with this Briton?"

Lady Ealdgyth floated into view, her pale skin wrinkled by a frown.

"If it is to heal properly, my Lady, the lad should not do much of anything till summer's end. I am afraid that you have a useless runt of a thrall on your hands." The surgeon spoke apologetically; it was annoying to feed a slave who couldn't work.

The Lady put one finger to her lips in contemplation. She stared thoughtfully at Evyn, who wished she would look elsewhere. He felt uneasy under her gaze.

"I suppose we could send him to Lewys," she finally said.

"Lewys! My dear Lady, you cannot be serious!" the surgeon said, smiling in polite disbelief.

"Why can I not be serious?" the Lady asked in her cool voice.

The surgeon stammered, "Oh . . . well . . . I really. . . . My Lady, please, Lewys is hardly a suitable choice," he finally blurted out.

Lady Ealdgyth turned her regal face from Evyn to her surgeon. "Are you questioning my judgment, Magnus?"

"I . . . um . . . of course not, my Lady. It is just that, well . . . it is just that . . ."

"It is just what, Surgeon?"

Evyn listened intently as the Lady Ealdgyth and her surgeon, standing on either side of him as he lay on the table, argued.

Who is Lewys? Evyn wondered. He slowly rolled to one side and sat up, but as he listened to the argument shooting back and forth over his head he forgot about his arm and leaned on it. The pain was searing, and he gasped. Both the Lady and her surgeon stopped speaking and turned to him.

"Magnus, can you make a poultice of cockleburr for him? I remember you used that for the Earl when he injured his knee."

"Yes," Magnus answered, resigned. "And I will give him something to help him sleep, as well." He opened his cupboard of herbs and ointments and mixed a paste in a bowl, using warmed water from a cauldron hanging over the fire pit. After dipping long strips of linen in it, he tied them firmly around Evyn's arm. He splinted the arm and nestled it in a sling tied around Evyn's neck. Evyn took a deep breath as the warmth soaked into his skin. Then, in another bowl, the surgeon mixed a potion, crushing the leaves of a yellow herb into some liquid.

"Drink it quickly, lad," he said, handing the bowl to Evyn. "It tastes awful."

Evyn sniffed it suspiciously. But he tilted the bowl to his lips, gagging as the bitter stuff slid down to his belly.

"He will sleep the rest of the day, my Lady," Magnus said.

The Lady stroked Evyn's head affectionately, but when he flinched she dropped her hand.

"Earl Tostig leaves for the north tomorrow," she said to Magnus. "I will ask him to take the boy as far as Aethelney."

Evyn's head began to swim, and the room grew dark around him. He allowed the surgeon to take his good arm and lead him to an empty cot in the sickroom. As he sank down onto the straw-filled mattress, his eyelids felt so heavy that he could no longer keep them open.

Who is Lewys? he wondered. *And where is Aethelney?*

The last words he heard were those of the Lady fading in the distance. "Yes," she said, more to herself than to her skeptical surgeon, "I think Lewys is just what the boy needs." Then everything swirled black and silent.

The next morning at dawn, the surgeon Magnus unwrapped Evyn's arm and smiled at his own skill. He applied a fresh poultice and wrapped it once more. "I'm sure I don't know why the Lady took such trouble over you," he said to Evyn. "From the looks of you, you'll never be much use to anyone."

In the yard, Earl Tostig's men readied themselves for a long ride. They scraped the dirt from their horses' hooves and tightened the saddle girths around their bellies. They slung their kite-shaped shields over the pommels of their saddles and mounted as the horses stamped restlessly.

Lady Ealdgyth came from the Great Hall, pulling her cloak about her shoulders. She gave Evyn a roll of parchment. "Give this to the abbot when you reach Aethelney."

Evyn tucked it inside his tunic with an icy stare. *Where is*

Aethelney? Why are you sending me away? And who is this rogue Lewys whom your surgeon distrusts so much?

She spoke with one of Tostig's mounted men. Yes, he would take the boy on double with him and keep an eye on him as far as Aethelney.

"Come on, lad," the young housecarl said.

Evyn placed his foot in the stirrup, and the agreeable housecarl pulled him up by his good arm. "First time riding with armed men?" he asked. When Evyn nodded, he said, " 'Tis no matter. You'll be safe at Aethelney. We're the ones who will see the fighting."

Evyn saw Earl Harold and his brother Tostig emerge from the Great Hall. Harold, with bowed head, nodded gravely to something Tostig had said. Tostig spoke again and laughed at his own words, and although Evyn could not hear what he'd said, he decided there was something cruel in the sound of his laughter.

The obliging housecarl turned in the saddle. "They talk of campaign plans, I reckon. There will be more fighting soon where we're going, against dangerous outlaws in North Wales. Harold means to bring peace to the whole land, and I know many Welsh will be glad of his help."

Earl Tostig mounted his dark horse gracefully, like an acrobat, and said, "With good weather, I will meet you in a week's time."

Lady Ealdgyth stepped forward and held the bridle of Tostig's horse, as though she was unwilling to see him leave.

"Woe to that man who breaks the peace. He will find himself caught between two sons of Godwin," Tostig said, shaking his glorious hair back from his face.

"I will come up from the south, and we will catch him in a vise," Harold said without smiling.

Tostig turned to the Lady. "Farewell to the loveliest squire in the land," he jested as she reluctantly handed him the reins. He signaled for the last of his scouts and housecarls to mount and affectionately saluted his brother.

As he did so, a raven dived from the sky. It cawed angrily and swooped low over Earl Tostig's head, so close that the powerful wings lifted his fiery hair. Its shadow darkened the Earl's face as it passed by. Evyn saw and shrank back. *Not another raven-shadowed man,* he thought. Such an ill omen: it always foretold misfortune. And Evyn knew now that it was not just the idle talk of old men. Had he not seen it happen to Morgan? But, strangely, the Saxons around him seemed not to notice.

Harold returned his brother's salute as Tostig spurred his horse ahead. Evyn peered at Harold's unsuspecting face. *He doesn't know.*

At Harold's command the gate swung open. The Earl of Northumbria and his men, perhaps forty of them all told, rode out along the road beside the river Exe. It was the same road Evyn had walked on with Uncle Morgan. *That seems so long ago,* Evyn thought. So long ago . . . almost like another lifetime. Then, without quite knowing why, he glanced back for one last look at Earl Harold and his Lady.

Throughout the morning, the housecarl talked a good deal. He was a Wessex man who had gone up to Northumbria when Tostig had been given that earldom. When they stopped at midday, he shared his rations with Evyn.

"The people of the Humber River region have Viking blood," the young housecarl explained as he broke a piece of bread and handed it to Evyn. "They are restless under a Saxon earl. They see Tostig as a foreigner," he said between bites. "Perhaps they will grow to love him. He's been known to charm the birds out of the bushes, but, between you and me, lad, sometimes he is a hard lord." The housecarl paused. It was not wise to say too much, even to a boy who couldn't speak. He was silent awhile. "For now," he said, changing the subject, "we must bring peace to the Welsh land."

After their meal they rode on, the river flowing quietly to their left. The housecarls in the vanguard sang a loud song, very bawdy, with many verses, until Earl Tostig, laughing and saying he could bear no more, called for silence. At sundown the air turned damp. They camped in a field, tethering their horses, posting guards, and pulling their cloaks tight as they found sleeping places near the fires.

The next morning, Evyn gritted his teeth in agony. A night on the cold ground had set a chill into his broken arm, and it ached as though the injury had just occurred.

"We rode far yesterday; with good fortune we will reach Aethelney Monastery in time for the monks' noon meal," the housecarl said.

When noon came, Evyn's broken arm throbbed painfully, and his legs ached from clinging to the horse's flanks. He hung on to the back of the housecarl's saddle with his good hand, trying to concentrate on anything but his arm: the rhythm of the horse, the smell of its coat, even the housecarl's occasional jokes. But the throbbing grew until it pounded in his ears. When he thought he could no longer bear it, the housecarl's voice broke through the pain.

"There is the monastery," he said, pointing off to the right at wooden walls and a tower rising from the crest of a small hill.

Aethelney Monastery was not a cathedral monastery, and

was therefore not large. Evyn saw at a glance that it was far smaller than the Lady's estate.

Tostig and his men turned from the main road, taking the narrower lane up to the monastery gate. The porter threw it open without a challenge, since Tostig was expected. His scout had arrived exhausted late the previous night with news of the Earl's intention to stop there. Entering, they found themselves flanked by stables on their right and a hostelry on their left. While their horses were being led to the stables, Evyn gazed at his surroundings and cradled his arm. Before them rose a two-storied church, its wooden doors roughly carved with stiff-limbed saints. Joined to the church was an arcaded cloister, a covered walkway leading to the monks' dormitory. The aroma of food indicated that the kitchen and dining hall were to the east. The monks filed past them on their way to their midday supper. As Evyn turned back, he saw the young housecarl smiling. "I told you we might arrive in time for a meal," he said.

The doors of the church opened, and the abbot came out and embraced Tostig.

"A thousand welcomes. We are honored by your visit."

"No, no," Tostig answered, "it is we who are grateful for your hospitality."

"You and your men must be hungry. Go on to the dining hall; our cooks have been expecting you. I will join you in a moment."

As the abbot turned to leave, Evyn remembered the Lady's message. He ran over to him and, as he had seen the pages do, knelt before him with the parchment in his outstretched hand.

The abbot read Lady Ealdgyth's letter and promptly sent

Evyn to the infirmary, where a stoop-shouldered little man who called himself Brother Alfred fed him and gave him a strong dose of mead to dull the pain.

"Rest is what that arm needs," the monk said.

There Evyn spent the weeks of high summer, the time of year called Litha. He sat in the sun lazy as a cat, or sometimes, if he was needed, he ran errands for Brother Alfred. He counted the stars at night and spent much time thinking. He thought of his mother. He missed her and her warm hands, and now, for the first time, he could think of his father as well. Since his father's murder and his own mutilation, Evyn had been unable to picture his father in his mind's eye. He often found himself going over his father's features. *He had black hair and gray eyes. He had a bright color in his cheeks.* But still he could not see him. It had been the same when his mother died. Now the memories flooded back like a surging tide. He remembered working beside his father in the fields. It was backbreaking labor plowing and harvesting, but his father had always made it pleasant with a song or a story. He could even hear the sound of his voice. He fondly remembered his little sisters with their constant giggling, the youngest peeking out from her pouch tied to their mother's back.

One evening at dusk, Evyn walked out to the orchard by the east wall. The sweet scent of half-ripened apples lingered in the air. He rested against the trunk of a smooth-barked apple tree, covered his face in his hands, and wept silently. The ones he loved best in all the world were gone forever, and that happy life was over. Evyn was dead, too. From now on he would simply be Shadow. *It is a stupid name,* Evyn thought. The dream of becoming a *storiawr* was gone as well. Now he must be content with being the water boy or whatever else was demanded of him. His face ran wet with tears, tears for the dead and tears for himself. *Weep tonight,* Evyn thought. *Begin a new life tomorrow.* A life that simply must be endured for as long as it was his destiny to live.

When the moon had climbed well overhead, his tears stopped flowing, and Evyn could breathe without the air catching in his throat. He wiped his face on his sleeve and returned along the moonlit path, leaving the fruity scent of the orchard behind him.

Once again Evyn began the slow process of healing. His arm and his heart had both been broken. Little did he realize that of the two his arm would heal faster. But each morning, as he knelt on the wooden floor of the church next to Brother Alfred, he prayed for courage. The silence of the monastery was soothing, and Evyn's heart and arm slowly began to grow whole again.

"My last apprentice learned all I could teach him and was sent off to a new monastery. It is good to have company again," Brother Alfred said as he hung a bunch of comfrey from the rafters one day. "Are you interested in learning about herbs? They are the secret to health, you know."

Evyn nodded. He knew only a few treatments the old women of his village had tried when his mother and sisters fell ill.

Brother Alfred took Evyn to the woods with him to gather sealwort, the tall woodland plant with bells of white flowers. They had filled their baskets when Brother Alfred cried, "Look! Over here wild garlic grows." The monk climbed through the thickets to reach the plant. "In the old days when the Romans were here, they said it gave a man courage," he said, filling his basket. "I know not if it be true, but some housecarls wear a necklace of garlic into battle. For myself, I think they would be wiser to say a prayer before they lift their swords."

Sometimes, while Evyn sat quietly in a corner, Brother Alfred made notes on his wax tablets, recording which herbs he had in his cupboard and which medicines needed to be replenished. Every afternoon the monk unwrapped the bandages around Evyn's arm and doctored it. At first he made a poultice from sealwort, soaking linen strips in it as the surgeon Magnus had done. One day, after a few weeks, Brother Alfred tapped his arm.

"Look, boy, the bruises have healed. Sealwort is strong for that. Tomorrow we will use sage. It will strengthen that muscle again."

Evyn looked at his arm. The bruises, which were at first purple and then a sickly yellow, had disappeared. But the skin was noticeably paler and the muscle far thinner than on his other arm. He flexed slowly and made a weak fist.

Brother Alfred laughed. "Do not frown, boy. Sage will do the trick for that arm. It is not too late. The muscle is weak, but it has not died. Do you know the old saying 'Why should a man die while sage grows in his garden'? It is true. Before Michaelmas comes, your arm will be mended." Evyn hoped Brother Alfred was right, but he soon found that he had little time to worry about it.

The next day, moments after the dinner bell had rung, the door to the infirmary swung open and three men were carried in on stretchers. One of the litter bearers wore a scarlet tunic with gold edging. His hands were caked with dried blood.

"These men," he said, nodding toward the injured warriors, "are Earl Harold's housecarls. There's been fighting in the west and St. Ethelbert's infirmary is full. Can you take them, Brother?"

"Yes, of course," Brother Alfred said. "It is our vocation."

The wounds were serious. Sword and broadax had done deadly work on the first two men, and the third man, knocked from his saddle during the battle, had a badly broken leg. Evyn watched Brother Alfred examine each man slowly and carefully, with gentle hands.

"Lad, fetch the cockleburr from the rafters and build up the fire," he said calmly. "We have much to do."

Far into the night, Evyn and Brother Alfred remained awake. Vespers rang as they cut away bloody tunics and bathed wounds in warm herbal water. Hours later the bells of compline rang, and the monastery slept, but Brother Alfred and Evyn did not rest. They continued to clean the filthy wounds, and then with splints and strips of linen they set the broken leg. When all was quiet except for the howling of wolves in the distance, Evyn sat by a feverish soldier, bathing his forehead with a cool, wet cloth.

The following weeks brought more wounded. Evyn learned to massage a wrenched knee and to apply a poultice so that the injury stayed warm and evil spirits could not enter. Sometimes the injured soldiers returned to battle with a hobble or a pink scar, but more often Brother Alfred called the gravediggers and another cross was erected in the cemetery.

One afternoon, as Evyn gently massaged the torn muscles in a soldier's leg, the man said to him gratefully, "You have the touch of a surgeon, boy."

Evyn shook his head modestly.

"No, it is true," the soldier insisted. "You are better than some of the field surgeons."

Evyn smiled. He was glad to learn these new skills which brought comfort to the wounded and earned him a place in the monastery.

One morning in the chapter house, where the monks always gathered to hear their day's assignment given by the abbot, Evyn was startled to hear his name called.

"Shadow," the abbot said briskly, "today you will make yourself useful in the scriptorium."

"A new assignment, perhaps," was all Brother Alfred whispered by way of explanation as they filed out of the chapter house.

The scriptorium was dark and still cool with night air as Evyn entered behind the other monks assigned there. It held an odd aroma of chemicals and herbs, oils and pungent powders. Evyn watched as one of the monks opened the shutters, flooding the room with muted late summer sunshine, for they needed every bit of light. Taking their places at long tables stacked with books, parchment, bowls of ink, and quill pens, they began their day's work.

Their vocation was to save knowledge. Once there had been many books in England. But when the Romans sailed from the island, barbarians came and set fire to the beautiful libraries. The books which were not burned were left to mold and crumble to dust. When Vikings landed in their longships, they destroyed many monasteries. They stole the monks' silver and gold chalices and burned their few books. But years later, Alfred, King of Wessex, and his warriors pushed the Viking hordes back into the eastern part of England. The King called for the old books, as many as could be found, to be copied, and for new books to be written. He called for a history of the Angles and Saxons to be recorded. So now each monastery had its own Chronicle of events wherein the battles and deaths, invasions and uprisings, whose son ruled which earldom, and even the weather were carefully recorded.

After a prayer, the monks began copying where they had left off the day before. One of the monks led Evyn to a corner where a basket was filled with dulled quill pens. He took out his paring knife and spent several minutes showing Evyn how to sharpen the point. Evyn took a deep breath. It would take the morning to sharpen each as precisely as the monk had done. He sat down on the floor and took up a pen and knife when the doors suddenly banged open.

Startled, Evyn glanced over to see a tall young monk rush into the scriptorium. His wild brown hair curled out in all directions from the edge of his tonsured head. His eyes, green as a cat's, sparkled with mischief, and his nose, which was hooked and far too large for his face, lent him a comic air. As he raced into the room, his monk's robes whipped about him like the cape of a mad wizard.

"Brothers, how goes the work?" he hollered with a grin.

Every monk in the room looked up from his copying, glad to have a second's respite from the eye-straining task.

The young man approached a table near Evyn, unlocked a cupboard, and carefully arranged pots of precious gold and rare pigments on the table before him. This was no apprentice who was using such costly paints. Evyn found himself staring at the young man, who was so unlike the other monks. His nose and unruly hair made him seem the jester, yet his brow was wide, the mark of a wise man.

The monk felt himself being studied and glanced up from his parchment, scanning the room till he found the eyes that watched him. Evyn turned scarlet; it was rude to stare. The monk cocked his head and looked at him, the way a hound does when something puzzles it.

"Put you in the corner, did they?" he said in a friendly

tone. "Come sit with me if it pleases you. There is room enough at my table."

He did not speak like the other Saxons. The lilt of his voice sounded familiar to Evyn. He hesitated, then scrambled up from the floor and took a seat on the monk's bench, spreading the quill pens and the knife before him on the wide table.

After a moment the young monk turned to Evyn again. "I have not seen you here before. Are you new to the monastery?"

Evyn motioned to his mouth and sliced the knife through the air in way of explanation.

"No tongue, then, lad? You cannot speak?"

Evyn shook his head.

"Oh . . . 'Tis a pity." His tone was heartfelt.

Evyn was relieved to see that the monk had not judged him as others had. He had not curled his lip in a sneer or made the usual remarks about worthless thralls.

"By your black hair I would say you are a Briton, am I right?"

Evyn nodded. He took his knife and a wax tablet from the table and etched a crude deer on it—Rhywallon's crest.

"Oh, from Rhywallon's *dyn*, are you? You are well met, friend. My kinfolk hail from near there." The monk's eyes sparkled with pleasure. "It is strange that we should meet here and not in our homeland."

At that moment the abbot entered to make his rounds, checking the work, seeing that no one, especially the young lads new at the monastery, slacked off in his duties. When the abbot left, the wild-looking monk nudged Evyn.

"You are the one they call Shadow?" he asked.

Evyn nodded.

"You have a task ahead of you," he continued.

Evyn obediently picked up the paring knife again and the next pen.

"No, that is not my meaning," he said. "My name is Lewys," he said in introduction. "The Lady Ealdgyth sent you here."

The conversation of midsummer between Lady Ealdgyth and her surgeon suddenly came back to Evyn. So this was the Lewys of whom Magnus was so unsure.

"Do you know how to read and write?" Lewys asked.

Evyn shook his head.

"I thought not; it is a rare skill. My gift to you, as an old ally," he said, cocking his head close to Evyn's as though they were spies sharing a secret. "Watch me carefully while I work. You will soon be familiar with the letters. I will teach you to read and write." Then he whispered in Evyn's ear, "I will even teach you Latin." With a flourish of bravado, Lewys boasted, "What the rogues stole from you, Lewys will restore. Of course, it is true that not many can read or write their letters, so it will still be a hardship to make your thoughts known. But with this skill you will be useful. You have seen the stewards keeping records, I do not doubt." Evyn remembered Lady Ealdgyth's steward, whom she respected so.

Lewys worked silently and meticulously. He unrolled the scroll of parchment before him, sitting at an angle so Evyn could observe him work. Then he seemed to lose himself in the small world of parchment and ink, forming his letters with incredible grace and beauty; and, it seemed to Evyn, with incredible ease, for the letters flowed from the tip of his pen as though an angel guided his hand. Evyn noted the monk with growing admiration, and this time Lewys was unaware of being studied, so complete was his concentration.

From that day, Evyn was at Lewys's elbow every moment. He moved his cot to Lewys's cell in the monks' dormitory. He sat by his side in the dining hall and shared his table in the scriptorium. And while Evyn remained silent, Lewys spoke constantly on every subject, from astronomy to herbs to the history kept in the monastery Chronicle. He had read every book in the library. Now he generously fed it all back to Evyn. As for Evyn, he found himself smiling and nodding and dreaming at night about the new skills he was learning by day.

After the first week of Holymonth passed, all of the monks worked together during the harvest. Day after day Evyn toiled by Lewys's side, gathering the barley that would provide their bread and gruel for the coming year. When the feast of Michaelmas came late in the month, they cut the flax, stacking it in cones to dry in the fields. The following week Evyn climbed the sweet-smelling apple trees inside the monastery walls. Brother Alfred had been right, Evyn thought, as he gripped the branches of the tree, his arm bearing his weight again. He tossed the fruit down to Lewys.

On days when it rained, Evyn and Lewys pulled up their hoods and fled to the warm scriptorium. At first Evyn merely watched over Lewys's shoulder as he copied from one open book to another. Later, Lewys would hand him a stylus and a wax tablet.

"Copy this," he would say after etching one or two letters at the top of the tablet.

Evyn would dutifully take the pen and copy till the tablet was covered with small letters. Often Lewys would shake his head and say, "Do this over." With a knife heated over a candle, he'd smooth the wax surface, erasing all of Evyn's scrawled letters, and Evyn would begin the task of recopying. When the trees on the hillside turned red and gold, Evyn began to put the letters together. Working with Lewys, he copied strings of words onto the wax tablet. Each time he completed a line, Evyn slid it to Lewys's side of the table. Lewys might look up from his own work and either nod approvingly or shake his head over some line that remained illegible.

Over the course of weeks, Evyn slowly realized that the curves, lines, and dots had begun to lose their mystery. There is *the,* Evyn thought, glancing over a sheet of parchment. There are the words *In this year* . . .

Finally, when the trees waved their bare arms and a thin frost covered the meadows, Evyn saw something that seemed miraculous to him. There, in the open book before him, lay the words *In this year (1053) Earl Godwin passed away; he was taken ill while he was staying with the King at Winchester.* Evyn touched the parchment gently with his fingertips. *I know this,* he thought, realizing that he had mastered a precious, almost magical, skill. *I know this. Earl Godwin was Harold's father. I can read.*

To a boy locked behind a wall of silence for so many months, it was a welcome gift. He could put his voice on parchment. One evening in the tiny cell they shared, he etched on the wax tablets, telling Lewys his whole story, and, for once, Lewys was silent and nodded as he read each line. Now Evyn could ask questions. There was so much he wanted to learn. Could he read the books in the library? Yes, of course, Lewys had answered. Evyn felt a growing happiness in his new life at the monastery. The monks welcomed him here. They valued his help. He had found a family.

Then, a week after Aethelney Monastery celebrated the birth of Christ, a bright-haired Saxon courier dressed in scarlet and gold galloped his lathered horse through the gates.

1063

During Yuletide, when peaceful men sit by the fire telling stories, fighting erupted in the western shires.

Evyn and Lewys watched with interest as the mud-splattered courier dismounted and quickly tied his reins to a hitching post. When the pale and weary rider asked to see the abbot, they gladly escorted him to the abbot's house north of the monks' dormitory.

"He wears Earl Harold's colors," Lewys said after the abbot had admitted the messenger and barred the door again, leaving Lewys and Evyn out in the cold.

Evyn touched his brow lightly, his sign for "Tell me more," or "I do not understand."

"I know not, Evyn," Lewys said, laughing. "The Earl of Wessex does not tell me his secrets. But I shall enlighten you on one matter." Lewys looked about, as though he was sharing a very grave secret and wanted none but Evyn to hear.

Evyn leaned forward.

"If we do not hasten to the dining hall," he whispered, "there will be no bread left for two ignorant hill Britons."

Evyn cuffed him playfully on the arm as they raced back down the path.

Later, when the platters of food were being cleared from the tables, the abbot finally entered the dining hall with the courier behind him. The messenger, only a little older than Evyn, had blond hair that fell in waves to his shoulders and sea-blue eyes, like so many of the Saxons. He held his head tilted back slightly as if scornful of the present company in which he found himself. He strode to the High Table and stood soldier-straight.

"Gryffin is on the march again," he said simply, pausing momentarily to see the unsettling effect of his words as monk turned to brother monk, open-mouthed in alarm. The courier, his nostrils distended like an actor, seemed pleased with the results of his delivery. He was taking a deep breath to continue his speech when the abbot spoke abruptly.

"He is a crafty swine," the abbot said, pacing back and forth with his hands clasped behind his back. "He marches in winter to gain the advantage of surprise."

The courier, clearly annoyed, again took breath to continue his speech.

"Go on, lad," the abbot interjected, as the messenger parted his lips to speak.

"Gryffin was born among the sea Welsh," the surly boy said between his teeth. "But he covets the silver mines in the hills, which are not part of the holdings granted to him by King Edward. He is marching inland through Carmarthen, burning all in his path on his way north to the mines."

No, not Carmarthen! Evyn thought.

Lewys put his hand on Evyn's shoulder, and for once his eyes were not smiling.

"Though it is midwinter, Earl Harold is readying his men. He says he will not wait for the thaw while farms are burning throughout the western shires. I am here at Lady Ealdgyth's bidding to ask for your prayers and to take the one called Shadow back to Exeter with me in the morning."

Evyn felt as though live trout flip-flopped in his stomach. *Not back to Exeter! Not back to the slave hut!* He had hoped the Lady had forgotten him. He had so hoped to be left with the monks. Evyn clenched his fists in anger. Did she really need one more thrall to do her bidding?

That night in the whitewashed cell he shared with Lewys, Evyn sat with his wax tablet on his knees, writing furiously while Lewys looked over his shoulder in amusement and a little irritation.

Lewys read the first line aloud: " 'I will not go back.' " He walked over to look Evyn in the face, and as he did so his huge shadow followed him around the candlelit room.

"Evyn, our lives are not our own. After all that you have endured"—Lewys's green eyes narrowed with intensity—"you of everyone here must know that." He paused, pressing his lips together in exasperation. "I am a monk. I answer to the abbot. By God's will he is my lord here in this life. But you were meant to live in the world. And, as God has made Harold Earl of all these lands, so he, Harold, is your lord. To serve God, you must serve Harold."

Evyn sneered and bent over his tablet again, his knife racing swiftly across the surface, forming letters. When he finished, he held the tablet up for Lewys to see.

" 'As water boy?' " Lewys read. "Ah, I see, the Devil's favorite sin—pride. You still fancy yourself a free man and a *storiawr*, do you? Are you too important to draw water? Does that not bring life and health to the people?"

Evyn scribbled again.

"So, they are not your people, you say. Tell me, Evyn, where are your people?" Lewys raised his voice sharply. He would be cruel, if need be, to make Evyn understand. "Your people are in a Carmarthen graveyard. That was your old life. You are no longer Evyn of Carmarthen. You are no longer free. You are a silent shadow now. Why God has allowed this I do not know. But I do know that now it is your duty to serve Harold, and if Harold's Lady needs a water boy, then that is your vocation, and you should fulfill it with holy pride, which comes of serving God."

Lewys paced the room again, running his fingers through the fringe of his hair, while Evyn sat sullenly hunched over his wax tablet.

"Do you know," Lewys said suddenly on a different tack, "that you have yet to make one sign of gratitude for all you have received from Harold's Lady? It was in her power to make you a galley slave or a mole burrowing in one of the tin mines. Instead, she gave you food and clothing, and kind words, too, I will wager."

Lewys reached the end of the little room and turned, his shadow darkening the wall behind him.

"When that bone snapped," he said, pointing to Evyn's arm, "she had her personal surgeon care for you. Magnus is surgeon to the noble family, not some ignorant midwife for serfs."

Evyn shook his head and turned away from Lewys, but he dogged Evyn like a rat terrier. Bending over the boy's shoulder, Lewys whispered, "She sent you to me to learn to read and write. It was by her instructions that I taught you. That was the message you carried from her."

Evyn looked up slowly. *Why would the Lady care so much for me that she would have me taught?* He reached forward and touched Lewys's forehead with his fingertip.

Lewys interpreted. "Am I certain? Yes, idiot, I read the message myself," he said, his eyes burning brightly. "I lived in her household for ten years," Lewys continued. "I was playmate to her sons and page at her High Table. I, too, am an orphan, but she treated me as if I were one of her own."

Lewys paused for a moment and then suddenly laughed, shaking his head at some memory. Half to himself he continued. "She was my champion. When I felt that it was God's will for me to come to Aethelney, she let me go with her blessing. When others laughed and said I was too foolish to be a monk, she encouraged me. She made the path here easy for me to follow." He sat down next to Evyn on the cot. "Go back, Evyn. The Lady Ealdgyth has shown you a great kindness; now it is for you to return to her gratefully. Show her the skills you have mastered here."

That night, Evyn stared at the thatched roof of the cell for a long time before drifting off to sleep. *So it was the Lady who has made it possible for me to learn my letters, and I have been so rude to her.*

When the winter sun set the next evening, Evyn and the courier rode into Exeter. Earlier, as they passed the Lady's riverside estate, Evyn kicked his horse toward the gate. But the courier said haughtily, "No, we are to ride on to the city." So, leaving Evyn puzzled, they rode farther downriver to Exeter. They galloped up to the arched gateway with its diamond-patterned tile work below the slitted openings for the archers.

"Who approaches Exeter?" the watchtower guard challenged.

The arrogant young courier proudly saluted, exposing a wide silver band on his wrist with the emblem of Harold's personal crest, the Fighting Man, engraved upon it. Satisfied, the guard called down to have the gate opened. Through the dark and deserted market streets they galloped, the lanes silent save for the sound of their horses' hooves ringing against the cobblestones. The shops were boarded up for the evening, their upper rooms dimly lit by oil lamps. Evyn imagined the merchants and their wives and children and servants huddled around an upstairs table for an evening meal or game of dice or knucklebones. Up another cobbled street they pressed on, the horses slipping now and then on icy patches. Evyn followed the courier down the cloth merchants' lane. When they passed the last shuttered stall, the lane opened onto a large square dominated by a huge three-storied Hall. Evyn reined his horse to a halt, his eyes traveling skyward, marveling at the splendor before him. This Hall was larger than anything he had ever seen. The foundation, high as a man's chest, was made of stone blocks mortared snugly together. These supported the upper walls of oak and stucco. There were massive crossbeams at each floor level, with diagonal buttresses of oak shoring up the joints. The exterior of the middle floor glowed in a cream-colored plaster wash with decorative arches painted across its length, while the topmost floor was of stucco and beam only. Its roof, edged in a crenellated wall, was crowned with a watchtower facing south, toward the road from the Narrow Sea. In the winter sky above, crystalline stars sparkled around a full-faced moon.

"Come quickly, boy," the courier called back condescendingly. "Have you never before seen a Saxon Hall?"

Evyn reluctantly kicked his horse forward, following the courier, whose loose hair lifted from his shoulders with each stride of his horse.

To the rear of the Hall were the stables, and at the sound of hooves, Harold's stablemen came out into the cold. Evyn dismounted, handing the reins to one of the men, and bounded after the courier, who waited for him impatiently five steps ahead. Once more the courier showed his arm ring with Harold's Fighting Man upon it, this time to the guards at the rear door of the Hall, and once more they were waved in without question. They climbed up a chilly stairwell to a chamber where the courier's knock brought the answer, "Come in." After leading Evyn into the chamber, the courier was dismissed. He brushed past Evyn on his way out. For his part, Evyn was glad to hear the arrogant lad's footsteps slapping quietly down the stairs.

The chamber was far larger than Lewys's cell but still small enough to hold the warmth of the fire. On one wall hung a heavy embroidered tapestry depicting a hunt. To the left of the tapestry a velvet curtain enclosed a small sleeping alcove. Before Evyn, in the middle of the room, a large table was littered with rolls of parchment. One was spread open, held down at the corners by an ivory drinking horn and two silver candlesticks. A man with honey-golden hair stood behind the table with the hearth at his back, so that the fire cast his shadow before him upon the parchment. After dismissing the courier, he placed his hands upon the edge of the table and leaned forward, studying the parchment.

At that moment Lady Ealdgyth, who had been warming her hands at the fire, stepped out from behind the Earl's wide shoulders. Her skin was as pale as the first time Evyn had seen her, and, although her face seemed thin and tired, her eyes were warm. In the privacy of Harold's chamber she had let down the luxurious coils of her hair, so that the deep auburn locks fell rippling down her back. Smiling, she said, "A thousand welcomes. We are glad to have you back for the last of our Yule celebrations." Evyn smiled in return, and the color along each cheekbone heightened.

Then the Earl lifted his gaze, and Evyn felt his silent scrutiny. When he had seen Harold at the midsummer feast and afterward when he took leave of his brother Tostig, it had been from a distance. Now he stood in the same small room as the Earl of Wessex, the man who was second only to King Edward, and it quickly became clear to Evyn why the Earl's housecarls admired him so. His eyes, clear and intelligent, watched him hawk-like. In color they were gray-blue like the sea before a storm, with lines under them as though he had spent a sleepless night. His forearms were hard with muscles, the veins running down like cords from elbow to wrist. A jagged white dagger scar showed above one wrist. Harold's master, King Edward, was too old now to lead an army, and, even had he been younger, he was not the kind of man who felt comfortable with a sword. No, it was to Harold that the safety of the country fell, and he did not shirk that duty. It was for him to uphold the Golden Dragon, the symbol of Wessex, and his own personal Fighting Man banner.

Though he was tired from the long ride, and hungry, for they had not stopped to eat, Evyn stood up straight, squared his shoulders, and returned the Earl's even gaze as his father would have wished him to.

"It is for another reason than enjoying the Yule celebration that you have been summoned here," Harold said.

"Gryffin has taken up the sword again. Last week he found two of my British scouts and hanged them. Those men were my eyes and ears there. They knew the country and the people. Your people, lad. Is that not true?"

Evyn nodded.

"Come here."

As Evyn approached the table, he saw traced on the new parchment the bare outlines of a map, and with a cold chill in the pit of his stomach he realized that it was of his homeland.

"Here is the city of Caerleon. It is not far from your people's settlement. Gryffin has marched through here." He pointed to a pass in the mountains. "I need you to show me what the land is like between these two points. Can I march an army through here?"

Evyn took a closer look. Yes, he knew the places. He had been to the market at Gower a few times, and the mountain pass where Gryffin had led his men was the only trail the old swine could have used.

Harold traced his finger across the soft parchment. "Can a column of mounted men pass through here, or is it too heavily forested?" As he handed Evyn a quill pen, he added, "My Lady tells me that you cannot speak, so you must draw a picture as best you can."

Evyn took the pen, and above the dot marking Caerleon he wrote in precise letters: *upland meadows.* He had camped nearby once with his father when they had gone on a hunt. Suddenly Evyn realized that Harold was staring at him and the pen poised between his fingers.

" 'Upland meadows,' " he read aloud. "So, we have a young scholar." He glanced back at his Lady, one eyebrow raised. "I was not told that you can read and write," he said, turning back to Evyn. "Write more."

Evyn took a small wax tablet that lay to the side of the map and carefully inscribed the following words:

I thank my Lady for sending me to Aethelney, where Brother Lewys taught me the letters.

He handed the tablet to the Earl, who again read it aloud. Then Evyn knelt and kissed the hem of the Lady's mantle. Lady Ealdgyth graciously raised him up. "You have learned well at the monastery," she said softly.

Harold stroked his mustache worriedly, and it occurred to Evyn that the Earl would be fighting in unfamiliar and treacherous territory. Ignorance could mean defeat and cost the lives of many of his men.

"Write more," Harold commanded. "Tell me everything you know about the country between these two landmarks."

So Evyn wrote until his hand cramped, describing everything from where a small marshy area bordered the river, to the large flat rock north of the trail which had always been called the Giant's Table. He wrote about Rhywallon's *dyn* nestled in the hills, and made a mark for it on the map. He showed where the woods thickened and the stream he and Uncle Morgan had crisscrossed in their flight from the sons of Gryffin. He showed, as best he could remember, the trail through the woods leading to the hidden cave where they had taken refuge, the cave with the large inner chamber.

Harold Godwinson stood behind Evyn, looking over the lad's shoulder. He occasionally asked a question or made a comment. Can horsemen go through here? How many men will the cave hold? How wide and deep is the stream? If the ice has broken, where is the best spot to ford it? Can it be forded here? He smudged the wet ink as he spoke, pointing to different spots on the map.

Lady Ealdgyth sent the guard at the chamber door for a stack of fresh tablets for Evyn to write upon, and, seeing that he was tired, she sent for food and drink, as well. While the candles burned low, Evyn pulled every bit of information that he could from his brain as Harold questioned him without ceasing. Sometimes Evyn nodded or shook his head. Sometimes he wrote. The night wore on until even Lady Ealdgyth put down the embroidery she was stitching as she sat by the fire and closed her eyes. Evyn's hand ached from writing, and the map grew blurred. But still the Earl pressed on. Is this settlement friendly to Saxons? Or, here, lad, is there often snow here this time of year?

It was not until the dripping candles had made a waxy mess over the table and the guard at the chamber door had changed that Harold finally said, "You have served me well, lad." Then he turned to the Lady, for Ealdgyth had stirred in her chair as Harold rolled up the maps.

"My Lady, I had not intended to interrupt the Yule feasting so soon, but from what the lad has told me, I will leave tomorrow. Two can play at this game of surprise. Gryffin must learn that he is not above King Edward's law."

Evyn felt sick at heart as he listened. Gryffin's sons would surely be with their father, and how Evyn had prayed never to see them again. Yet Lewys's words echoed in his soul: *It is your duty to serve Harold.* And in a way it was an easy command, for Evyn found himself drawn to the Earl of Wessex—the man whose voice held both soft music and solemn authority.

Evyn took the pen one more time and wrote: *My lord, I pray you, give me leave to serve you on this campaign.*

Harold read the plea aloud and smiled at the Lady over Evyn's bowed head. This campaign would be of dash and ambush, calling for the expertise of his elite housecarls. A hill boy untrained in arms would be a danger to himself and to others. Harold shook his head over the note and started to speak when the Lady put a finger to her lips, imploring him with her eyes to say yes. Harold grinned at his own weakness. He had never been able to resist her.

"As you wish," he said to both the woman he loved and to the strange boy before him. "Perhaps you will serve me well there, but as I am weary of calling you lad, I think you should write out your name."

Evyn's stylus sliced through the soft wax:

E . . . v . . . y . . . n . . . of . . . C . . . a . . . r . . . m . . . a . . . Then for a moment his hand froze as he recalled Lewys's words. This was the time to start his new life. He scratched out what he had written and carefully wrote *I am called Shadow.*

The rest of that night Evyn slept in the Great Hall below Harold's chamber with the servants and housecarls. In the morning, Harold's steward brought him a heavy scarlet tunic edged in golden yellow. Evyn pulled it over his head. It was cut for a man and fell below his knees with the shoulder seam hanging down over his arm. The belt was of matching scarlet cloth, and Evyn wrapped it around his waist twice, knotting it snugly at the side with the sash swinging at his hip the way he had seen the young courier wear it.

The steward laughed. "A bit big, perhaps, but you will need it when the icy winds blow." Then he gave Evyn a satchel of food and a wolfskin cloak.

Outside in the square the sky was still wine-dark in the west, but a pink band lightened the east. The early morning sparrows whistled from their hidden nests in the eaves. The housecarls said little, Evyn noticed, and spoke in hushed whispers. Evyn kept to himself, his thoughts on Carmarthen. *Perhaps I will see Uncle Morgan,* he mused. Would it be too much to hope that his uncle might have the silver to buy Evyn's freedom? He sighed and shook his head at his own foolishness. Did he dare wish it? Could it be possible that he might become free once again?

Two hundred riders, mostly seasoned housecarls, thundered down the road with perhaps a dozen cooks, squires, and a few nimble scouts adding to their number. This was the small, professional army on which Harold depended, not the clumsy, slow-moving fyrd, the national army counted in the thousands, composed of ordinary farmers, shepherds, and tradesmen who were obligated to serve for a determined number of days each year.

"No," Harold had said, "Gryffin is too swift and cunning for the fyrd. It will take speed and cleverness to catch that wild boar."

On the sixth morning, while the squires kicked dirt on the campfires, Harold conferred with his scouts and captain. Their breath came in cold, white puffs as Harold crouched on the hard ground, drawing maps in the earth with a sharpened stick. At his instructions the three scouts sprang onto their saddled horses and raced into the hills. They knew of friendly landholders in the borderlands who would gladly quarter Harold's men in a Hall or barn as they traveled through the country. They also knew which towns had taverns where information concerning Gryffin's movements might be bought.

As it turned out, it took little cunning to find Gryffin. Once they reached deep into Wales, each day brought cries of, "Smoke on the horizon!" Day after day they followed the odor of smoke and blood as they came upon one burned-out settlement after another.

Evyn knew that it would be an agonizing task to tell Lewys that his village had been burned to the ground, the survivors scattered in the hills. He angrily tossed a charred piece of wood away as he stood among the smoldering ashes of his friend's childhood home.

The next day brought more heartache.

1064

With cunning Harold confronted the enemy.

The next morning, as Evyn slung the saddle over his mare's back, Harold called to him.

"Shadow," he said, "come ride by my side. We are nearing Carmarthen, and my scouts' knowledge of the area is scant. I need you to be my scout now."

By midmorning they approached the little market town called Gower. From there it was less than a day's ride to Rhywallon's *dyn*. Evyn wondered what they might find as he buried his fingers in his horse's thick mane for warmth.

"We ride through Gower with a purpose," Harold explained. "No doubt Gryffin has his spies, and I want him to know I am trailing him." But Harold slyly instructed his men to break into smaller groups and ride through casually to hide their true numbers.

The cries of the merchants and the hum of the crowd in Gower reached them even as they climbed the last hill before the crossroads. Although a bitter wind blew down the lane, a large and noisy crowd had gathered to do their weekly bartering. No sign of strife or plundering scarred Gower. It was week's end, and the lanes bustled with buyers and sellers. A cloth merchant hawked his fabrics—"Flemish wool here"—and farther on, a row of saddles set up on trestles caught the attention of the wealthiest buyers. A kettle man clanged his pots and pans together while women pulled their husbands over to see his wares. They lingered for some time as Harold spoke to one or two merchants.

That afternoon, long after they had left Gower behind, Evyn smelled smoke. When they cleared the woods he saw a billowing cloud of smoke on the horizon, drifting lazily to the east. Evyn kicked his horse into a gallop and sped ahead of the others. As he crested the last hill, he saw what he had been dreading: the smoldering ruins of Rhywallon's Great Hall, the stockade fence flattened to the earth in piles of blackened timbers, and huts and workshops reduced to heaps of charred embers still glowing red.

Evyn's mare raced up the lane past the rocky ledge, his old haunt for memorizing verse. He leaned forward against his horse's neck and pressed her on, harder and harder. Suddenly he reined her to a staggering halt. Bodies littered the yard. Men, women, and even children, armed only with their farm implements, had fallen against the invaders.

Evyn swung his leg over the saddle and leaped down. He ran frantically from one body to the next, checking each for a pulse or shallow breath, as Brother Alfred had taught him. He hoped for at least one survivor, but there were none. Gryffin had had no pity.

Where the entrance to the Great Hall had been, two bodies lay awkwardly sprawled on the ground. One, face up, was the master, Rhywallon. By his side lay one who had died with him. A man who had had the courage to stay and fight, a man of average height with shiny black hair. Evyn knew before he sank to his knees and gently turned the body over that it was his Uncle Morgan. The handsome face was serene in death, the skin pale, the eyes closed lightly as though he were dreaming.

Evyn cradled his uncle's body, the man who, though he had betrayed him, had been kind at times and charming always. It occurred to Evyn as he smoothed his uncle's hair back from his face that he had forgiven him long ago. The feeling of rage that had burned in him all last spring was absent. He felt only the keen grief at the loss of his last kinsman. *Now I am all alone,* Evyn thought. And, almost as an afterthought, he realized that his last chance for freedom had died with Morgan.

"Do you know him, Shadow?" Harold asked, breaking the silence that had surrounded Evyn like a pool of water.

Evyn started. He was surprised to see the Earl beside him. He had not heard Harold's black stallion gallop into the yard. He had not felt his presence at his shoulder. The question slowly settled into his brain . . . *Do you know him?* Evyn took his dagger and scratched letters into the dirt: *My uncle. The last of my kin.*

"I am sorry they are gone, lad. It is a heavy blow."

Evyn felt Harold's warm hand clasp his shoulder, and it seemed to him that a small measure of the Earl's strength seeped into him.

Evyn then became aware, as if waking from a dream, of the clamoring sound of horsemen surrounding him as the housecarls trotted their mounts into the ruined yard. Though the bridles jangled and the saddles creaked, it was quiet, for the men did not speak. It was a somber thing to realize that these poorly armed villagers had been hacked down. It was the kind of dishonorable act that trained warriors could not forgive.

Harold's captain, Hakon, a man of thirty years with a wide, expressive mouth, the corners of which were now turned down in distaste, dismounted and waited for orders.

Harold turned first to Evyn. "Shadow, the earth is too frozen for ground burial; we must burn the dead. We will have a funeral pyre tonight. Later we will send a priest here to consecrate the ground."

That night, after the funeral pyre had burned down, Evyn slept fitfully on the hard ground. He felt the spirits of the dead all about him. Once he woke around midnight. He sat up, huddled in the wolfskin cloak the steward had given him. Harold and Captain Hakon crouched before a campfire, questioning a third man whom Evyn recognized as one of the scouts. A map, stretched on the ground, fluttered in the wind. Harold pointed to it and then twisted around and pointed north. The scout nodded. Evyn heard only muffled whispers, and although Harold gestured freely, Evyn could not read his meaning. Soon he found himself sinking back down onto his shoulder, and his eyes closed again.

In the gray light before dawn, Evyn heard Captain Hakon walking among the sleeping men, calling them to wake. He gathered half of them and said, "Ready yourselves quickly. We ride back to Gower."

The men whispered among themselves. It was unlike Harold to give up the chase with his quarry so near.

"No, no," the Captain said, sensing their doubt. "Some of us return to set down a false trail for Gryffin to follow."

The men exchanged knowing looks and laughter. This was more like the Harold they knew from many campaigns.

Moments later, Harold walked among the men. Pouches of sleeplessness rimmed his eyes, but his hair was combed back neatly from his face and his eyes were wary as a hawk's. He had passed his fortieth year now, and several days in the saddle were more telling on him than they had once been. Evyn saw that Harold favored his left leg, though the Earl refused to show any sign of pain on his face. His brow was smooth, and a smile played on his lips.

"Shadow," he said, taking Evyn's arm and leading him away from the others, "you told me of a cave with room to hold a hundred men. My scouts are not familiar with it. You must lead the way to it now."

Evyn panicked. He had been there only that one time when Uncle Morgan saved him. They had ridden by night through thick woods for hours, and Evyn had been half delirious with pain and the oncoming fever. He would never be able to find it again! An icy gust of wind tickled his neck, and Evyn shuddered from the cold. It was an impossible request. But Harold had not asked him: he had simply said, "You must lead the way." Even without understanding Harold's plan, Evyn knew instinctively that everything depended upon finding that cave. He felt his throat constrict. He held one hundred lives in his hands. If he could not find the cave, it could mean disaster, perhaps another massacre. Why had the Earl of Wessex gambled everything on him? Why had he put such confidence in a thrall of another race?

Evyn felt the Earl's piercing gaze as he waited for some sign from him. He nodded weakly.

Harold clapped him on the shoulder. "Good. Go mount up. You will ride up front next to me." Then he strode off to where the captain stood with his half of the men gathered around him.

"Here, be Harold for a few days," the Earl said as he tossed his plumed helmet to his captain. "But don't ruin my good name," he added playfully.

Hakon chuckled as he caught the helmet and slid it over his head. Then the men understood. "Harold" and his men were retreating; Gryffin would be lulled into thinking that he and his troops could safely travel the narrow roads again without fear of ambush. In the meantime, the real Harold would be hiding in a cave with the other half of his soldiers.

Captain Hakon, who looked surprisingly like the Earl in his distinctive red-plumed helmet, climbed onto Harold's famous black stallion, Thunder, completing the ruse. His men quickly saddled their mounts and swung their horses' heads to the south, following him. The real Harold watched in satisfaction and then turned his borrowed horse north, gesturing for Evyn to ride beside him.

They rode in silence as Evyn led the way across the common field where Rhywallon's sheep had once grazed, then up the slope and into the woods. He was glad of the quiet. He needed to concentrate. Where had Uncle Morgan ridden that night? They had headed north and then east, he remembered, along a narrow and overgrown forest trail. But that had been spring, when the forest had been crowded with new green growth, and now it was midwinter and the woods were barren. He led them as best he could recall, first north, then east. There was the stream. He recognized the anvil-shaped boulder where they had crossed.

Evyn led the way now with more confidence. He remembered to cross back a furlong farther upstream and pick up the deer trail leading deep into the woods. But soon he felt completely lost. The path disappeared. He nervously tightened his grip on the reins as he looked about, wondering if he would find the trail again.

On and on they rode, winding their way up the wooded hillside. A biting wind sliced through their cloaks and woolen tunics. The bare branches swayed overhead, and the ground bore white patches from a recent snowfall. Evyn's knuckles cracked and bled from the cold. He felt keenly aware of the horsemen following behind him, waiting for his lead. It seemed to him that he and Uncle Morgan had ridden along the edge of a ravine shortly before they had reached the cave. But there was no ravine in sight. Evyn stopped, and all the riders behind him halted, so that the only sound was of saddles creaking as weary horsemen, cold to the bone, stretched in their stirrups. To worsen their plight, the sun had hidden itself behind a heavy blanket of clouds, so that Evyn was no longer sure whether they were heading northeast. No doubt Gryffin knew the lay of the land. Chances were he even knew of the cave. Perhaps his scouts had seen them already.

Evyn rested one hand on the pommel and the other on the stern of his saddle. He stood in his stirrups as the other riders had done and peered into the woods in each direction. The earth, dry and frozen hard, was carpeted with dead leaves, which blew before the wind like an army of chattering mice. To their left a few fallen tree trunks slanted down the hillside, banking the piles of leaves. The men, knowing they rode through enemy territory, remained silent.

A strange thing happened at that moment. The sun broke through a small keyhole in the clouds, casting a single ray down into the woods. It came from behind Evyn's shoulder and fell in an unwavering line of silver light. The cold air caught in Evyn's throat. Could this be a sign? He followed it, guiding his horse through the trees, to where the ray struck the forest floor. There was the trail, and beside it the hillside suddenly slipped away steeply, down into a rock-strewn ravine.

Evyn turned in the saddle and waved, signaling the others forward, and Harold spurred his horse into a trot with the housecarls close behind. At the ravine's edge they slowed and rode cautiously in single file, giving the horses time to find their footing.

By the time the last rider reached the spot where the light had fallen, the first rider, Evyn, found the mouth of the cave.

"Work well done," Harold said to Evyn as the Earl dismounted. "You have the makings of a scout."

Evyn took their horses and tethered them to a nearby tree. He ducked into the cave with Harold a step behind him. Evyn showed Harold the small upper chamber where he and Uncle Morgan had stayed. Then they returned to the mouth to get a torch and explored the rest of the cave, past the first chamber, down a narrow slope. The air within felt far warmer than the biting wind in the forest, and Evyn pulled off his cap. He led the way, holding the torch before him. On either side water trickled down the rough walls, glistening like jewels in the light.

When they reached the second chamber, Evyn raised the torch over his head, lighting up a huge cavern. The light bounded across the roof of the cave, leaving dark crevices here and there where the rock dipped inward. To their right, stalactites gleamed like a row of crystal staffs. It was as Evyn remembered—there was plenty of room for Harold's men. The Earl straightened his back and paced off the area. At the far side he crouched down by a little pool, dipped his hand in the water, and licked the moisture from his fingertips.

Once outside again, he called two of his scouts to a quiet spot, and after nodding at his instructions, they rode back down the trail. Quickly then, before dark settled over the hill, the men dragged off their saddles and bridles, their kite-shaped shields and their weapons, bows and arrows, battle-axes and swords. They took the sacks of food from the pack animals. All this they carried down into the inner chamber. Afterward, Harold chose five men to herd the horses farther up into the hills.

They headed off in the cold with their caps pulled down over their ears and their cloaks wrapped tight, while the rest of the men crept into the cave to play dice and eat bread and apples by torchlight. They cast lots for guard duty and the long wait began.

Although Evyn was relieved to have found the cave, his thoughts were busy with Gryffin and his sons. *Are they nearby?* he wondered. *Will they remember their promise of revenge? Yes, of course they will.* Evyn knew that men like these did not forgive the death of a brother. Though he was innocent, he would be held responsible. No doubt they were the ones who had killed Morgan. After getting his rations, Evyn sat by himself in a dark corner pondering all these questions.

Harold's men, eager to lift their swords and fight at his side, grew bold and asked him his battle plans, but Harold only said, "For now, we wait."

By the evening of the third day, the housecarls began to grumble, and even Harold paced restlessly. They had heard nothing from their scouts, and with each passing day the odds of their being discovered increased. The men were bored and grew tired of eating stale bread and apples. They quarreled over their games of dice. They wanted to try their luck hunting for a deer or wild boar, but Harold forbade it.

"The hour has not yet come," he said sternly.

When midnight came and it was time to change the watch, Harold told the two relief men to sleep on. "I am wakeful and will take your turn guarding the mouth of the cave." After he crept up the slope, the men whispered among themselves that they had been fools to grumble under so fine a lord as Harold. "Has he ever asked us to do anything he would not do himself?"

When the cave was filled with the sound of men snoring and turning in their sleep, Evyn, too, crawled to the upper room as Harold had. The nightmare visions which stole upon him in the dark often made sleep unwelcome, and the stale air of the cave made his stomach turn.

It was colder where the night air penetrated at the mouth of the cave. Evyn felt it on his face. He sank down at the back wall of the upper chamber, perhaps twenty feet from the entrance where Harold crouched. The Earl peered into the darkness, watching for any sudden movement. Evyn dared not come any closer. He pulled his knees up to his chest and tucked his cloak around his ribs for warmth.

Although he dreaded sleep, Evyn finally rested his head against the cave wall, his eyes closing. Within moments sleep overtook the tired boy with a spinning sensation.

They came upon him standing in the lane, the rain falling on his head, trickling down his neck. The upraised dagger. The struggle.

Evyn gasped for air. He opened his eyes and was lost in inky darkness. *It is only a dream,* he thought, taking a deep breath and releasing it with a shudder. He'd had the same nightmare night after night since last spring. *It is only a dream.* With an effort he loosened the muscles of his shoulders, which had grown taut as a bowstring.

Harold, still motionless, remained at his post. He peered into the dark, crouching like a wildcat waiting to pounce. Moonlight glinted off his drawn sword. At that moment, a stone's throw from the cave, a twig snapped. Harold instantly sprang to his feet and rushed out into the black night. Dry leaves crackled underfoot, and Evyn heard a thud, then a man's groan and the sound of tussling.

Paralyzed by fear, Evyn found that he could not move. Unchecked terror filled his heart. Was it Gryffin and his sons and soldiers? Had they followed their trail here to the cave?

Another thud sounded, followed by the grunt of a man who had been thrown to the ground. Harold needed him. He must help. The Lady had sent for him, and Lewys had urged him to serve Harold well. But fear encircled his heart, squeezing the courage from his veins and freezing his limbs. His breath came quickly and in shallow puffs. His constricted lungs ached painfully. Sounds of the struggle echoed in the upper chamber as the muffled noise of two men grappling continued. A sapling swished as it was bent and then released, the thud and whoosh of air as a man fell to the ground, winded. Then a frantic whisper: "My lord, it is I."

Silence followed, then quiet laughter. A moment later two forms darkened the cave opening as they ducked inside. Harold threw his arm affectionately on the shoulder of the "intruder." They collapsed on the floor of the cave, chuckling softly.

"My lord, you nearly killed me," Harold's scout said after he'd regained his breath.

"I thought you were one of Gryffin's men," Harold explained. "Why did you not whistle as we'd agreed?" he asked as he brushed the dry leaves from the neck of his tunic.

"My lord, I confess," the exhausted scout said sheepishly, "I lost my way. I thought the cave was farther up the hillside."

There was a pause, and then Evyn heard the scout again. "You say the lad, the one who cannot talk, had been here only once before, and yet he found this place with barely a stumble. He must have his wits about him, though he is speechless. There are many twists and turns in that trail."

"Aye, I intend to keep him in my service." Then changing the subject, Harold said, "But come, tell me all you learned of Gryffin's movements."

"He will be at your mercy soon, my lord," the scout said.

And though he continued speaking, Evyn heard no more of the conversation, for he burned with shame. Harold spoke well of him, yet the Earl did not know what a coward he had brought along. Evyn thought of the scout and of the housecarls sleeping deeper within the cave, each one willing to give his life for Harold. Only Evyn bore a coward's heart within his ribs. It was no excuse that the scout had been a Saxon, for if it had been one of Gryffin's men, Harold might be dead now. Gryffin's sons had been right when they called him a rabbit. *That is what I am,* Evyn thought as he descended quietly into the lower part of the cave, *a fearful, wide-eyed rabbit.*

At dawn, Harold shook each sleeper. "The time has come. Gryffin is walking into our trap. He plans to ride south this day through a narrow pass not far from here. Quickly, now, see to your armor and weapons."

The housecarls donned their heavy coats of ring mail. They slid their conical helmets over their heads, pulling the nosepieces down, and fastening the chin straps. They slung their full quivers over their shoulders and fitted their bowstrings. They sheathed and buckled on their swords and daggers.

To Evyn, Harold said, "Assist me with my mail shirt."

Evyn was startled. That was a squire's duty, and he was

but a lowly thrall. But he quickly ran to where Harold kept his armor and dragged out the heavy mail shirt. The overlapping iron rings clinked together as he hoisted it up and held it open for Harold to slip his arms through. The Earl of Wessex buckled the leather fasteners down the front, then held out his hand for the helmet he had borrowed from his captain earlier in the week and slid it over his golden hair. His face, masked by the low iron brow and nose guard, assumed a grim demeanor. The planes of his jaw and cheekbones became lean and harsh in the dim light of the cave, as though chiseled from quarried stone. His curved nostrils flared back like a wolf's. Hesitantly, Evyn drew out the exquisite sword for Harold. Its jeweled hilt shone and its blade bore the name Gyrngras. Harold sheathed it along his hip. Then he took the broad-bladed battle-ax and slid it under his belt.

It seemed to Evyn that all the power of the Saxon people was concentrated behind the muscle and bones of the Earl of Wessex. *This is why they will die for him*, he thought.

One of the housecarls brought out the Fighting Man standard and unfurled it. The banner rolled down on its cross-shaped frame, revealing a warrior, stitched in gold upon a scarlet field, raising a two-handed sword resembling Gyrngras. It would be planted on the battlefield.

"Are all ready?" Harold asked his standard-bearer.

"All are ready, Sire."

"Then let us fill our hearts with courage for combat."

Outside, a few of the brightest stars still shone. But dawn approached, and the sky quickly grew lighter as they climbed the hill, following Harold and the standard-bearer as they made their way west.

An hour passed as they traveled in silence. Then a wolf's howl broke the stillness of the woods. Evyn thought it odd to hear this creature of the night cry out by day. Harold turned his head to catch the sound, and his standard-bearer pointed northwest. Harold nodded in agreement, and they struck off in that direction with the contingent of housecarls close behind. They had covered another furlong when the wolf's howl pierced the air again. Harold adjusted his direction and continued toward the sound. They climbed down a gully and up a rock face, grasping saplings to ease their way. A third time the cry of the wolf broke the midwinter peace of the forest. They were very close to the sound now. Harold quickened his pace and the noise of chain mail clinking grew as his men followed. They reached a pine-covered hilltop overlooking a ravine and another hill of pines opposite. There, in a treetop, half hidden by the thick green needles, scarlet and golden-yellow flashed. It was one of Harold's scouts waving his cloak to catch their attention. He lifted his head and howled like a wolf one more time.

In the distance, they watched the scout descend quickly, branch by branch. He scrambled down his side of the hill, hopped rock to rock across the bottom of the ravine, and climbed to where Harold stood with his men.

"Sire," the scout said, pointing in the direction of the tree he'd descended, "Captain Hakon waits yonder with the rest of your men. Gryffin approaches now from the north."

Harold climbed atop a rock so that his hundred housecarls could see him. "You have fought hard for your King to make the countryside safe," he said. "You have fought hard for me. I know. I have seen the wounds you have borne in the past." He paused. "If I am counted powerful in Wessex and across King Edward's realm, it is because you have made me so. The King once said to me, 'Harold, you stand above all other men.' I said, 'No, Sire, I want nothing more than to stand shoulder to shoulder with my men. I am nothing without them.' "

Harold gazed from face to face. Most had been with him many years.

"Now we are to face Gryffin, and these are familiar hills for him, while we are in strange country. Fear not, for by God's Holy Cross we will defeat him. When this day is over, those men who sleep in their beds in Exeter and Winchester and Dover and London will count themselves as less than men because they were not with us here today. They had no part in protecting the people from a ravaging beast."

Harold led the men over the ridge to where a pass widened into a small meadow bordered by steep hills. They met Hakon there and the housecarls under his command.

"You are well met, friend," Harold said to Hakon.

Hakon grinned, his wide mouth cracking his face in two. "Your ruse is working. Gryffin walks into your trap."

"If it works, it is by God's hand," Harold answered. "Quickly now, hide your men."

The captain took the other men and hid with them in the woods, out of sight of the pass, just over a hilltop.

To Evyn, Harold said, "Climb this tree, and watch and listen. Later you will write an account of the battle for the Aethelney Chronicle."

Evyn scaled the tree. After he found a perch high up among the needled limbs, he watched as Harold assembled his housecarls into the terrible shield wall. The men stood shoulder to shoulder, their shields pulled up to their chins, their swords or battle-axes drawn. The men aligned themselves three deep and more than thirty men wide. When Harold was satisfied, he drew his own sword, Gyrngras, and took his place in the center of the impenetrable wall.

Soon Gryffin, flanked by his sons and soldiers, thundered through the narrow pass. He spotted the Fighting Man standard thrust into the hard earth and Harold with his men drawn up in formation. As Gryffin jerked the reins of his horse and raised his arm to signal a retreat, he saw the trap that had been laid for him. Already Hakon and his hundred men blocked the pass behind him in a second stout shield wall.

"I fear you not, Harold," the old man called out with hatred. "This is my land, and my numbers are greater than yours. You are foolish to face me here."

The Welshmen dismounted rapidly. The horses, slapped out of the way, scuttled up the steep hillsides snorting and neighing in panic. The two Saxon battalions began to close in on the Welshmen, Harold from the front and his captain from the rear. Gryffin drew his heavy sword, striking the first ferocious blow like a cornered boar. Sword clanged against sword and thudded against shield. Wounded men cried out and fell to their knees, their lifeblood spilling across the frozen ground. Harold led his men with ease and authority, a single shouted command bringing the right flank charging or the left flank swinging close in a vise. Evyn marveled at the discipline of the housecarls. When Gryffin fell under a Saxon sword, a shout of triumph rose among Harold's men. Seeing their leader dead, the Welshmen fled. They had followed him for the gold he gave, not from any sense of loyalty.

"Let them go!" Harold called as a few of his men left the shield wall in pursuit. "It is only Gryffin and his sons I want."

Many scratched and scrambled their way up the hill and escaped into the forest. Gryffin's two sons fled as well, and

Evyn recognized them, for in their panic they had torn off their helmets and dropped their heavy shields. But Harold ran them down. These he had promised his own justice.

Gryffin's dark-haired son turned wildly like a wretched animal and slashed at Harold with his sword. But the weapon missed its mark, and Harold thrust with his own sword. It was a swift and deadly blow, and he fell on the spot, his limbs shuddering once, then falling limp. The fair-haired son, seeing his father and brother cut down, turned in anger. Harold was alone on the hillside, unprotected by his men. Gryffin's son crept up behind Harold quiet as a serpent, ready to strike, and only Evyn could see him from his treetop perch. His heart pounded like a hammer against an anvil. Harold would be struck down from behind without a chance to raise his shield in defense. Without thinking, Evyn, who had uttered no sound since last spring, when he had shamed himself before his uncle by trying to speak, howled a quick and piercing wolf call as the scout had done. All in the moment it takes to blow out a candle, Harold glanced up as Evyn pointed to the enemy creeping behind him. Harold wheeled around as the Welshman raised his battle-ax and brought it crashing down. Springing back, Harold caught the blow on the rim of his shield, the hide and wood shattering in his hand and exploding into useless splinters. In the next instant, as the battle-ax finished its downward swing, Harold brought his own sword down on his enemy. A shrill scream filled the air as Gryffin's son cried out, fell to his knees, and died.

Harold breathed deeply and surveyed the meadow below. His Saxons possessed the field now. They had routed the rebels, and with Gryffin and his sons dead, the plundering of Wales was at an end. The English pulled off their helmets and banged their shields on the ground joyfully.

"Out! Out!" they roared as they stomped their feet while the last few rebels ran for their lives.

As Harold sheathed his sword, he called up to Evyn, "Once more you have served me well. It is in my mind that you have discharged the debt which another incurred. The thrall ring around your neck comes off tonight. You have earned your freedom."

1064

In this year the Earl of Wessex patrolled the Narrow Sea.

In the spring of 1064 the fighting in Wales ceased. Evyn learned from Lewys that the hill people returned to their settlements and began to rebuild. King Edward, though his beard was snow-white, enjoyed fair health and even joined Harold in the hunt now and then. As before, Harold's stalwart brother Gyrth ruled East Anglia, the gentle Leofwine held Kent and London, and the beguiling Tostig, ever charming, ever ruthless, governed Northumbria. Harold, exerting a power and authority beyond anything he had attained before, ruled the rich land of Wessex with its rolling downlands and fertile plains. To his north, young Edwin, the untried son of Alfgar, held the hills and valleys of Mercia.

In the months following the Battle of Carmarthen, for that is what Harold's raid into Wales came to be called in the Chronicle, Evyn returned to Aethelney and wrote down all the details of the battle. He enjoyed this work. For once, he did not feel the handicap of his silence. Pouring his thoughts onto the parchment, he watched with pleasure as the ink dried before his eyes. This work brought recognition from the monks, for they knew the self-discipline involved in learning the letters. It was a worthy task to preserve the history of the kingdom. Lewys, watching over Evyn's shoulder, nodded approvingly at what he had written.

"It is good. Now all those who come after us will know what happened."

The monks plowed their fields and cared for the newborn lambs. The apple trees burst into a swirl of white blossoms thicker than in any year before, and the early return of the swallows foretold a pleasant summer. Peace settled over England, and Evyn foolishly thought it would remain.

One day in late spring, Evyn received a summons to appear before the Earl, and once more he headed south.

While Evyn rode through the streets of Exeter, Harold set his chessboard on the table in his chamber. Tostig, who sat across from him, shook out a large, upturned pouch. Carved wooden playing pieces tumbled over the table. Picking them up one by one, he mused as he set them in their correct positions upon the board.

"How fares the King?" Tostig asked, holding the largest playing piece.

"The King is well," Harold answered, slightly amused by his brother's artificial wit. "He wishes me Godspeed for the naval maneuvers this summer."

"That is good," Tostig said, placing the king on his square. He picked up another piece from the scattered jumble, a feminine figure. "And how fares the Queen?" he asked, peering at Harold from under his long lashes.

"When I saw her last, she was in good health but still sad

to be childless," Harold said as he placed his own king upon the board. "She misses you much. You know you have always been her favorite."

"If time allows, I will stop in London on my way north to York. I long to see her," Tostig said.

"And now it is my turn to ask you," Harold said as he found a bishop in the crowd of playing pieces before him. "How fares Ealdred, Archbishop of York?"

Tostig chuckled with affection. "His brows remain thick and black, though there is much white in his hair now. He is well and promises to hunt with me next month." He turned a bishop over in the palm of his hand, admiring the fine workmanship of the piece before placing it on the board. He became thoughtful. "The cathedral school grows in numbers and renown under the Archbishop's guidance. We will be a land of book-reading men soon if Ealdred has his way. He is both learned and prayerful, but not so prayerful as to be useless. The northerners respect him."

"You would be wise to seek his advice, then," Harold said.

Tostig shook his head, and the fiery red hair shone like the plumage of an exotic bird. "Nay," he answered, "he would have me cut the taxes. He says they are too burdensome for the people, but I told him it cannot be done."

"*'Nay'!*" Harold repeated with a laugh, echoing his opponent's foreign expression. "You speak like a northerner now."

"It is a dialect easily learned by a Saxon, but the Northumbrians still see me as an outsider. I cannot conquer their distrust. I see them watching me with suspicious eyes."

"To ease the taxes would win you many friends," Harold counseled.

"It is not friends I need," Tostig said curtly, slamming his bishop down. He grasped the next figure and held it up in Harold's face. "It is knights I need—and stronger forts, too," he said as he placed the rooks in position.

Harold said nothing as he lined his pawns in shield-wall formation before his king. It was fruitless to counsel this stubborn earl when he was in this mood.

Footsteps sounded on the stairs, and a moment later Evyn stood in the open door.

"Come in, Shadow," Harold said.

Evyn entered with a quick stride; he was glad to be there, glad to be near the Earl of Wessex again. Then he saw Harold's guest and stiffened. *Tostig!* He had wished to avoid this raven-shadowed man. He could not shake the feelings of distrust he held for Harold's brother.

Tostig looked up from the board and said, "Brother, your pawn has arrived."

"No longer a pawn," Harold replied; "only a little less than a knight."

Evyn genuflected respectfully before Harold.

"I see you have cut your hair like a Saxon," Harold said in that rich tenor which reminded Evyn of fire-warmed mead. "It becomes you. The women will have their eyes on you now."

"He looks not like a Saxon to me," Tostig retorted icily. "He is far too small and black. It is in my mind that you should throw him back, Brother, and wait for a bigger catch."

"Pay him no mind, Shadow. The Earl of Northumbria bears a sharp tongue today. I have called you here because the lad who served me as squire passed his eighteenth year. He is a man now, and will go to serve his father. So I find myself in need of a squire, and the Lady Ealdgyth recommends you."

The Lady Ealdgyth recommends you. Evyn could barely take in the Earl's words.

"You will stay here under the tutelage of the squire master," Harold continued. "He will teach you how to sit a horse correctly, and how to wield a sword and battle-ax, and the bow and arrow if you wish. I will be sailing this summer, and you will accompany me and learn one end of a longship from the other. You have been a farm boy first, a clerk second. Now you have the chance to learn the skills of a soldier. A warrior's life is an honorable one. But this is your decision; I will not command you to do it."

Evyn felt the blood rising in his cheeks. This is not what he had expected to hear. He had thought he was being recalled only to serve in the Lady's household again.

"I am asking you to be my squire, and you will be required to take the oath of loyalty to me. No man, if he is wise, does that lightly. The oath binds you to me in a special way. You must remember that my enemies, and I have many, will be your enemies. I have far more powerful foes than the likes of Gryffin. There is Harald Hardrada of Norway, who battles for the pleasure of killing. And there is Duke William in Normandy, who ever seeks to enlarge his territory. He is kinsman to our King Edward, and he covets our land. They are both far more dangerous than the puny Gryffin. You had but the merest taste of battle last winter in Carmarthen.

"Is it in your heart to serve me, to take my enemies as your enemies, and my friends as your friends?"

Evyn knew that the Earl did not overstate the danger involved, yet his heart lingered over Harold's words: *The oath binds you to me in a special way.* Evyn knew that to be true. A good squire became an extension of his lord's arm. He kept his lord's weapons sharp and his armor clean. He groomed his lord's horse. When they traveled or campaigned, it was the squire who packed and unpacked, seeing to it that all was done as his master preferred. All this he could do for Harold.

Evyn's heart seemed to stop beating. He recalled his cowardice in the cave when Harold mistakenly wrestled with his scout. Only Evyn knew of his own timid heart. Would he now have a chance to make amends, to serve Harold bravely?

Evyn nodded his assent, and Harold smiled.

"Good. Now off to the squire master with you. He has his instructions, and you have many things to learn."

As Evyn left, Tostig slid his pawn forward to begin the game. "Your new squire is a lad of few words," he said maliciously.

Harold did not bother to look up from the board. "Better that than to hear foolish gibberish and complaints. You know the proverb: He who is never silent talks much folly."

Harold moved his pawn forward, and then one of his knights in answer to Tostig's second move. Tostig picked up a bishop and eyed the playing board through slitted eyes. After a few moments he put it back and jumped his knight instead. Move, countermove, a pawn was captured here, a rook changed hands there. Twice Tostig slid his other rook forward with a laugh, cornering Harold's king, but each time Harold escaped with a strategy Tostig had not foreseen. Sometimes the Earl of Wessex played cautiously, sometimes with a recklessness that surprised his opponent. Even so, Harold could not press an advantage over his brother. He found himself playing from a defensive position. Why did it seem that Tostig chased him across the board? He had never before played so aggressively.

The opponents lapsed into silence, contemplating the

various moves open to them after each turn, barely aware that the light from the unshuttered window grew dim.

"You are more skillful than I remember," Harold said after an hour passed.

"It would please me more than you know to say I bested you," Tostig answered.

But Harold, who was the master of many games, would not allow his king to fall into checkmate. He parried each move Tostig made while the Earl of Northumbria watched in growing frustration.

"I am weary of this game, Brother," Tostig said at last. He left his seat and stared out the window for a long time.

"It is not like you to quit," Harold said, after an uneasy silence.

Tostig returned to the table, but neither man enjoyed the rest of the game. It wore on overlong and ended in a draw.

During late spring and early summer, Evyn worked with greater concentration and precision than he ever had in his life. With the other squires, he learned how to grasp a long sword, thumb topmost along the hilt for greater strength. He learned how to use a shield for balance and to block an enemy's blow. He practiced with the short bow and arrows out in the fields against the straw targets. In the afternoons he rode till he could command a horse with the touch of his knees. Sometimes the young housecarls stopped to teach wrestling and hand-to-hand combat. In the evenings when it grew too dark to work outside, Lady Ealdgyth took Evyn and the other squires aside and continued the lessons in etiquette that they had begun as pages.

"The lady is seated first, then the man. They share the drinking cup, but each sips from his or her own side. Like this . . ." The Lady Ealdgyth demonstrated as the squires and pages clustered around her. "The gentleman gives the choicest morsels of food to his lady partner, and all quarrels are set aside while guests sit at the host's table."

Time sped by quickly for Evyn. He grew taller, although not as much as he would have wished, and his shoulders widened. His muscles became hard from the daily practice. He was not the strongest of the young men, nor the most skilled with weapons, but he achieved mastery enough to avoid ridicule. His feelings for the English changed. Because they were beloved by Harold, Evyn grew to love them as well. Their lore became his lore, their heroes his heroes, and their enemies his enemies.

Harold kept his word and took Evyn with him that summer to patrol the Narrow Sea. They set sail from a sheltered bay, but an hour after the Earl's sleek new longship left the harbor, a sudden storm blew up, darkening the sky. The huge sail snapped back and forth as a wild gust of wind barreled in from the west, and the green coast of England disappeared in the thickening mist.

The wind turned cold and grew stronger with each passing moment. It roared in their ears and whipped Evyn's hair till his face stung. The waves swelled into green mountains topped by swirling yellow foam. They slammed into the ship, each one higher than the last. The pilot shouted orders from the stern, but Evyn could hear nothing, so great was the noise of the wind. Then a stinging rain broke from the skies, pelting their heads. Evyn's hair clung in wet strips on his forehead and neck, and the water trickled into his eyes and down his back. The horizon lay shrouded in rain and mist in all directions. They crashed through the water with no way of knowing how far off course they were or in what direction they were blown. Harold did what he could to reassure the men, staggering from bench to bench as the ship rose and dipped. But it was not until hours later that one of the housecarls jumped to his feet and cried out, "Land!"

There, in the gray light of dusk, on the starboard side of the prow, a jagged rock loomed from the sea. The ship, helplessly riding the thundering waves, was thrown against it. The crunch told them of the gaping hole in the starboard side. Water gushed in, flooding the deck, and the longship suddenly lurched to one side. The next wave cascaded over them, carrying away six men. Evyn grabbed a coil of rope and tossed one end to the closest man as he thrashed in the water. But the next wave came upon them like a powerful waterfall, and Evyn was thrown into the cold water. The sea closed over his face, and he saw the light above grow dim as he sank into the icy depths. Water filled his boots, turning them into weights. *So this is how death comes, with darkness and the cold penetrating to your bones*, he thought. His lungs felt as if they would burst.

Suddenly a strong force pulled him to the surface. His face broke from the water, and he gasped for air, choking and coughing. A wave crashed over his head, shoving him toward a cluster of dangerous-looking rocks jutting sharply from the water, but the force that had pulled him up kept him safe from harm. Someone gripped the neck of his tunic. It was Harold, his golden hair the color of wet sand. There was no sign of the longship.

"Do not struggle against the water," Harold cautioned breathlessly. "Ride it, and it will carry us in to shore."

Evyn jerked his head toward the horizon. Pinpoints of light flickered there from oil-soaked torches. He thought he heard the sound of horses, made nervous by the storm, whinny excitedly. A moment later he felt pebbles under his feet as the waves pushed them toward the stony shore.

Then, with one last burst of strength, Harold pulled his young squire up onto solid ground.

Evyn lay on the wet stones for what seemed like a long time, so welcome was the firm earth beneath him. When he finally rolled over and sat up, he saw eight or ten of their number near him. Several of the rowers survived, and four or five housecarls crawled on their hands and knees, spitting up water. Evyn was glad to see Hakon among them.

Evyn looked around—surely they must be somewhere near Hastings, or perhaps farther east, near the city of Dover. People along the southern coast were all Saxons and under Harold's jurisdiction.

Evyn shivered with the cold. Dusk was turning to starless night when he heard a horse whinny again. Up along the grassy dunes, a line of riders watched, several of them holding torches. How glad Evyn was to see them. But as they rode forward he saw that they wore their hair shorter than Saxons, and several sported a kind of long, pointed cap Evyn had never before seen.

Harold faced the riders squarely, returning their suspicious stares with his own unflinching gaze. Though his clothes hung heavy with seawater, his hair tangled and matted around his face, the Earl of Wessex radiated the strength and dignity that earned him respect from his men and fear from his enemies.

"What land is this and who is your lord?" he asked the front rider.

1064

In this year a storm left Earl Harold shipwrecked . . .

The horseman, a young man with a long thin nose and a small mouth, turned to his companions and spoke in a strange tongue. The comment, which brought laughter, was spoken in a fluid language all softness and trills, far unlike the rolling, melodic cadence of the English tongue or the rounded vowels of Evyn's people.

Hakon and the few housecarls who survived formed a defensive circle around Harold and drew their short daggers, for their heavier weapons had sunk to the bottom of the sea with the longship. Instantly the riders, who far outnumbered Harold's men, unsheathed their long swords or nocked arrows in their bowstrings, taking aim at the Saxons.

"Drop your daggers, men," Harold said. "This would make a foolhardy fight. It is in my mind that they mean us no harm. While the custom along this barbarous coast seems not to be the hospitality due to shipwrecked men, neither is it murder. I suspect it is a ransom of gold that will please them most."

The housecarls obeyed, letting their daggers clatter upon the stones at their feet. Harold unclasped the band of gold circling his wrist. Tossing it up to the leader, he said, "Tell your lord that this is a gift from Harold, Earl of Wessex."

The treasure proved him a powerful and wealthy man. King Edward would pay much for his safe return.

"That should buy our safety for a time," Harold explained quietly to his own men.

The rider greedily fingered Harold's gold bracelet and parted his thin lips in a smile. He held it up and shouted to his companions who surrounded the tiny band of Saxons, motioning for them to follow. Harold spoke reassuringly to his men. "For now we must follow the holy words: *Be as harmless as doves and as wary as serpents.*"

Before they had gone very far, a second group of horsemen approached at a gallop. The leader, a portly man with an old scar dissecting one eyebrow, spoke to Harold's captors in the same strange language, finally dismissing them. He eyed Harold cautiously, then wheeled his horse about and, with his bodyguard surrounding the Saxons, led them along a westward road.

"That is Count Guy of Ponthieu," Harold whispered to Evyn. "Though he is courageous, there is not one drop of honor in his veins."

After a march of several leagues, Evyn made out the dark outline of a fortress looming on a hilltop. Built of stone, it was massive and more heavily fortified than any of the Saxon forts he had seen. They crossed a drawbridge over a wide moat dug around the base of the castle. After a few shouts were exchanged, the iron gate of the portcullis rose, and the English preceded their captors through the courtyard to a towering keep. There the strangers prodded the prisoners as they descended narrow, circling steps to a dungeon. Walls of cold, damp stone bound them in, and the rank smell of mold suffocated them.

The guards opened an iron-clad door in the heart of the tower and, after searching each man for hidden weapons, rudely shoved them within. The door slammed shut with a resounding clang and the bolt was thrust into place. That was followed by the sound of the guards speaking in their strange tongue. Harold listened intently.

"As I thought. This is Castle Beaurain," Harold said after the guards went away. "It is held by Count Guy of Ponthieu. He is Duke William's vassal."

"So we are in a stew, are we not, my lord?" Hakon asked dejectedly as he ran his fingers through his unkempt hair.

Harold sat down on one of the wooden benches ringing the dungeon and smiled ruefully. "Perhaps—perhaps not. We will see how quickly the news of our capture flies. It is in my thoughts that Count Guy will probably apply to King Edward to see how much gold he can demand in ransom for an English earl. If the saints are with us, we will see the soil of England soon." Harold stretched his bad leg before him. He motioned to his men to sit. "Now it is time to rest and gather what strength we can."

The men sank down. The chill seeped into their bones, and their stomachs growled with hunger. No one dared speak of what might happen if the saints were not with them.

Evyn, too, was cold and weary. His teeth chattered, and he folded his arms tightly across his wet tunic to keep from shivering. He thought of those men whose pale faces and flailing arms were claimed by the sea. He had been among their number until Harold pulled him to the surface, to air and life. He watched as his master bound a field bandage around the gashed arm of one of the rowers. Evyn took a stone from the dungeon floor and scratched thin white letters upon the wall, touched the Earl, and gestured to it.

" 'Thank you for saving my life.' " Harold looked up from the letters solemnly. "It was a debt I was glad to repay."

Later, Harold spoke soft and comforting words to ease the fear that chewed at the hearts of his men. One by one they fell into an exhausted sleep.

On the third day the guards talked nervously on the other side of the heavy dungeon door. Harold shook his head in exasperation. "I can make out so little of this foreign talk. They are expecting someone to arrive soon."

"Perhaps a courier with the ransom money," Hakon offered, his wide mouth spreading in a hopeful smile.

"It is too soon for Gyrth or even King Edward to gather any sizable amount and send it here. I do not know," Harold said quietly, smoothing his mustache.

Early on the morning of the fourth day, their captors roused the band of Englishmen, herding them up the stairs and into the glaring sunlight. Count Guy, with a grim expression made all the more menacing by his scarred eyebrow, led them to the city of Eu on the Norman frontier. Though they were given fine Norman horses to ride and were spoken to through a courteous interpreter, at Eu they once again found themselves in the castle keep. There they waited and waited.

Around noontime on the next day the sound of hooves clattering upon the cobblestone courtyard filtered through the small high window. They heard jangling bridles and the noise of men dismounting and dusting themselves off.

Somewhere outside, a man growled orders in a deep voice ill matched to the soft language Evyn heard from the guards. There was silence then, and the anxious prisoners strained their ears in vain. The moments passed so slowly that even Hakon finally slumped to a bench, clenching his fists in silent agony.

Clanging sounded on the stairs, as if many men were descending the narrow stone steps. On the other side of the door came the same growling voice, in a tone that suggested the speaker was well accustomed to giving orders and being obeyed immediately. The bolt slid back, and the iron door swung wide with a creak.

A huge man, with the light at his back, stood framed by the door. He planted his feet far apart in a warrior stance with his arms akimbo. His hair, palest orange and stiff as a boar's bristles, was cut very close to his head and shaved high up his neck. He wore a mail shirt of unsurpassed quality, his waist girded by a long sword with an elaborate ruby-encrusted hilt. His height and breadth dwarfed the guards behind him.

His eyes, shadowed by pale but bushy brows, flitted from face to face as though searching for one man in particular. When they rested on Earl Harold, his gaze froze, and he asked, "Who among you is Harold of Wessex?"

He spoke in Latin, the common language of the Church.

Harold drew himself up to his full height, and although he was two hands' breadth shorter than the newcomer, he was an imposing man with the agile body of an athlete. Evyn was proud to notice that the sea-stiffened clothes and tangled hair of his master did nothing to diminish his dignity.

"Who asks for King Edward's Earl?" Harold replied in his masterful voice.

"King Edward's cousin," the answer shot back arrow-quick. But just as quickly the growl of the newcomer softened. "I, William, Duke of Normandy, welcome Harold of Wessex, King Edward's good servant. I apologize for the rough treatment. Rest assured that Count Guy has felt my wrath. We are not all barbarians ignorant of the customs of hospitality. If you and your men are well, and it is my fervent wish that that be true, then we will leave here at once."

Hakon, who, unlike the other housecarls, knew Church talk, heaved a sigh of relief and grinned. But Harold, cautious as ever, bowed courteously. There was a stiffness in his manner that spoke of wariness.

He is on his guard, Evyn thought.

With the Duke's next words, the smile slipped from Hakon's face.

"You are in my custody now," the Duke said. "May it prove gracious to you." Although the red-haired Duke bared his teeth in a smile, the emphasis was unmistakably upon the words *my custody*.

At that moment Evyn understood what Harold had already sensed, that they were all caught in a dangerous game. Were they simply to be tossed from one captor to another? Rulers often played clever games with hostages, and it was not uncommon for a highborn man to spend his life as a prisoner after falling into the wrong hands.

Harold turned to his men and spoke in the English tongue. "We are guests of Duke William now. Conduct yourselves in a way to bring honor to your people so that it may be said that the Saxons are proud and forthright. But when questioned, guard your speech and say no more than is necessary."

To Duke William he said in their common language, "We gratefully accept your hospitality."

. . .

Thus began a tense summer for Evyn. They immediately set out for the Duke's stronghold at Rouen. Evyn rode up front at Harold's side, while Hakon and the other housecarls were kept in the middle of the mounted procession. On the first day the column of riders wound its way through the forests of Normandy, surrounded by broad-leaved trees of oak, beech, and hornbeam. Always the Norman knights hemmed them in, keeping their hands on the hilts of their swords. Evyn knew that they regarded Harold as their enemy.

On the second day they rode past fields thick with wheat and barley. Sheep crowded the rolling hills, the lambs bleating for their mothers. In the afternoon they passed a caravan of merchants traveling to a summer fair. *This is a wealthy land,* Evyn thought.

The Duke, who was fond of his own conversation, talked overlong. He asked many questions, most of which Harold parried with polite excuses. When Harold proved too quiet for the Duke's wishes, William turned to Evyn, asking, "Squire, will you join your King's fyrd when the time comes?"

Evyn made the sign to indicate he was mute.

"My squire cannot speak," Harold explained.

Duke William drew back in distaste. "I will not abide a mutilated man in my own entourage."

At noon on the third day, under a glaring French sun, they reached Rouen. Their first sight of the city included the severed heads of men who had incurred the Duke's anger. These he had placed at the gates as a warning. Behind the gory heads, the walls of the city rose higher than Exeter's. Soldiers patrolled the gates and kept watch from the top of the walls. Rouen was heavily fortified by a man who trusted no one. Within, the city buzzed like an angry beehive—merchants, tradesmen, peasants, and soldiers poured through the streets. Rats ran through piles of stinking garbage, and scavenging dogs roamed in every alley, while beggars clustered at each corner pleading for alms. The Saxons' host, blind to the ills of his dukedom, took great delight in pointing out the marvels of his city.

"My dear Earl Harold, what think you of my markets? They overflow with goods brought from afar: fine leather from Italy, figs and oil from the Holy Land, and thick wool from Spain."

Harold answered politely and then retreated to his only defense: silence.

That was their welcome to Normandy. From the moment Duke William's broad silhouette filled their cell door he treated the English with unbearably smooth courtesy but always with a touch of mockery and even a hint of deceit. Evyn's skin grew cold whenever he was forced to be near the Duke, and that was often. As Harold's squire, he was expected to be at his master's side at all times, and Duke William rarely allowed Harold out of his sight.

The days crawled by with a terrible slowness. Midsummer turned to high summer, the time the Normans called August after the Roman custom, and still they were detained at the Duke's court.

Evyn longed to escape. *If only there were some way to slip away, to bribe some fisherman to take us back across the Narrow Sea, to England and freedom.* But Duke William kept a constant guard on the tiny band of Englishmen.

Each day the Duke asked in his gruff voice, "Will the Earl of Wessex honor me at my table?"

And each day Harold answered, "If it pleases the Duke."

Evyn stood behind Harold's chair throughout each torturous meal, noting how little his lord ate. Harold sipped the strange drink made from apples which the Normans called cider. Only Evyn saw that it was distasteful to him and guessed how much his master longed for the warmed mead of his homeland.

One day in late summer as they sat idly at table, the Duke's Hall noisy with conversation, a Norman messenger raced in, knelt before his master, and began to whisper the tidings he carried.

"Speak up, man. We keep no secrets from the Earl of Wessex," the Duke growled.

The messenger, startled, repeated his news. "M-my lord, there is an uprising in Brittany. Conan, Count of Brittany, and his people are revolting against your rule."

The Duke sat back so heavily in his chair that the wood creaked. His face grew dark with rage and his eyebrows drew together in a frown. He clenched his teeth so that the muscles in his jaw worked tensely.

The Duchess Matilda placed her tiny hand on the Duke's arm. "It is ill news, my lord," she said, her eyes wide with concern.

He rudely snatched his arm from her gentle touch and drew a breath to shout at his wife when he stopped, suddenly aware again of Harold's presence. Instead, he picked up his drinking bowl, gazing at the liquid within as he thought. The frown lifted from his face, and a cruel smile twisted his lips.

"No, it is not ill news at all, my Lady. On the contrary, it affords an opportunity for our guests to see more of our beautiful country. It seems to me," the Duke said slowly and deliberately, "that this disturbance can be turned to our advantage. I have as my guest the ablest general in the northern world." He turned to Harold. "Surely you would not refuse me the privilege of your companionship on this campaign, along with your advice on military matters."

Quick-witted as his master was, Evyn saw that Harold was taken aback, his usual eloquence momentarily gone. Nevertheless, he remained composed and lowered his head as if to say, "As you wish."

The Duke roughly pushed his chair back. "Good, it is settled. We ride west tomorrow. Of course, your squire may accompany you, but I think it best that the rest of your men remain here. I use the sword to deal with rebels, and I do not wish to expose my guests to unnecessary danger." With an artificial bow to Harold, he strode from the Great Hall.

That night in his small chamber, hung with silks and velvets, Harold sat in contemplation as Evyn unlaced the Earl's boots and slid them from his feet.

"Shadow, he is sly and dangerous," Harold said. "He means to have me killed in battle in Brittany. He covets England and longs to sit on King Edward's throne. If I die, he would have an easy path climbing over the backs of the English people. We are walking through a treacherous swamp here, and it will take all our wits to stay alive and return to our island home."

Evyn placed the soft leather boots to the side of Harold's chair and looked up into his master's face. The lines under Harold's eyes were more pronounced, and there was a faraway look in his gaze. Evyn knew that his lord was considering the courses of action open to them. They were frighteningly few.

"By Christ's Holy Cross," Harold said softly, coming out of his reverie, "if it is God's will that we return safely to England, then we will do so. If it is His will that we end our lives here, then it must be with courage and honor, is that not right?" He looked Evyn directly in the eye. "I have had many lads serve me as squire over the years, but I tell you most solemnly that it is your quiet companionship and thoughtful ways that I have treasured most. Are you with me?"

Evyn nodded, and not since the day he had taken his oath of fealty had he felt so strongly his affirmation of service to Harold. He rose and straightened the cloak Harold had tossed over the bench. How foolish he had been when Gryffin and his sons lay dead on the field. Evyn had thought himself safe, that he no longer had enemies. Now that he was Harold's squire, caught in bonds of loyalty, the Earl's enemies were his own. It seemed strange to Evyn then that although these new enemies were more powerful, he no longer felt paralyzed by fear. He increasingly saw the Earl, with his calm manner, as an echo of his father, whom he missed so terribly. Though the morrow brought uncertainty and possible death, Evyn fell into a deep and peaceful sleep that night.

There was no dawn to speak of, for heavy clouds rolled in across the Narrow Sea, covering Normandy in a thick fog. When the city's early morning bells pealed, Evyn woke and dressed. He set out Harold's riding clothes. As he stood at the chamber's tiny window, he heard the first rolling booms of thunder far to the west, foretelling a long day of hard rain. While Evyn stared across the thatched rooftops of Rouen, wondering whether he should wake his weary lord, there came a knock at the door.

Evyn admitted one of Duke William's chamber men, who said, "Hurry and ready yourselves. The Duke intends to leave now."

Minutes after Harold awoke, he and Evyn made their way to the courtyard and mounted their borrowed horses. Duke William whipped his stallion to a fast gallop as they rode over the bridge crossing the Seine River. Traveling westward out of the city, the Norman army, both mounted men and foot soldiers, began the week-long journey to Brittany to face the rebel forces. Before the hour was out, the rain began. It fell first as soft droplets, but soon turned into a stinging downpour. It rained all day long, all night, and for the next two days and nights. But the Duke made no concession, though his men suffered much.

Toward week's end the rain eased, but when they reached the banks of the river Couesnon the swollen channel surged with water. It was flecked with foam, and torn branches clogged the surface.

"It is far too dangerous to ford the river here, my lord," Duke William's scout reported. "We must ride upriver five leagues to the next ford."

"My fury grows with each passing moment," William responded, angered beyond all reason by the delay. He cruelly jerked his reins and spurred his tired mount upriver.

Hours later, when they reached the next ford, the Duke's face grew red with rage. The river still surged high. Two of his infantrymen, sensing the Duke's impatience, ventured to test the current.

"It is still dangerous, my lord," the scout cautioned.

"Let them cross," William answered, his eyes trained on the two soldiers wading into the water. He took his gaze from his men for a moment and turned to Harold. "Normans make the best soldiers in the western world. See how eagerly they race to battle."

But at that moment one of the men slipped and was swept away with the current past the spot where William sat on his stallion. The soldier's head broke above the muddy water for an instant, long enough for the terrified man to scream for help.

William appeared embarrassed that one of his men should have failed in his attempt to cross.

"Fool! That he could not keep his footing."

But Harold did not hear. He leaped down from his horse and rushed to the water's edge. Evyn, without stopping to think, followed his master. They raced along the riverbank, keeping pace with the drowning man. As they ran, Harold untied the belt at his waist, ready to toss the end to the Norman soldier. But as he broke the surface of the water again, Evyn saw with alarm that the man's eyes had rolled back in his head; he could do nothing to help himself. Without breaking stride, Harold threw the belt to Evyn, bolted ahead, and dived into the churning water. He grabbed William's man, now limp and heavy, and pulled him to the surface. Evyn tossed one end of Harold's belt to him a moment before they would have been swept out of reach downriver. Wrapping the other end around his wrist, Evyn clutched a riverbank sapling to steady himself as the belt was jerked taut by the current pulling at Harold and the Norman. Evyn's hands were rubbed raw as he grasped the sapling. Just as he felt that the force of the river would pull them all away, Harold found his footing, dragging himself and the Norman soldier to safety.

The Norman lay deathly pale and motionless. *It is too late,* Evyn thought.

But Harold rolled the man over onto his belly and pounded on his back. There was no response. Harold continued, though his own chest heaved for air. William, who had dismounted, and the other Normans reached them now. A small crowd formed around Harold as he stubbornly fought for the man's life. At that moment the man's body shook violently and a gurgling noise erupted from his throat. He coughed, and his chest rattled. Then he vomited all the river water he had swallowed, gagging for a long time till his face grew pink once more.

The Normans were amazed by this Englishman who brought the dead back to life. Had they not seen the man dragged cold and lifeless from the water? Yet here he was, coughing and gasping for air before their eyes. They were impressed by Harold's courage and strength, and touched by his concern for a foreigner, a lowly foot soldier. *"L'Anglais est très courageux,"* they said.

Duke William shook his head cynically. "You carry the heavy responsibility of keeping King Edward's southern coast safe, yet you risk your life for a Norman foot soldier. That is not wise, my friend."

Harold lifted his head as one of the Normans draped a cloak over his dripping tunic. "You are wrong," he said, and for the first time Evyn heard his master speak from the heart to his captor. "A wise general knows he can do nothing without the men who risk their lives for him."

Duke William raised one eyebrow in disdain and strode away.

1064

. . . and he and his men spent many weeks
at the Norman court.

After that, the Duke's soldiers treated Harold with the greatest respect and admiration, and William dared not endanger his English guest in a dispute between Normans and Bretons. The Duke crushed the rebellion swiftly with no offer of negotiations, spilling more blood than was necessary. Uncharacteristically, William spoke not one word to Harold on the ride back to Rouen, and Evyn worried that Harold's act of heroism, which bought them temporary safety, might have turned the Duke against him with venomous hatred.

"His silence worries me, Shadow," Harold said one evening a few days later, as they sat in the Duke's orchard. "He is cunning. Being trapped here all this time has been like grasping a wriggling asp. He will use force or guile to achieve his ends." Harold closed his eyes and rested his weary head against the trunk of a small apple tree.

In the morning, without warning, word was sent to Harold to ready himself and his men for another journey. This time their destination was Bonneville-sur-Touques, where Duke William's noblemen had requested a council.

When Harold told his captain, Hakon smiled delightedly. "Bonneville-sur-Touques . . . that is a port city. He has grown tired of us and dares not besiege his cousin King Edward with ransom demands. We are to be sent home finally."

"I hope you are right," Harold said as he pinned his cloak at the shoulder. "But I dare not trust him."

Everything William now did bore out Hakon's speculation. They rode west for two days in great pomp with crowds cheering them along the way. When they reached Lisieux, they boarded a wide river barge. William insisted that Harold travel by his side throughout their journey, and now on board the boat, in contrast to his silence on the ride back to Rouen, the Duke spoke, about the most inconsequential of subjects. Harold, for the safety of his men, played his end of the charade. He smiled at the Duke's jokes, chatted amiably, and revealed as little information as he dared.

"I trust that your harvest was abundant last autumn," the Duke rumbled. "A country is only as strong as its dinner table, and a famished people find it hard to defend themselves."

"The English have enough to eat and appreciate the concern you feel for them," Harold answered.

"And your forests are plentiful. I imagine you have a surplus of lumber, perhaps for building longships or forts. I understand you have a fine wooden fort at Pevensey."

There was no such fort there, only the stone ruins of an ancient Roman fort. Harold saw that William was attempting to trick him into verifying his scouts' reports, trying to tease out of him the best place for an invading army to land. But Harold was too wise to be so easily fooled.

"King Edward is a good king. He defends his people with many forts along the coastline."

"Yes, of course, it would be a terrible disaster were England to be invaded by her enemies," William growled.

Like all good generals, Harold sensed when to take a defensive stand and when to go on the offensive. So for the first time he seized the conversation and steered it away from his weak spots, aiming to keep William on guard.

"You never confided the nature of the uprising in Brittany. Have your Breton subjects been misled by their Count?"

Evyn watched Duke William stiffen. He reckoned Harold was the first ever to speak so candidly about weaknesses in the Duke's own realm. William's face grew red with anger. "You chat lightheartedly about sensitive Norman matters of state." His voice rose as he spoke, and Evyn sensed that the Duke was ready to erupt in fury. But then his tone changed to a condescending pleasantness as if his revenge against this popular and eloquent Earl could wait.

"It was a small matter," he said. "There is no need to trouble yourself with it." He stood abruptly and made his way on steady legs to the prow of the barge, where he remained for some time before returning to his guest.

Evyn faced the riverbank where the willow trees dipped their long fingerlike branches into the water as the barge lazily floated past. In their shade, the first of the autumn leaves glided like tiny yellow and scarlet boats. A trout leaped from the placid water, causing a splash and a growing ripple.

"Soon we will reach the city," William said.

They passed the tanning district situated on the outskirts

of Bonneville-sur-Touques. The smell of decaying animal flesh hung heavily on the air. Evyn was reminded of the whispered talk in the narrow hallways and cramped servants' rooms in the Duke's castle in Rouen. It was said that William was the grandson of an ordinary tanner. This tanner had a lovely daughter, Herleve, whose beauty captured the heart of Duke Robert. Though William's father accepted him as his son and heir, Robert never married Herleve, and so the Duke's enemies called him William the Bastard behind his back.

Soon they spied the towers of the city rising above the flat line of the river. The cry of sea gulls reached their ears. Women carrying large wicker baskets of laundry threaded their way down a path leading to the river. Many were already soaping and rinsing the clothes, their skirts tied above their knees as they waded into the water. Tunics, mantles, and chemises lay stretched over bushes to dry. The younger girls laughed and sang as they tended little brothers and sisters.

"You will see the harbor when we round this next bend in the river. I think you will find it interesting," William said.

Evyn eyed him coldly. His physical presence was so intimidating that his officers and courtiers, even his wife, Matilda, cowered before him. *It is not that way with Harold*, Evyn thought. One could be honest and fearless before the Earl of Wessex. He looked to Harold, who sat on a cushioned bench. His master gazed pensively at the sun-sparkled water as it dripped from the swinging oar blades.

At orders from the helmsman, the portside rowers lifted their oars while their starboard companions, with long sweeping strokes, turned the prow of the wide barge eastward around the river's bend. As they straightened, and the portside rowers dipped their oars again, the harbor and city swung into view. Sea gulls circled the fishing boats as the day's catch of eel and herring was brought in and hauled ashore. But what caught Evyn's eye was the sight of a tall-masted English longship.

Hakon jumped to his feet. "Look, my lord, it is the *Wave Rider*!"

Harold stood also, shading his eyes from the sun's glare reflecting off the water. It was indeed the *Wave Rider*, and the few Saxons lining her deck cheered when they spotted their Earl unharmed.

Tears sprang to Evyn's eyes; he was so glad to see the men of his own island again. He wanted to dive into the blue water and swim to the longship, so impatient was he to be sailing for England. Harold, too, was touched and put his arm around Evyn's shoulder. "We shall celebrate soon," he said quietly.

"See, I have brought you safely to your own people," William said.

"We are grateful," Harold said formally. "When I reach England, King Edward shall hear of your kindness."

"I hope you are not so eager to be rid of us that you must make haste for England. I have planned a final feast for you on Norman soil. There are men here I wish you to meet."

Harold hesitated. He wanted nothing so much as to be free of this treacherous Norman Duke. But he was not so foolish as to truly see himself as Duke William's guest. No, he and his men were still hostages. Harold was sure of it when he saw that the *Wave Rider* was manned by weaponless oarsmen, a gray-haired pilot, and a helmsman too young to have grown a mustache.

"I shall not keep you long," the Duke promised. "I want only to bind the ties of friendship between us."

"It must be as you wish," Harold said.

All of Harold's party except the Earl and Evyn were dismissed to their longship to await their master. William and his escort took them to the ducal Hall, which stood on high ground not far from the waterfront. The doors stood open and the tall narrow shutters were thrown back so that shafts of mote-filled sunlight punctuated the interior. As they entered, the trumpeter sounded a blast, and the Normans within turned their attention to the Duke and his guests. William's men fell back to allow him room to pass. Harold followed behind with Evyn at his shoulder.

The Normans came to the Duke one by one, bowing obsequiously.

First came Odo, William's obese half brother, who had been named Bishop of Bayeux. Evyn had never seen anyone who looked less like a bishop, with his pouty lips and sleepy eyes. "I was glad to hear that you crushed the Bretons," he said.

Then the Duke's other half brother, Robert of Mortain, bowed his greeting. Behind him was the only man, so they said, that William trusted completely, his adviser and seneschal William Fitzosbern. He ran the Duke's household and administered all his lands for him. Though he had passed his prime and his shorn hair had turned gray, Fitzosbern retained his cold warrior's glance. With him came old Roger of Tosny, Fitzosbern's father-in-law. Then followed a succession of faces representing the great families of Normandy: Richard Fitzgilbert, Hugh d'Avranches, Hugh de Montfort, and Maurilius, Archbishop of Rouen.

Harold forced himself to smile and bow graciously as he was introduced to the great men of the realm, who could provide William with soldiers, ships, and horses. It was the Duke's plan to impress upon Harold the wealth and power of Normandy, and Harold saw his purpose. This was not a cordial parting; this was William displaying a captured general to intimidate his hostage and to amuse his noble vassals. When the long procession of Norman landholders dressed in their imported silk tunics ended, the Duke said, "Shall we eat?"

A legion of servants carried course after course from the kitchen: mutton and pork, salted eel, bread, cheese, apples, and apricots from the south, and, as always, the Norman cider.

Evyn fidgeted restlessly. He thought only of the ship in the harbor. But Harold remained controlled. He ate slowly and complimented the food. He answered all questions put to him. He even sipped the cider.

After the meal the toasts began, and, because Duke William had introduced Harold as his trusted ally and adviser on English matters, the salutations were warm and polite. Harold sat erect and courteous through it all, while Evyn grew flustered and longed to be aboard the *Wave Rider*.

Finally the Duke rose and, raising his goblet, said, "It has been our privilege to enjoy the company of Earl Harold of Wessex for these past two months. We are loath to part with his company. I speak for myself, my family, and the lords of Normandy in my wish for closer ties with England. We seek to bind ourselves to our cousin Edward with cords of love. And so it is with solemn pleasure that I announce the betrothal of my daughter Agatha to Earl Harold of Wessex."

The color drained from Harold's face, and his arms fell limp at his sides. A marriage betrothal! To deny this would be an insult to William and his daughter. It would never be forgiven.

"And to strengthen those ties further, Harold has agreed to be my man in England, to pay me tribute, and to acknowledge me as his lord. When my beloved cousin Edward dies, I will take his place on the throne of England. To make these agreements formal and binding, Harold has asked to swear the oath of fealty here before you as witnesses. Then we will all wish him Godspeed on his journey home."

With a gesture, William sent the page at his elbow from the Hall. A moment later the lad returned, bearing two ornately jeweled reliquaries to be used for the oath-taking.

"The last two months have shown me that the Earl of Wessex is an honorable man. What he speaks is the truth, and you have heard me say that he has agreed to all that I have said. So, before you, my brothers, my friends, and my allies, there is no need for an oath-taking. But in our negotiations Harold insisted upon this. This is to protect Harold," William said condescendingly, with his hand upon his chest. "The Duke of Normandy needs no such protection," and his laughter rumbled through the Hall. "There is no need to fear, my dear Earl, I will not promise my lovely Agatha to another man."

Oh! How furious Evyn grew. He wanted to leap onto the table and shout, "*Liar!* Everything he says is a lie!"

He cursed the day he lost his tongue. But, voice or no, he would not stand idly at his master's shoulder and allow him to endure this betrayal. There was a way to silence this vile Duke forever. Evyn stared at the small dagger Harold had used during the meal. It rested on the tablecloth before him. If he acted quickly, he could save Harold from this treachery. He would kill the Duke for Harold's sake. He knew how to do it. Had not Hakon taught him? Evyn snatched at the gleaming knife, but Harold instantly clamped his hand upon the boy's wrist.

Only one man saw what took place between the Englishman and his young squire. William did not falter in his speech, but his eyes flickered to the table where Harold grasped Evyn's wrist inches from the dagger.

"Yes, my friends," he said, his bulky chest puffed out. "These English have grown very dear to me."

Evyn found himself helpless in the grip of the man he most wanted to help. He strained against Harold till the color rose in his cheeks; the dagger was so close. The Normans in the cavernous Hall remained unaware. A bowl of apples hid Evyn's hand and the dagger from their view. William's noblemen had filled their bellies and were drowsy. They could never dash to the High Table in time to save their Duke. But Harold made no move to release his hand, and Evyn's fingertips grew cold and tingly. All the while, droning in the background, William rambled on, speaking of the Earl's many fine qualities.

Finally Harold tilted his head back slightly and whispered to Evyn, "This is neither the time nor the place. God is our witness to this villainy. We must be content to return to England and see to it that this knavish Duke is never allowed to land."

As he spoke to Evyn, Harold studied the crowd of Norman counts and landowners listening to William's speech. Without exception, their eyes were on their Duke.

Then Harold looked Evyn in the eye until his squire finally nodded obediently. Satisfied, the Earl released his hold.

"I see our English friends are eager to sail home, so we will delay only for these formalities, and then we will see them off," William said, taking Harold's arm, as he would a child's, and leading him to the reliquaries. Although this was a coerced oath and not legally binding, Harold had no way to prove that it was an unwilling pledge without endangering all his men. Evyn watched helplessly as Harold placed one hand upon the box on his right side and the other hand upon the box on his left. He repeated in tones barely above a whisper the conditions William set before him. This was an oath, a mortal matter before God, and Harold knew that oath-breakers were condemned to eternal fire. "One does not take an oath lightly," Harold had said to Evyn once. And now, for the sake of his people left undefended in England and for the safe release of the men with him here in Normandy, Harold repeated William's words, his hands trembling as they rested lightly upon the boxes.

"I, Harold Godwinson, Earl of Wessex, solemnly swear to accept William, Duke of Normandy, as my overlord. I will accept William as the lawful heir to the English throne should King Edward die childless. I pledge my betrothal to Duke William's daughter Agatha. I will use my power and wealth to ensure William's succession to the throne, and I will keep a garrison of Duke William's knights at Dover Castle at my own expense. So help me God and all the saints."

Taking the boxes, William held them aloft one at a time, turning so that all might see their jeweled brilliance. Opening the lid of one, he exposed the contents first to Harold and then to his own vassals. Harold became sorely alarmed. Other men might foolishly shrug it off, but Harold of Wessex was not a foolish man. There within the box was no mere scrap of cloth worn by a holy priest but the bones of a saint, and an oath sworn on bones was the most binding.

Harold's face, which was white as ashes, bore a stricken expression as though he had drunk poison.

This will kill him, Evyn thought.

Harold stood frozen in place, distraught over his actions. As a Christian, he knew that to forswear an oath would place his own soul in mortal peril, and it would drag his country into war with Normandy, but to keep such an oath would be traitorous to his people.

Earlier, Harold sensed Evyn's thoughts when he snatched at the knife, and now Evyn felt the Earl's pain. He ran to his side, and with his right hand he grasped Harold's arm and with his left he made a fist over his heart. It was the Saxon sign for courage.

Harold drew himself up to his full height. Without speaking a word of farewell to his "host," he left the Hall with Evyn.

1065

. . . though he spoke with the greatest eloquence, Harold could not persuade them.

Immediately upon their return to England, Harold visited the King in London. There Edward was supervising the last details of his magnificent new church, Westminster Abbey. It rose, stone by stone, above the thatched rooftops of London.

Closeted in the King's private chamber, they conferred for several hours while Evyn wandered the crowded Hall and bustling passageways of the palace. When they emerged for the noon meal, Harold told everyone about the terrible storm. For diplomatic reasons, since the King was half-Norman by birth and education, the story Harold told was less than the whole truth. William had been a gracious host to shipwrecked sailors and nothing more.

Later that same day, Harold and Evyn rode five leagues north of the city with the Earl setting a recklessly fast pace on a barely broken stallion. They thundered through the Chiltern Forest with its gigantic oak trees, their path carpeted with the first of the autumn leaves. As they raced through Waltham's open gates, the Lady Ealdgyth Swan Neck ran from the Great Hall, tears streaming down her pale cheeks.

As she reached Harold's stallion, she cried in a broken voice, "My darling! I thought you were dead . . . and then we heard that you were being held hostage. I didn't know what to believe."

Harold leaned down and tenderly swept her up into the saddle before him. He whispered sweetly in her ear, his mustache brushing her cheek. She turned and gazed at him, the tears glistening in her eyes. Without another word, she threw her arms around his neck like a young girl. During the days that followed, there was laughter and music whenever he was with the Lady. Only Evyn saw his troubled face when the Earl thought he was alone.

The last days of Holymonth came and Evyn received permission to ride to Aethelney Monastery. He longed to see Lewys, and he planned to help the monks with their apple harvest and further his studies while he was there. The merchants' caravan with which Evyn rode made its way west. The autumn fog rolled down into the valleys across the wooded hillsides, and the drizzle fell without end. It made for a long journey, but Evyn's weariness disappeared when the tower of Aethelney loomed through the mist. The bells pealed at the approach of visitors. When Lewys saw Evyn among their number, he pulled his friend off his horse and wrapped him in a crushing hug.

The seasons passed quickly. Autumn raced by, spreading her golds and russets across the hills of England till the last of the red apples went into storage. Then winter found Evyn, his scarlet cloak pulled tight against the chill, in the scriptorium practicing his letters and writing an account of

Harold's summer in Normandy in the monastery Chronicle. The end of yuletide he spent in the infirmary with Brother Alfred, caring for those who lay ill with the winter fever. The stoop-shouldered monk continued teaching him about healing and herbs. When the spring sun melted the last of the snow, Evyn left Aethelney and returned to Exeter, where Harold was overseeing the minting of coins. Hakon was there, too, and promised to instruct Evyn further in weapon skill and horsemanship. So May, which the Saxons called Threemilki because that was the time the farmers milked their cows three times each day, found Evyn in a field with a sparring partner, practicing the parry and thrust of shield and longsword.

When autumn came again, Harold and Evyn traveled to Harold's fortress at Northampton, where Lady Ealdgyth waited for them.

"He has grown a hand's breadth surely," the Lady exclaimed when she caught sight of Evyn leading his horse to the stable.

Evyn grinned and saluted. He was fond of Aethelney, and he loved Lewys, but this was his place. To be at Harold's side was where he belonged, serving him however he could.

Harold clapped one arm around Evyn's shoulder and said, "Let us see if the cook will feed us."

As they strode up the lane toward the Great Hall, a sentry posted on the catwalk shouted, "My lord, many riders approach from the north!"

"Come with me, Shadow. We shall see who visits," Harold said.

They climbed the ladder leading up to the catwalk and gazed out over the brown fields of the estate. The river Nene disappeared like a ribbon in the distance. On the horizon, perhaps half a league beyond the river, a line of black-clad riders kicked their mounts into a trot as they neared Northampton's walls.

"It is Earl Edwin, is it not, Sire?" the sentry asked.

Harold shielded his eyes from the brightness of the noon-time sun and squinted at the distant horsemen.

"Yes, it is Earl Edwin, with his brother Morcar by his side, if I am not mistaken."

Edwin was the son and heir of his late father Alfgar, Earl of Mercia. Though he was barely out of his teens, he was not a foolish young man. He kept good counselors and governed Mercia wisely. And, although there had been some bitterness between their fathers, Harold and Edwin got on well.

"My lord, look," the sentry said, pointing. "He rides at the head of a great army!"

The streaming banners of Mercia crested the rise at Edwin's back, followed by the azure banners of Northumbria. The standard-bearers led a vast army, numbering several thousand men armed with round shields and battle-axes. At that moment Edwin raised his arm to halt the great army riding with him and, in a show of trust, rode ahead accompanied only by his younger brother, Morcar.

Harold climbed down the ladder of the catwalk and met them at the gate.

"Earl Edwin, you were a boy when I saw you last. Now I see you are a man. Come sit by my fire, and tell what news you bring."

"It is very grave news we carry," Edwin said as he dismounted.

The young Earl was tall and slender, with brown hair soft as a wren's feathers. His face bore the solemn expression of one who has grown up too quickly, his brows drawn together in one worried line. "My brother and I need your counsel."

Morcar slid off his horse. He was not as tall as Edwin, nor as broad through the chest. That would come in time. The tips of his ears stuck out through his fine hair.

As they retired to a private chamber, Evyn turned to leave.

"No, Shadow, you are to remain here," Harold said.

Edwin hesitated to speak before Evyn. But when Harold asked, "What has happened?" he began.

"The harvest was poor in Northumbria this year. The rains fell hard and long, and much of the barley rotted in the fields before it could be brought into the barns. The people have barely enough to hold them through the winter. But Earl Tostig has refused their requests for mercy. He has exacted an even heavier harvest tax than in years past. He wears gold on his arms and fur-trimmed cloaks while the women and children of Northumbria starve. After he left last week to join the King for hunting in the south, the men of his earldom rose up against him."

Then Morcar, younger and more impetuous, took up the story. "They slew Tostig's housecarls and looted both his treasury and his armory. My lord Harold, much blood has been shed on both sides."

"We do not come here to defend rebellion," Edwin interrupted. "But this revolt was born of a long-suffering desperation. King Edward has not heeded the cries of the Northumbrian people. He loves Tostig too much to see the injustices he has committed. Harold, you know what we say is true. The Northumbrians are a stubborn and hotheaded people. They have proclaimed Tostig an outlaw and invited

Morcar to be their Earl." Edwin, who had been speaking quickly, now stopped for a moment before adding, "They say they will kill Tostig if he returns."

Harold turned to the young Morcar. "And what was your answer to them?"

"I said that this was a serious matter and that I desired the counsel of men of wisdom and power. Though King Edward may see it as rebellion, we see it as justice. I am inclined to accept their offer, and to show our purpose we have joined our Mercian militia with that of Northumbria. Our Welsh allies join us, too."

"Because you came to me alone and unarmed, I will not harm you," Harold said. "But this is a serious story you tell. I will not allow my brother Tostig to be made an outlaw."

"Harold, we do not come with ill will toward you. But our neighbors in Northumbria have suffered for ten long years under Tostig's greed and cruelty. King Edward has been deaf to our pleas. It is as if we are strangers in our own land. But King Edward knows you; your sister is queen, and you can speak for us. You know the law; you know this can be done. It is in your power to resolve this quarrel."

"I am not of a mind to speak against my own brother," Harold said abruptly.

"Perhaps you fear the House of Godwin will be weakened with Tostig gone," Edwin answered. "But that is not so. You, Gyrth, and Leofwine control all of Wessex, East Anglia, and the London shires, and if you negotiate a fair peace for us with the King, we will vow to be your allies in all your undertakings. The House of Godwin will not be weakened."

"You are better off without him, my lord," Morcar said.

Harold turned on him savagely. "I will forgive that remark because you are very young, Morcar, but see to it that you do not utter such words in my presence again!" Softening his tone, he added to Edwin, "I know there is truth in your accusations against Tostig. If you find it agreeable, I will entreat him and King Edward to come and meet us at Oxford. Let us strive to avoid more bloodshed. To show my good faith, I will provision your men on the condition that most of your army remain here while we ride on to Oxford to negotiate a peaceful settlement. It is an evil thing when those who are countrymen fight with one another. It weakens the whole kingdom and leaves us prey to foreign invaders."

After exchanging glances with his brother, Edwin spoke for both. "Let it be as you say."

After Edwin and Morcar left, Harold said, "Shadow, fetch parchment and ink. I want you to write a message for me and carry it personally to King Edward at Britford."

Evyn wrote the dispatch on the finest parchment to be found in Northampton's storerooms, folded it, and watched as Harold dripped hot wax on the outside and impressed his seal upon it. Evyn slid it into his courier's pouch, knelt for Harold's blessing, and then ran to the stables, where a horse was saddled for him. Hakon and a troop of mounted warriors waited to escort him.

Three days of hard riding brought them to the hunting lodge at Britford. There King Edward, tall and thin and white-haired, like a snow-covered sapling, received Evyn and Hakon. Norman courtiers surrounded the King at the High Table. Evyn knew them by their shorn hair and hesitated when he saw them. They were good for nothing but empty flattery. Perhaps there was truth in what was said, that the King favored these foreign-born Normans over his own people.

Tostig sat at the King's side. A circlet of gold confined his famous red hair. Evyn could not help remembering the way that fiery hair had stirred under the wings of the raven. *He is a cursed man*, Evyn thought. Tostig eyed him indolently as though he could read his mind, turning his gaze only at the sound of the King's voice.

"Hakon I know," the King said as he placed a joint of venison on the trencher and wiped his mouth delicately with a napkin. "He is Harold's right hand as Harold is my right hand, but who is this new squire?" the King inquired of Evyn.

"This little one is Harold's dumb shadow," Tostig said derisively. "Harold sends his greetings in the care of a mutilated thrall."

The color, born of anger, rose in Evyn's face. He knelt before the King and gave him Harold's note.

The King took it and read it slowly and silently. When he had finished, he placed it in Tostig's hands, saying, "This concerns you."

Evyn watched as Tostig's eyes flew over the parchment.

Still handsome, still haughty, Tostig had changed not at all since the first time Evyn had seen him that summer evening in Lady Ealdgyth's Hall more than two years before. Harold had changed, Evyn thought. His wisdom showed in the gray hair at his temples now, and his bad knee pained him more than it used to. But Tostig seemed forever young and foolish. He expressed no concern for his people, neither the native Northumbrians nor even the faithful housecarls slain on his behalf. No, his thoughts were on his treasury and his pride.

"Sire," he begged the King, "give me an army, and I shall put down this insurrection swiftly before the winter snow flies. The Northumbrians must not be allowed to raid with impunity."

"No, Tostig," the King said gently as he took the parchment back and read Harold's message once again. "Harold counsels wisely. It is not in my heart to plunge the kingdom into civil war."

Suddenly the King began coughing violently. It seized him in a terrible spasm, and he bent over and put his hand to his chest. Gasping for air, the King loosened the ties at the neck of his fur-trimmed tunic. His cough was dry and raspy, like stones rubbing against each other. Evyn had heard that kind of cough in Brother Alfred's infirmary; he knew what it meant. King Edward was gravely ill.

"Get my lord a cup of mead," Tostig ordered.

A moment later the King straightened. His face, usually so pale, was red with exertion, and his eyes watered.

"My thanks, Tostig," the King said hoarsely, as he sipped the mead which had been brought to him. "I am all right now." He paused as Tostig, Hakon, Evyn, and his Norman courtiers looked on worriedly. "It is nothing," he concluded, waving them away. "Go and prepare yourselves to depart for Oxford tomorrow."

When the royal party reached Oxford six days later, Harold greeted them, while Edwin and Morcar waited anxiously in their tent.

"Are you with me, Harold?" Tostig asked with a charming smile. "It will be like old times when we defeat these rebellious Northumbrians." He embraced his older brother.

"Yes," Harold answered, "I am with you, but I am for peace in the land, too. I will not raise the sword against Northumbria."

When he heard that, Tostig dropped his arms and stepped back. His nostrils flared. "Your words are arrows in my heart," he said bitterly and walked away.

Later that day, most of the members of the witan, the King's council, arrived in small groups. Some rode west from London and Dover, others north from Winchester. Thanes from Ringmere came from the marsh country, and the Sheriff of Chepstow arrived from his city in the west. The pink sunset and starry night bespoke fair weather on the morrow, and Harold suggested an outdoor council at a natural amphitheater not far from Oxford's Hall. In the morning, hostages were exchanged to ensure the safety of all involved. Then the men assembled and seated themselves on the hillside overlooking the river.

Harold spoke first. "We come here today, not to seek violence, no, not even to seek justice perhaps, but to seek a lasting peace for our kingdom. For when we war among ourselves, we become like sheep lost in the hills, an easy prey for the wolves beyond our shores who seek the destruction of England. Yes, friends, I say England though we are Angle and Saxon, Jute and Viking, Briton to the west, Pict to the north. Though we are many tribes, we have become one people governed by the same laws, from the marshes of Kent to the rocky coast of Carmarthen, from Hastings in the south to the Great Wall in the north.

"Now the Northumbrians come before us with a grievance against their Earl."

Here Evyn noted that Harold refrained from saying Tostig's name or claiming him as a brother, determined to be objective. Evyn looked out at the softly undulating hills sloping down to fields and river-bordered meadows. The last vivid hues of autumn splashed the countryside with color before gray winter arrived. Over his head a cloud of starlings winged their way south.

Turning back to face the gathering, Evyn studied those around him. Edwin listened to Harold's words closely, his manner solemn beyond his years. Morcar leaned against his brother's side; they were never willingly apart. King Edward, seated on a chair which had been carried outside for him, rested his thin hands with their long fingers loosely on his lap. Tostig, sullen and brooding, paced behind the King's chair until Edward gestured for him to sit. He sat reluctantly, nervously twisting the rings upon his fingers. He was willing to plunge the kingdom into civil war over his injured pride, while his brother was summoning all of his skill, and power, and eloquence to avert that possibility. Harold's courage and selflessness set him apart, for it was becoming clear that his greatest concern was the welfare of the people.

"I appeal to you, the thanes of Northumbria, to lay down your weapons and to entreat your Earl for forgiveness for your insurrection. He is bound by laws as you are and will relieve the suffering caused by heavy taxes."

But all of the Northumbrians shouted their dissatisfaction in unison.

"You do not know the danger you invite when you divide the kingdom so," Harold warned. "Our enemies will laugh at us when they hear of our quarrels. They will say, 'The English cannot rule themselves, so we shall do it for them.' They will kill our men and carry our women and children away to the slave markets. Our fields will run with blood. Our skies will be rent by wailing—"

"Tostig is an outlaw. We will not have him as our Earl," one brave thane shouted amid "Hullahs!" of support from his fellow northerners.

Harold raised his hand for silence, and the men quieted. "These differences can be solved by—"

Another Northumbrian interrupted. "My lord Harold, we have talked for ten years, and Tostig has refused to listen.

We are united in our desire for Morcar to be our Earl. Though he is young, we believe he will rule well."

Despite Harold's eloquent pleas and the respect in which he was held by the northerners, they would not be moved from their decision.

Harold faced the King and the members of his witan who had gathered round his chair and said, "Though it grieves me much, it is apparent that the thanes of Northumbria are united in their feelings against Tostig. I would not have the blood of many spilled over an injury to one man, though that man be my own brother. I know Morcar will act in the King's interests and in the interests of his people. My counsel is to let it be as they wish."

Tostig jumped to his feet so quickly that his hair flew back from his face. He shouted, "Is this how it is to be—with Harold second-in-command of the whole nation while I am forced into disgraceful exile?"

But no one paid any attention to Tostig, for at that moment King Edward began coughing violently. Squires were sent scrambling, one for the surgeon and one for a cup of mead for the King, who appeared very weak.

Tostig took advantage of the confusion to confront Morcar. "Enjoy your earldom, little brat," he whispered. "By God's Bread, I vow that you shall not hold it long." Then he brushed past Morcar, who was clearly shaken by the oath, the tips of his ears turning crimson.

"Brother," Harold called as Tostig elbowed his way through the throng.

The Northumbrian thanes, seeing Tostig's fury, made room for him to pass. Harold followed through the crowd's wake. When he reached Tostig, Harold placed his hand upon his brother's shoulder to halt his progress. Tostig whirled around defiantly, his dark eyes glittering. "Do not touch me!" he said in a shaking voice. "I hold you responsible for this, Harold, so spare me your golden-tongued wisdom." He wrenched himself free, gathered his wife and children and the few retainers still loyal to him, and fled.

Evyn saw Harold turn dejectedly. His master's face was lined with disappointment. This parting was not what Harold had wanted. But he had known that it was a possibility, and he had planned for it. Evyn saw the Earl of Wessex scanning the crowd until he seemed to find the face for which he searched. A young man stared back at Harold. His clothing was of good cut but neither rich nor elaborate, and his face was ordinary, too, except for the long, thin black eyebrows that arched curiously over his watchful eyes. It appeared to Evyn to be a face which would easily blend into any crowd. He had been waiting for Harold's signal. When the Earl of Wessex nodded to him, he nodded back across the sea of heads between them. He turned on his heel and followed the path Tostig had taken.

When Tostig left, the Northumbrians raised a victory shout, hoisted Morcar onto his horse, and paraded him around as a victor. They thanked the King, who rested comfortably now, and promised to be lawful subjects to him.

Later that day, as Evyn was putting Harold's few belongings into his traveling pack and Harold sat wordless in a corner of the room, a messenger knocked and was admitted.

"The King sorrows over Tostig's exile but sends his thanks to you for avoiding violence. He also requests that you accompany him to London and be by his side when he dedicates his Westminster Abbey during the Yule feasting."

"I will do as the King wishes," Harold said, little realizing how soon funeral bells would break the stillness of a London dawn.

1065

In this year the King took ill in London not long after Earl Tostig was exiled.

"Slow your pace. The King is weary," Harold called to the front riders in the long procession of servants, courtiers, and housecarls as they made their way back to London.

They took the road following the river Thames as it flowed gracefully toward the sea. On its glassy surface, the last of the autumn leaves glided along, dotting the water with yellows and browns and a few bright scarlets. Thick schools of salmon swam upriver to lay their eggs in the quiet streams where they had hatched. The water shimmered with their movement.

But few in the procession noticed the beauty of the placid Thames, for England's King often coughed until he gasped breathlessly. Finally, with the assistance of his courtiers, he slid off his white horse with its royal trappings and rode inside his curtained litter for the remainder of the journey. Upon reaching his Westminster palace, he took to his chamber, where the Queen, Harold's sister, and his Norman surgeon cared for him.

After Harold was satisfied that the King was comfortable he left, taking Evyn with him. As was his custom each year, he visited all the large towns and cities of Wessex. He meant to renew ties with his people, to sort out differences in the moot halls, and to see for himself how the harvest went in each shire. Hurriedly, to beat the winter snows, they rode southeast to Dover. Later, following the coast roads, they visited Hastings, Bosanhamm, and then inland to Winchester, Harold's boyhood home. They stopped for a week to rest there and continued to Exeter. On the first day of December, they set out for Bristol. During their journey, the winds grew cold with the promise of freezing rain. Evyn noticed that Harold's limp worsened with the change in weather.

By the time they reached Bristol, Harold had difficulty hiding his condition. He closed himself up in a quiet room away from the noise of the sheriff's Great Hall. His knee throbbed, and each movement brought excruciating pain.

Evyn wrote on his slate: *I have a little training in medicine.*

"Then do what you can for me," Harold said through clenched teeth.

Evyn searched out the midwife. With some difficulty, he made himself understood and gathered the necessary herbs and linen bandages. Then he went to the kitchen and fetched a bowl of hot water. By the time he returned to the upper guest chamber, Harold had removed his soft leather boots. His breeches lay tossed over the back of the bench. He slumped forward, resting his head in his hands upon the table before him. As Evyn entered the room, Harold dropped his hands from his face, exposing the agony etched into his features.

"Ah," he said with a sigh of relief, "it is only you, Shadow." He could not bear to have anyone else see him like this.

Harold sat back in his chair stiffly. He closed his eyes and rested his head against the carved tendrils of the chair back.

Evyn had never seen his master in such pain. Quickly he crushed the dried herbs so that the particles slipped through his fingers into the bowl of hot water beneath. Then he soaked the linen strips in the mixture, turning them over to wet them thoroughly. He wrung them out carefully, and as he applied them to the sore knee, he saw the cause of his lord's suffering. There, on the inside of Harold's leg, stretched the inflamed gash of a poorly healed wound. *A battle-ax,* Evyn thought, staring in horror at it until Harold opened his eyes and managed to smile weakly at the boy's astonishment.

"I got this long ago," he said. "It still bothers me when the weather is poor, or if I do much riding."

Evyn was embarrassed when he saw how courageously Harold bore his pain, while he, Evyn, had allowed fear and doubt to be his constant companions. How he wanted to become a man like Harold. Evyn worried that his cowardice would overcome him as it had that night in the cave.

In the simple sign language they had developed between them, Evyn asked the question he'd been pondering for so long: "*What gives a man courage?*"

Harold understood immediately. "Do not think that courage is the absence of fear. Even the bravest warrior trembles with fear at times," he said. "It is not easy for any man to face death or to endure more pain than he thinks bearable. And do not be misled by old men or foolish young housecarls with their silly charms."

He reached forward and poked at the leather thong around Evyn's neck with the villagers' charm for courage swinging at the end of it.

"It is not with garlic cloves, my friend!" Harold said, summoning a smile. "There is no magic herb that makes a man brave. Courage is knowing that what you do is necessary. Don't doubt yourself, Shadow. There is more valor in your heart than you realize."

That night Harold slept deeply for the first time in weeks. After two days and several more of Evyn's treatments, his knee could bear his weight. Before a fortnight passed, when a crisp frost covered the fields and the roads were frozen into hard ruts, Harold and Evyn, escorted by twenty housecarls, left for London.

They rode hard, arriving in time for the Christmas feasting and the dedication of the new abbey church. The square before the church swarmed with admiring visitors from all over the country. Fourteen years ago the King had set the cornerstone, and since that time he had poured every extra silver penny he had into the building of this church. The central tower over the transept, where the wide arms of the T-shaped church crossed, rose over one hundred feet into the air, soaring above the tile and thatched roofs of London. The deafening music of iron bells from the tower drowned out the talk below. The outside walls of the abbey boasted row after row of statues of the saints, each wearing a white crown of snow.

"There is St. Peter—the one holding the keys," Harold shouted in Evyn's ear, pointing out the church's patron. "There is St. Alban, the first British martyr, whom the Romans killed for professing Christ. There are the four Gospel writers, each holding a book and quill pen."

They climbed the steps of the abbey, and as they entered

the dark interior, Evyn pushed his hood back and squinted down the long nave. The people instantly made a path for the Earl of Wessex, his squire, and his housecarls as they proceeded toward the altar. There King Edward sat on a throne at the foot of the steps. He wore a long elegant robe in the Norman style and a cloak lined with spotted ermine. The Queen stood at his side, and she pulled the collar of his cloak up about his neck so that only his sunken eyes and the crown pressing against his white hair could be seen.

After Archbishop Ealdred dedicated the abbey, the King retired to his chamber in the palace, and his people saw him no more. Harold, admitted to the inner chamber, conferred with him several times over the following days, leaving Evyn to wander the corridors of King Edward's palace. Though it was Yuletide, the Great Hall was quiet. No one desired the usual raucous merriment of the season with the King so ill. The servants whispered uneasily, and the Norman courtiers, so distrusted by the native English, kept to themselves.

The New Year came on a day of howling winds, and all remained indoors. Courtiers, housecarls, and servants crowded the Great Hall, but Edward remained cloistered in his chamber. Sometimes the surgeon would emerge, but he refused to answer their questions. On the fifth day of the New Year, Edward died. For the first time, the death knell for a king tolled from the tower of Westminster Abbey.

Evyn watched suspiciously as the Normans of Edward's court huddled in whispered conference. He decided to follow one man who left the group. The Norman quietly stole down passageways and back rooms to the royal stables. He saddled a horse and took the road leading south.

He goes to tell his Duke, Evyn thought. *He goes to tell him we have no king.*

The Queen wept inconsolably. Her lord was dead, and he had given her no son to rule in his place. Harold came to her side and drew his sister to him to comfort her. Issuing orders as he caressed her veiled head, the Earl of Wessex took command. The Saxon thanes eagerly welcomed Harold's leadership, while the Normans watched him grudgingly over their shoulders.

"Send for the men of the witan. Their presence is needed now," Harold said. Couriers bowed and raced from the Hall, streaming out in all directions from London to gather the great men of the realm whose counsel and vote were crucial to the election of a new king.

"Send for Archbishop Ealdred, too," Harold said.

Another courier raced away on his mission.

The next day the funeral procession began from the King's chamber where Edward's body—washed, anointed, and dressed in robes edged with fur and threaded with gold—lay wrapped in the finest linens from the royal treasure chests. The pallbearers hoisted the open litter to their shoulders and carried it through the rooms of the palace. They proceeded out into the streets where the people gathered for one last look at their sovereign. King Edward the Confessor was buried, as he had wished, before the altar of St. Peter within Westminster Abbey.

When the final prayers had been said and the body committed to its tomb, Harold rested his hand on Evyn's shoulder. "Now the witan will meet in Edward's Great Hall," he whispered, "to choose a new king."

For a king to die childless foretold disaster for the country. In the past, earl had risen up against earl, each wrestling for greater power, thus leaving the kingdom weak and a temptingly easy prey for foreign invaders. It was necessary that the matter be settled quickly and that the new king be crowned and anointed by Archbishop Ealdred, the most respected churchman in England.

Later that afternoon, members of the witan began to arrive, still dressed in their mud-splattered riding clothes. First Eadric of Dover, who had been lodging in London over the Yuletide, strode into the Great Hall, followed by his brother Edmund. Then Aelfric came. Though he hailed from the West Country, he, too, had been in London. Two hours later, Eadwulf pushed open the doors of the Great Hall and curtly dismissed the retinue that had escorted him from Ely. He was fresh from the saddle and still smelled of his horse.

While Eadwulf shook the horsehair from his cloak, Archbishop Ealdred and several Northumbrian thanes entered. Ealdred strode into the Hall ahead of the others. With his proud, high-boned features and toughened hands, he looked more like a grizzled general than a monk. He was a soldier for God, he said. His hooded eyes, dark and wise, betrayed no emotion at the news of the death of the half-Norman king. Draping his arm around Harold's shoulder as a father would, he led him to a quiet corner of the Hall. He had words to say to Harold he would have no other hear.

Finally Harold's brothers, Gyrth and Leofwine, marched in together an hour later.

"Shadow, wait outside. I will need you soon," Harold said.

When the members of the witan had seated themselves, Harold dismissed the servants and barred each set of doors to the Hall from the inside.

From his place on the other side of the doors, waiting with the royal servants, Evyn heard only muffled voices. Evyn recognized Gyrth's low voice but could not make out his words. Harold's voice, with its wider range and distinct pronunciation, carried farther. Soon the servants grew bored and scattered to the kitchen to sit by the warm fire. Evyn alone remained in the corridor to await the decision. *How can they leave?* he wondered, his stomach knotted with anticipation. *Who will be the new king?*

"It is urgent . . ." he heard Harold say.

Then followed a low rumble of tangled voices of various pitches and tempos. Then Harold again: "No, this must be done quickly. There is no—"

Each time Harold spoke, one or two others broke in like sword thrusts to disagree. Evyn could tell by their tone, if not their words. He imagined the smiles of disbelief and condescending reassurances each time Harold called for an urgent decision. But then the weight of the argument began to surge the other way when Gyrth added his voice to Harold's. And even Leofwine, who much preferred to remain silent, shared his thoughts. But it was not until Archbishop Ealdred spoke that absolute quiet reigned in the Hall. Evyn could hear his own breathing. The men of the witan knew that Ealdred had no interest in power, that it was the people's welfare he kept closest to his heart. They revered him for his fairness and wisdom. He was no power broker striving to place one man above another or one family against its neighbor.

Evyn closed his eyes and pressed his ear against the door and concentrated all of his attention on what the Archbishop said.

"Edward's only heir is his very young cousin, who is somewhere on the Continent. He has not been educated to rule. He does not know the English tongue. He is a mere boy. It would take weeks to find him and weeks more to bring him here safely and anoint him as king. Edward's only other relative is William of Normandy—"

A curse cut through the air followed by the crash of a cup against the wall as someone vented his anger against the hated Norman.

"And we all know," the Archbishop continued calmly, "that he has no love for the English. His sole intention is to plunder the country for his own benefit. No, I will not anoint William king. Then there is Harald Hardrada of Norway—he they call Hard Counsel, for he is fierce and unforgiving. He may reassert his fragile claims to the English throne by calling upon the promises made between our King Harthacanute and King Magnus of Norway many years ago. But it is in my heart that he bears no love for the English. Our people will not willingly put on the Viking yoke again. So, no, I will not recommend Harald Hardrada.

"But I will argue here on behalf of one of your own. A man who is England born and bred, a man with years enough behind him to rule with a strong hand and with years enough before him to serve the country long and well. He is a man who has proved he can lead us in war if necessary, but who knows, too, how to keep the peace. His knowledge of the law is well known. He is famed for his diplomacy. For those who doubt his wisdom or impartiality, I will say to them that I was with this man last autumn when he was forced to choose between his country and his beloved brother. I speak for Harold—I argue for Harold. Harold is England's hope now."

There was silence for a moment followed by a half-hearted argument from one of the Northumbrian thanes, as Evyn guessed by his accent. But he was cut short when it became apparent to all the members of the witan that Ealdred spoke wisely. "Though it is unusual for an earl to assume the kingship, it has been done before," the Archbishop explained. "Harold, with his ties to Danish royalty through his mother and his long years of service to the King, is the obvious choice among you." A series of affirmations rumbled through the Hall, some more enthusiastic than others. But all finally agreed that Harold Godwinson should be their King.

Footsteps approached and the heavy oak door swung open—it was Harold. England's new King, still dressed in somber clothes for Edward's funeral, appeared taller than Evyn had thought him, his shoulders straighter. The lines had vanished from his face, and he seemed more handsome than before, as though he had finally assumed the position for which he had been born. Awestruck, Evyn clumsily dropped to one knee.

Harold pulled him up by the neck of his tunic and set him on his feet again. The new King laughed out loud and cupped the boy's face in his hands as Evyn's father had often done when he was delighted about something.

"Go now and pack our things. We ride for Northumbria at dawn's first light."

That evening, darkness fell over the quiet city, and the wintry drafts shook the tapestries in the empty Halls and chambers of the royal palace. The people walked through the new-fallen snow to Westminster Abbey. They had seen a dedication and a funeral there, and now they came for the coronation of a king.

A lone figure entered from a side chapel and knelt in the darkness before the altar. His body, silhouetted by the dim light of the beeswax candles, remained motionless, as though caught in a trance. He was crowned with shimmering golden hair that covered his neck and fell forward as he bent his head in prayer.

Climbing the steps to the altar, Archbishop Ealdred turned and faced the man kneeling before him. The incense bearer swung the silver censer, and perfumed smoke rose from its lip. The fragrance filled the sanctuary and gradually drifted across the heads of the people. Ealdred began the ancient ritual that bound a king to his country.

"Harold, son of Godwin, will you be our King?"

"I will."

"Will you love and protect the country and all her people?"

"I will."

"Will you protect her from treachery within and from invasion without?"

"I will."

"Will you rule wisely, taking counsel from the witan and the earls of the kingdom?"

"I will."

"Then I anoint you King Harold II." Ealdred took a little container of blessed oil from one of the acolytes, dipped his finger in it, and traced a cross on Harold's forehead. "May God guard you from harm and protect you from evil. Amen."

With great reverence, the Archbishop took the pearl-encrusted crown from an acolyte, held it above Harold's bowed figure for a moment, and then placed it upon his head.

Harold rose and turned to face his people, his own beloved English. Evyn, as he stood among the throng, saw both pain and glory in the new King's face.

It was not until later that evening, as Harold met with Ealdred and Gyrth and Leofwine, that Evyn caught the first hint of what troubled his master.

"I am riding for Northumbria tomorrow," he said, warming his hands before the fire.

"The people are cold toward you there, Harold," Gyrth

cautioned. "The memory of Tostig's cruelty is still too fresh."

Leofwine, who sat at the table with his pale blond hair shading his face, looked up from the chess game he had begun earlier. "Is it necessary, Brother? You know there has been murder in those parts during these last few weeks. They bear no love for the Godwinsons."

"No, my friends," Ealdred said before Harold could speak. "Harold is right. The Northumbrians and Mercians need to see their new King. It has been many years since a king has traveled north. Edward always made the northerners come to him. It will gladden their hearts to see Harold on his first state visit coming to them." Ealdred turned to Harold. "You have nothing to fear from Edwin and Morcar. They have kept the vow they made to you last autumn to be your allies in all things."

"It is Edwin and Morcar whom I most wish to see," Harold said as he turned from the fire and faced the Archbishop. "Does their sister remain unmarried?"

Evyn glanced up from the wooden chest he had been packing with the last of the clothes Harold would need for the journey. Harold's words twisted in his brain.

Does their sister remain unmarried?

His sudden movement caught Harold's eye, and the stricken look upon Evyn's face must have angered the new King, for he said, "That is enough, Shadow. Go now. You may sleep with the squires in the Great Hall tonight."

Stunned, Evyn stared at his master, but Harold guarded his thoughts behind a stony face, waving Evyn away with his hand. As Evyn closed the door behind him, he set his lips together angrily. Harold had never before spoken to him so curtly. The boy spent a restless night and slept little.

The morning dawned cold and clear. Harold, Ealdred,

Evyn, and a large entourage of well-armed housecarls rode out from London. Their horses snorted white plumes of frosty breath as they thundered across the silvery landscape. By midmorning they reached Waltham, and there they broke the ice on the shallow stream to water the horses. Harold bade them remain where they were as he rode inside the gates of Lady Ealdgyth's estate. Evyn clenched his jaw as the King departed. *What kind of betrayal does he plan?*

The King was gone only long enough for the men to dismount and eat a hurried breakfast of bread and dried pork. When he returned, he signaled for Evyn to ride by his side but said not one word to him. At sundown they reached the monastery of St. Albans. There the abbot welcomed the new King warmly.

All day long, Evyn's blood had simmered, and though the winter air was cold, his face remained hot with anger. *Oh! How cursed I am to have lost my voice when I most want to vent my anger. What did Harold say to the Lady? Has he betrayed her love? Does he plan to wed another?*

They ate a simple evening meal of bread and cheese. Since the King ate in silence, no one else dared to speak. Evyn sat at the end of the table and picked at his food.

Soon they retired to their guest chambers: Ealdred to the monks' dormitory, the housecarls to the dining Hall, Harold to the abbot's own guest room. Evyn followed him and performed his duties with a sour taste in his mouth. How disappointed he felt. He had thought Harold perfect in all things. Was not loyalty the greatest of the Saxon virtues? How could he betray the woman who had borne him his children?

Harold sat speechless as Evyn slid the King's muddy riding boots from his feet and put them before the fire to dry. He folded the King's scarlet cloak and draped it over a chair.

He wiped spots of mud from the plumed helmet and set it on the table. But he did all this without once looking into Harold's face.

"I know well what you are thinking, Shadow, and I know that no explanation I can give will satisfy you. The Lady is your benefactress, and it is your duty to defend her honor. But I will explain. I plan to marry Edwin and Morcar's sister, as you have already guessed."

Evyn looked up with hate in his eyes.

"You are right to look at me that way. It will be a public humiliation for the Lady Ealdgyth to have another made Queen in her place. And none deserves the honor more than she, for she has remained by my side through the most difficult times."

The King's face grew dark and rigid. The wide brow shadowed his eyes, so that they seemed like empty caves. His voice lowered to an iron-cold depth Evyn had never before heard. He spoke bitterly.

"I am not some village lad who, when he sees a pretty girl, can go to his lord and say, 'Lord, this girl pleases me. I would that you would give her to me for a wife.' I do not have that freedom. I am the King now, and I can no longer act upon my personal feelings. I must do what is best for all of the people. When a king from the south takes a queen from the north, it unifies a country of many peoples. Don't you see, Shadow? A marriage alliance will save many lives."

Evyn shook his head, confused.

"If you are unwilling to sacrifice everything for England, begone," Harold said coldly. "*This* is what I must do. I do not ask you to do more than I ask of myself."

It pains him more than I had ever reckoned, Evyn thought. *He does this not to hurt the Lady but to care for his people.*

Evyn took the wax tablet upon the table and wrote *How fares the Lady?* She had been in his thoughts all day.

Harold closed his eyes; when he opened them again they glistened like the gray-blue of the sea. "The Lady's courage is that of the strongest warrior. She agrees that this is a chance to bring a lasting peace to the land." He paused. "Shadow, do not misunderstand. The Lady is my common-law wife. It is not a binding union. I am free to marry in the eyes of the law and in the eyes of the Church. Ealdgyth knew this when she came to me. I have always needed to be free to make a political marriage. The Lady is the daughter of a merchant. She has no armies at her command, whereas the sister of Edwin and Morcar is nobly born. I need her brothers and their armies as my allies. This marriage will weld the country together. I am two people now; I am the King and I am Harold. This is not a marriage for Harold. Harold is still wed to the Lady Ealdgyth—she is first in my heart. But I can no longer think only of myself or only of Ealdgyth."

He rubbed his eyes and ran his fingers through his rumpled hair. After wedging another log into the fire, he sat on the bench before the hearth. The flames played upon his face, warming his skin and lighting his hair and mustache.

"If you wish to be dismissed, I will release you. You are welcome to return to Aethelney. But I tell you, I treasure your company, and I value your skill. Clerks know nothing about caring for a man's armor, and squires know nothing of letters. You bring healing and relief from my pain. I would not willingly do without you. Yet you remain a mystery. Shadow, I do not even know the name your father gave you."

Evyn realized that he had unclenched his fists while Harold spoke. The King had shared his thoughts with him and had trusted Evyn with the secrets a man most wishes to keep in his heart. He had shown Evyn that he was merely a man, like other men, who could not always do as he desired.

Evyn bent down and wrote with his fingertip in the ashes at the edge of the fire. He shared the secret he had kept so long in his own heart. *I am Evyn.*

1066

And while they slept a restless sleep in York,
a longship crashed through the waves
on her way to Norway.

Twelfth Night had long passed, and the feasts celebrating the beginning of the new King's reign came to a close. Within weeks, Evyn and all of Christian England would tighten their belts as the days of Lenten fasting began. This was the hungry time of year. The sun lengthened its journey across the sky, the snow melted from the hillsides, and the streams ran with icy water.

Evyn chose to remain with Harold. For, although he still saw himself as an outsider among the Saxons, and his lack of courage continued to gnaw at him, Evyn felt strongly that he belonged by the King's side.

When they reached the great merchant city of York, the King's courtesy and generosity won over all of the northerners, including Edwin and Morcar's sister, who accepted Harold's marriage proposal with a shy smile. She was still young, with a small face and a pointed chin, and she stood less than Harold's shoulder. The people approved of the marriage and fondly referred to her as "the little Queen."

Harold correctly foresaw that the marriage would unify the country. But he had also explained to Evyn that his heart remained with Ealdgyth—she whose fate had been entwined with his own since childhood, she who was so nearly his match in wit and talent. Harold would do what he could to make his new Queen happy, but there was only one woman able to bring joy to Harold, and she lived in the south at her Waltham estate.

So it came as little surprise to Evyn that as soon as the marriage negotiations could be settled and all the long councils with the great men of the north concluded, the King commanded his retinue to leave for the south. The Queen would remain in the north in the home that she knew.

They rode south under low skies swollen with heavy clouds. Their journey took them across the deserted and windswept moors, all covered in gray and purple. Above the line of riders a kestrel, with feathers like rows of arrowheads, hovered high overhead.

But Harold did not see it. He rode hard and fast, keeping his eyes on the road before him, not the sky above. He knew where he wished to be, and Evyn drove his horse to keep up with Harold's great stallion, Thunder. Seven days later they reached Waltham.

Once they rode through the gate the King laughed often. The Lady Ealdgyth touched his heart, making him joyful once again. They went for long walks in the orchard, stopping now and then to inspect the buds which promised an abundant harvest. She showed Harold her new jewelers' workshops where the artisans hunched over their tables, fashioning bits of gold and silver, shaping the brooches and pins and jewel-studded hair combs that made England famous among kingdoms. In the afternoons she took Harold's hand and led him through her stables to see the new colts on their wobbly legs. Evyn saw that when his master was with her his footsteps fell lightly, and worries did not cloud his face.

A fortnight later Harold returned to his headquarters in London, and his smile came less often. Evyn could not help noticing the change in his master. The man who was now King of England had always been of a serious nature, never fully escaping from the heavy burden of responsibility he had carried as an earl. Bred from birth to rule, he accepted the role fate had dealt him. But before, he had made time for jokes and games of chess and hunting in the forests. Now he spent his days studying maps and poring over lists of stores of food and weapons. He spoke only of the possibility of war. Always, it seemed, his brother Tostig was in his thoughts and on his lips.

"I wait for news of Tostig," Harold said to Evyn one morning after he had listened to the court cases in London's moot hall. "He's made his winter quarters in Flanders, his wife's country. She has land there. Perhaps he'll settle down and be content."

Evyn wrote upon an unused tablet on the table before him: *He is a proud man. He will not stomach this disgrace.*

The King read it and smiled ruefully. "You are a good judge of men," he said, pacing to the window and staring out over the city to the swiftly flowing river beyond. There the skeletons of three new fighting ships cast their striped shadows at the edge of the harbor. The King rested his hands on either side of the window as he gazed at his city.

"I fear Tostig," he said, so quietly that Evyn barely heard the words. "And I fear for him."

As was customary, Harold had proclaimed the King's Peace for all the land during the weeks of Lent. Those who feuded laid down their weapons upon pain of death.

"I will have no murder during the season of prayer," Harold said. And in England Harold's peace was kept. But the King brooded over the turmoil just beyond his control. What did his brother plan?

One afternoon after a week of rain, Harold's thanes coaxed their King away from his table littered with maps and armory lists.

"I have not the time for hunting now," he protested.

But they persisted.

"Perhaps you are right," the King finally said, knowing they would trouble him till he relented. He rolled the map up and called to a servant. "Have my horse saddled. I will hunt today."

An hour later, Evyn found himself riding at the back of a pack of huntsmen. He felt the excitement pulsing with an ever-quickening beat as they cantered their horses out through the gates, past the city walls, and over the fields brown with last year's stalks.

The trail entered the woods between two towering oak trees, their branches covered in new buds. The royal insignia had been carved into both trunks as a warning to trespassers and poachers.

The King's forest was of old oak with some clusters of pine and beech. A breeze kept the branches overhead in constant motion, throwing a web of dancing shadows across the forest floor. They followed the trail down into the secret part of the woods. Evyn heard a thrush call out to its mate, which answered from some hidden spot deeper within. In the lower places, the path grew spongy, and the horses left deep hoofprints. The smell of damp earth was thick and heavy. The master of the hounds led the way on foot with the four dogs straining at their leashes. Their coats of short dark hair rippled over powerful muscles. Sniffing nervously at every log and rock, they soon picked up the scent and a wild howling began.

"They are on the scent!" the hound master cried over his shoulder, unleashing the animals. The hounds bounded over fallen tree trunks and scrabbled up the hillside, through the drifts of old leaves. Their baying and yelping, which at first echoed throughout the thick woods, grew fainter as they disappeared into the forest.

"Halloo!" the horsemen shouted as the chase began. They ducked under low branches and jumped their horses over fallen trees as they followed the dogs.

Harold leaned over Thunder's neck, his cloak streaming behind him. Soon he took the lead, the other hunters fanning out in his wake, separated by trees and underbrush. Urging their mounts on with wild cries, they crashed through thickets, recklessly leaped over ditches, and splashed through the streams.

Evyn, too, spurred his bay and loosened the reins, allowing the spirited animal to choose his way through the woods. The horse's long neck pumped up and down so that his mane flew back, slapping Evyn's hands with each long-legged stride. The cries of the hounds redoubled, sounding far ahead to his left. Evyn tightened the reins, turning the bay toward the dogs. He heard the men shouting in the distance and the cry of the hound master as he called to his animals.

Suddenly a wild boar crashed through the thickets in front of Evyn, his tiny eyes glistening with rage. His tusks dripped lather as he swung his head back and forth. His hooves, big as a man's fists, cracked twigs and struck up earth as he charged. Three arrows protruded from the boar's side, all good hits, but the beast would not die easily. Evyn felt his heart leap up within his chest, and he froze in the saddle. The bay whinnied fearfully and reared on his hind legs. The boar charged but veered away at the last moment to avoid the flying hooves. Diving into a thicker part of the woods, he disappeared as quickly as he had come. Evyn stared after the retreating animal as his heart pounded.

"You would do well to have drawn your dagger, friend," a voicc said quite near to him. "A wild boar can easily knock down a horse, and you might have found yourself in dangerous combat with a mean-tempered beast."

Evyn twisted in his saddle to see a man, mounted on a white mare, merely an arm's breadth from Evyn's shoulder. It shamed him to know that someone had seen him freeze with fear. The man was a stranger to the hunting party, but he wore the familiar scarlet and gold of Harold's men. By his coloring he was neither golden Saxon nor black Welsh, but could claim the blood of any race. His face was ordinary, but his long arched eyebrows, black and expressive, lent his face interest and an air of good breeding.

The man eyed Evyn's own scarlet tunic with a knowing smile, and one eyebrow arched higher.

"Take me to your master, boy," he said. "I have news he will want to hear." His manner was dignified, yet he was no kinsman to Harold nor one nobly born but one of the King's men.

Evyn remembered then. He had seen this fellow once before, only for a moment, but he was sure it was the same man. He had been in the crowd at Oxford, at the great council meeting by the riverside when Tostig had been outlawed. It was he who had nodded obediently to Harold from across the crowd and followed the angry Tostig in his flight into exile. Here was the spy Harold had waited for so long.

Evyn nodded respectfully and spurred the bay toward the next hill, where the noise of yelping hounds grew in frenzy. The stranger rode at his side and made no further comment. When they reached the cluster of hunters, they saw the boar on his side, panting heavily. Of the three arrows that had found their mark, Evyn noticed with pride that two had come from Harold's quiver. The King hopped down from Thunder's back, drew his long dagger, and mercifully slit the boar's throat. The animal snorted once and then lay still. "It is a good size," Harold said, glancing up at his companions.

When the stranger signaled to him, Harold immediately wiped the bloody dagger on the ground and sheathed it. "Friends, take the boar back for me," he said. "There is one here with whom I would speak."

Harold beckoned for Evyn to follow him as he swung up on Thunder's back. He led them to a quiet clearing in the woods, a little space of new, untrampled grass enclosed by tall pines. They dismounted, and the King motioned for them to sit on a large rock outcropping at the base of three pine trees.

"I heard nothing for so long that I feared you were dead, Thorketil," the King said to the stranger.

"No, Sire. But each time I wished to leave, the Earl Tostig made fresh plans, and I thought it best to see his intentions."

"How goes it with my brother?" the King asked.

"He is well, my lord. But that is the only good news I bring," Thorketil said apologetically.

Harold settled himself on the rock. It seemed his spy had a long tale to tell. Thorketil drew a deep breath and continued. "Last autumn his wife's brother, Count Baldwin of Flanders, welcomed Tostig for the love he bore his sister. There Tostig nursed his grudge against you. He holds you responsible for his disgrace. When the news came of King Edward's death and your election to the throne, Tostig raged like a wild beast. A month later, when we heard the report, carried by merchant ships crossing the sea, of your alliance with Edwin and Morcar, he became so furious that none dared approach him. He slept little and wandered Count Baldwin's Hall through the long night hours, while the rest of the household slept."

Harold rested his chin on his folded hands and stared at the ground before him. His jaw tightened, and Evyn knew that the King was disappointed. Thorketil paused for a moment, and it seemed to Evyn that the spy did not wish to tell the rest. But then he spoke again as if he was resolved to serve Harold as he had been instructed.

"Tostig's heart turned black," Thorketil said, "and he promised to have revenge on you. Your brother is determined to return. He has a dangerous plot in mind. He lays his grievances before any who will listen.

"In Flanders he kept nothing secret. Many times he steered the talk to his own troubles. At table he often said, 'My brother has wronged me. I will crush Harold and take back what is mine.' Or if he passed a group of Baldwin's young knights, he would tell them, 'I am gathering an army. Join me and I will give you land in England.'

"A few promised to come with him, but not many, for

Baldwin told him he did not have the means to make war on England. He gave him a few ships, but that was all.

"Finally, in frustration, Tostig loaded his ships and sailed east for Denmark to visit your cousin King Svein. I managed to hire on as an extra ship hand. Once in Denmark, he pressed his cause anew, begging again for more men and ships with which to launch an invasion.

"He said to King Svein, 'I will give you all I have in England if you, like the great King Canute, will take a Danish army to win the realm of England.'

"But young King Svein only said, 'I am so much less a man than King Canute was that I can scarcely hold my own country against the Norwegians.'

"After that, Tostig sulked. He slumped in his chair and stretched his legs out before him. He spoke to none and turned his head away from those who would comfort him."

Suddenly Thorketil broke off from his tale. "Forgive me for speaking so bluntly, my lord."

"No, Thorketil, I would have it no other way," the King said. "Go on."

"Then I heard Tostig say, 'If my friends will not help me, I will go to my friends' enemies. If Svein is so frightened of the Norwegians, then I want the Norwegians for my allies.' He sailed to Norway, and I took ship for London."

There followed a pause before Harold spoke. "It is well known that King Harald Hardrada of Norway has long coveted England. My brother Tostig is charming and will surely convince the Norwegians to gather a fleet to invade. There are two important questions that remain: Where will he land, and when?"

The spring wind sighed mournfully through the top

branches of the pine trees, and clouds scudded across the sun so that the shadows of the three men disappeared in a gloomy haze.

"Those are questions for which I have not the answers, my lord," Thorketil said, and the spy's long, arched eyebrows drew together in a worried frown.

1066

All that summer, Tostig raided the coast of England, from the Isle of Wight to the Humber. Finding refuge at the Orkney Islands, he waited for his ally, King Harald Hardrada of Norway, to join him.

The next months were like a game of blindman's buff, waiting blindfolded for the blow to come, not knowing when or where it might land. But this was no mere game, and the players were not children. Tostig played for nothing less than Harold's death, with the kingdom as the trophy. Yet Harold refused to play the fool to Tostig's deadly joke. He would not wait idly for it to end one way or another, and he filled his days with planning England's defense.

Harold established his military headquarters in London. The city's central location and great size made it ideal. The Thames connected it with much of the country, and merchants from many lands docked their ships there, carrying valuable information as well as cargo. It was a loyal city now, for after Edward's death most of his Norman followers had left the country.

While in London, the King entrusted Evyn with important messages of state. Soon the entire court grew aware of Harold's attitude toward his squire, and Evyn found that he was no longer mocked in the passageways, and the stable boys no longer spat when he led Thunder in to his stall for the night.

He was still shunned, however. The other squires, all sons of noble families, never included him in their games of dice or wrestling, but Evyn had grown used to being the outsider. He knew that with his black hair and pale skin he would always stand out as different from the golden Saxons. They treated him with the respect due to the King's squire, but never with warmth.

One evening not long after Holy Week, as they ate in the Great Hall, hung with banners of all the great families of England, a mouselike monk asked Harold to come to the rooftop watchtower. Evyn followed the King as he left the Hall. Up the twisting stairs they climbed till they reached the lookout, open to the sky and large enough for four men.

"There, my lord," the monk said, pointing skyward and twitching with fear.

Above in the starry heavens a huge ball of fire trailing three white tails like foamy spray lit the sky. It appeared as large as a full moon, and its light shone over all of London. Evyn gazed upward until his neck stiffened. He had heard of this strange star before. A man might see it once in his lifetime. Lewys had shown him drawings of it in Aethelney's library. Although it was beautiful beyond all telling, it was an evil omen, and some said it foretold death and the fall of kingdoms.

Harold reassured the nervous monk. With a clap on the man's shoulder, he said, "Look, Brother, how gracious the heavens are to dazzle us so. It celebrates the beginning of my reign." But from that day on, he redoubled his efforts to protect the kingdom.

In late spring, amid intermittent showers, the royal court traveled south to Dover, where Harold ordered the building of five new longships. With the chalky white cliffs jutting into the sea at his back, Harold knelt on his good leg in the damp sand of the beach, the local shipwrights looking over his shoulder.

"Make them sixteen oarlocks long with a steering pole of oak," Harold said, sketching in the sand. "They are to be manned by a seasoned crew of warriors, well armed and experienced in sea-fighting."

On to Hastings they rode, and then to Portsmouth, where he ordered more ships. At Exeter he instructed the minters to strike a new silver penny. They smashed the old molds carved with King Edward's likeness and created a new coin—one side bore Harold's likeness adorned with the pearl-studded crown he had worn on his coronation day. The reverse side bore the simple word *PAX*—Latin for peace.

Harold made Hakon his general. Though he would always consider himself Harold's personal bodyguard, more often now Hakon traveled to far-flung parts of the country to train troops and be where Harold could not. He had recently returned from East Anglia to meet Harold at Exeter.

"I want an accurate militia count from every shire," Harold said as he and Hakon inspected a herd of horses. "I may need to call up every man in the fyrd." The stablers made the horses trot on their lead ropes around the enclosure while Harold leaned against the fence and watched. Hakon jumped down from his perch now and then to check a mare's teeth or the hooves of a colt ready to be broken to the saddle.

"There are more than thirty shires, my lord," Hakon remarked as he climbed back up to his seat on the fence. Turning to Evyn for sympathy, he added, "I will spend my life in a saddle."

Evyn grinned. Hakon had a knack for making the gravest situation light.

"Each shire reeve is to make a full accounting," Harold continued. "I want to know how many lads have reached the fighting age of sixteen and what weapons they have at hand." Harold pointed out a lame horse as its handler led him in front, and waved it away. "Start with the coastal shires. They will feel the invader's sword first. They must be prepared."

"Surely, my lord, you don't fear Tostig?" Hakon asked. "Though he is brave, his skill is less than yours."

Harold glanced away from the horses in surprise. "I fear Tostig more than any other man," he said sternly. "A good general can outwit his foreign enemies if fate is on his side. But I cannot outwit Tostig. As boys we studied under the same masters, and as young men we fought in the same campaigns. He knows how I think and what I will do."

"But if Tostig returns, he must fight an offensive war, which is difficult, while we need only maintain our defenses," Hakon argued.

"Yes, Hakon, that is true, but it is to Tostig's advantage that he will strike the first blow. He will choose when and where that shall be, while we must be ready and watchful and constantly on guard. I have little doubt that we can muster an adequate fyrd from the men of our country. But how long can we provision them? How long can the villagers be away from their fields? The crops cannot be left untended all summer. The sheep cannot be left without their shepherds."

When and where . . . that is the dilemma, Evyn thought. Harold knows that Tostig is coming. He knows that Tostig has gained the alliance of the mighty Harald Hardrada of Norway. But when and where were unknown. It was not possible to patrol the entire coast till winter closed in again, and it was too late for a spy to get close enough to know Tostig's plan. So the long, nerve-shattering watch began.

During Threemilki the news that Harold dreaded arrived. An English merchant returned from Normandy with the news that Duke William was building ships and calling up all the knights who owed him service.

Harold drew a deep breath when he heard the message. A lesser man would have left the crowded Hall to brood in solitude. But Harold, in his clear voice, said, "Let the watch patrols be doubled along the southern coast and increase the naval surveillance in the Narrow Sea from the Isle of Thanet to Exmouth. We shall guard our flank from that Norman dog." Then, as though the threat of a Norman invasion was nothing more than an annoyance, he called for the storyteller to begin a tale.

That night Harold called his thanes together for a meeting. He heard the counsel of each man before issuing the warning they all expected. "Be wary. Our enemies are descending upon us like a plague. Tostig lurks," the King said slowly as he paced. "I know not where, but he is waiting to strike. No doubt he will come with Harald Hardrada at his side. Now the treacherous Duke of Normandy sharpens his sword, too, and builds longships to run up on our beaches. Go home. Warn your people. Tell the men to sharpen their battle-axes. Tell the women they must sow the crops this year."

The kingdom stiffened for the expected blow. Throughout the shires the men kissed their wives and children goodbye, and the ranks of the fyrd began to swell. Blacksmiths sweated over their hot work from early morning to dusk, forging the battle-axes and spearpoints that would defend the nation. The lords of each village rationed the barley and wheat to provision the army, and the royal housecarls drilled the militiamen in battle skills.

And they waited.

Then, one day not long after, men on watch spotted Tostig's longships as they entered the harbor on the Isle of Wight. But even as Harold raced there with his troops, listening impatiently to tales of Tostig's plundering, his beguiling brother disappeared over the waves, sailing eastward.

Harold returned to London disappointed. There news arrived daily, sometimes hourly. Tostig's small fleet had been spotted off the Sussex coast. His men had raided the city of Hastings before escaping in their ships again. The next day a rider rushed in breathlessly, reporting that Tostig occupied Sandwich near the southeast tip of England. Harold, with his housecarls and militia, galloped to Kent, but Tostig was gone when their horses clattered into the town square. Women wept in the streets, for besides stealing whatever they could carry off, Tostig's men had kidnapped many and murdered those who opposed them.

"It was terrible to see, my lord," one woman cried as she wiped the tears from her face with the corner of her veil. "He took my brother and his two sons at swordpoint and all of the other men down at the harbor. He forced them to board their ships and join him. He has a fleet of nearly sixty vessels now, my lord."

Harold stood on the shore, staring at the empty sea while gulls shrieked over his head. The wives and children of the kidnapped sailors crowded around him, hoping for answers.

"By God's Holy Cross, if it is in my power I will free your men," he told them. They put their trust in the King and went back to their homes to wait.

"If only I could speak to him," Harold said quietly to Evyn when the others had left the harbor. He squinted at the bright horizon, searching for the ships that had long since sailed from view. The frustration of the previous weeks told on his worn face. There were dark circles under his eyes, and his features seemed tired and pinched, like those of a man who has endured much hardship. "I feel certain that I could persuade him to lay down his sword," he said.

Evyn turned sharply from the sea to his master. How could Harold be so blinded by his love for his brother? Did he not know that Tostig would rather drag the country into ruin than set aside his grievance?

"What are you thinking, Evyn?" the King asked.

Evyn bent to the wet sand where the foamy sea lapped at their feet. With the edge of a little shell he wrote: *You will have to kill him.*

Harold stared at the words for a moment. Then he looked at Evyn accusingly, and in a voice bereft of its usual kingly authority he whispered, "But he is my brother."

The next wave washed the words away, and Evyn promised himself he would never write of it again.

During the weeks that followed, it became clear that Tostig's anger would not be spent until he defeated Harold and regained his earldom. After Sandwich he struck at Norfolk, where Burnham River flowed through the salt marsh to the sea. Not long after that he stopped on the south shore of the Humber River, bringing his men far inland to see the lay of the land. But this time Edwin and his local militia caught them on open ground, slaying many of Tostig's men before the disgraced Earl could escape to the safety of his ships. The renegades then attempted to land in Yorkshire, but there young Morcar, who now bore the title of Earl of Northumbria, met him in a skirmish and freed the kidnapped sailors from Sandwich. Tostig fled with only twelve ships. He sailed north to Scotland, where his friend King Malcolm gave him shelter for the summer.

The time called Litha came and the women and children worked the farms as best they could. The hazy days of midsummer lengthened, and still they waited. Weedmonth followed, when the heat of the sun was at its strongest. Thistles sprang up in the fields, choking the crops, for there were too few laborers. The men from the heartland grumbled at their southern posts far from home. "While we sit and wait, our crops wither," they said.

The quartermaster came to the King. "Food grows scarce in the storerooms. I can no longer feed this army."

Harold sent riders to all the monasteries, and the monks responded by sending the fyrd their surplus and sometimes more, so that they went hungry in order for the King to keep his army assembled and ready for duty. But even that was not enough.

Harold dared not disband the fyrd. His housecarls alone, though well trained, were far too few to oppose the invading forces Harold knew would come. Yet each day reports arrived from the heart of the country that the men were needed to harvest what was left of the crops. But Harold refused to release them from their duty. "The danger has not passed," he said.

Weedmonth drew to a close, and Holymonth began. The crops that survived the weeds rotted in the fields for want of harvesters. The time of the fyrd's duty came to an end, and still Harold refused to release the men. Open grumbling broke out in the ranks. Their obligation had already been met, had it not?

"We must not sleep yet," Harold said.

And as always, Tostig eluded him.

Back in London, Gyrth argued strategy with the King.

"Our brother Tostig licks his wounds in Scotland."

"Yes, I know. No doubt he is waiting for Harald Hardrada and his army to join him. We must keep the fyrd in readiness."

"This plan will fail, Harold," Gyrth countered. "You cannot keep the fyrd waiting for months at a stretch. Most of the men are not soldiers. They are farmers. You've already extended their time. They must be allowed to return home to harvest the crops—it is hay time already. If you don't, the people will starve next winter. Keeping the fyrd ready before an invading army has even landed has never before been done."

"If I disband the fyrd and Tostig invades with Harald Hardrada at his back, he will surely devastate the land," Harold said bitterly. "Tostig and Hardrada won't be satisfied till we're all dead on the battlefield. Then William of Normandy will cross over and pick our bones clean."

Finally, in the second week of Holymonth, Harold reluctantly dismissed the fyrd so that the men could return home for the last days of harvest.

Evyn rode with the King and his housecarls to Dover

with the standard-bearer carrying the scarlet-and-gold Fighting Man banner before them. There the King announced that the men were free to return home for the harvest. After sending word to all of the coastal cities that the fyrd was dismissed, Harold ordered his fleet to seek harbor in London. That day he stayed in Dover and watched with concern as his soldiers left the city for their inland homes, their satchels slung across their backs.

At sunset he and Evyn climbed to the watchtower above the harbor overlooking the chalky cliffs. Evyn leaned against the railing and listened to the breakers rolling in and the cry of the gulls. The cool wind soothed his sunburned face. The last traces of sunlight painted the water blood-red at the horizon. They peered across the Narrow Sea toward the land of Normandy and its neighbors, Flanders and Ponthieu, so close that a longship could cross in half a day's time. Suddenly the wind changed from northwest to south. What had been a warm, late-summer breeze became a cold, damp blast from the south. The white-capped waves rolled high, crashing across the beach with growing force and a roar that made it difficult to hear.

Evyn pursed his lips and blew while making the hand sign for rain.

"Yes, you are right, Evyn. A storm comes this way. My knee tells me so," the King said, shifting his weight to his good leg. "We must pray that the fleet reaches London safely."

But it was not Harold's fate that his fleet should arrive unharmed in London. Thunderclouds billowed up from the south, and by midnight the sea became a churning whirlpool. Those vessels caught upon the open water sank along the coast from Thanet to Sheppey. The next morning, planks and torn sails washed up on the beaches of Kent.

Gathering his housecarls, Harold rode to London, wondering why God had turned against him.

As they approached the city, two of the King's scouts met them.

"We have news, my lord," one shouted from a distance as they raced their foam-flecked horses toward Harold. "Tostig has sailed again. He left Scotland with Harald Hardrada."

"How many ships have they?" the King asked.

"Their fleet is three hundred strong, and all the ships are fully manned."

The horsemen pulled their mounts up sharply as they reached Harold. "My lord, they sailed down the east coast of England and into the estuary of the Humber River. They rowed their ships far inland, all the way to Riccall. That's less than half a day's ride from York."

Speaking more to himself than anyone else, Harold said, "This time Tostig will not raid and flee like a Viking pirate. He has an army behind him now."

Harold spurred Thunder into a fast gallop toward London, and Evyn and all of the King's men followed. The trees flew past them in a blur. Harold turned to Evyn as they crouched low in their saddles, the wind in their faces. "We needed to know where and when he would strike—now we have the answers."

There could be no worse news. Much of Harold's navy lay at the bottom of the sea, the men of his fyrd had disbanded and left for their scattered villages, and provisions were scarce. He had sworn to protect his country, and now he was powerless. But he would not give up.

"With God's help I will defeat the enemy," he said once he'd reached the Great Hall in London.

Before he'd even dismounted, he had sent a dozen riders

to recall the fighting men of the shires near London. To other couriers he shouted, "Go to Earl Leofwine," and "Find my brother Gyrth." Within the hour five hundred housecarls formed ranks outside Harold's London Hall in full armor, their shields slung over their shoulders.

To the resounding thunder of many feet, the army began the long march. North of the city, Leofwine, with his housecarls and the local militia from the area, fell in behind. At nightfall, by the light of torches, Gyrth met them at a crossroads with his troops from East Anglia. The army, snaking its way north, grew ever larger. All along the old Roman road to York thanes appeared, mounted on fresh horses and well armed, ready to do battle. With them came their men of village, town, and farm.

They followed the paved road called Ermine Street as it cut through the great Chiltern Forest with its massive oaks. After they left the forest, they passed through meadowland for many leagues and finally stopped for the night. The next day they entered the Bruneswald Forest, through which flowed the river Nene, and marched until after sunset. On the fourth day, they trudged footsore through the marsh country of Lincolnshire as they turned their faces toward York.

"We tread upon Northumbrian soil now," Harold said when they reached the Humber.

He sent scouts ahead to seek out the Earls Edwin and Morcar.

They reached Tadcaster on Sunday night and pitched their tents by starlight, but they rested little. In the middle of the night an exhausted scout arrived and was immediately escorted to the King's tent. Before dawn lit the sky, Harold gave orders to strike camp, saying, "Edwin is in York. We must leave at once."

And so the men, who had slept as though they were dead, roused themselves, making their way to York in the half-light of dawn. There they came upon Edwin's bedraggled army in their hastily erected tents outside the city walls.

On hearing that the King had arrived, Edwin emerged from his striped pavilion. His eyes were hollow from sleeplessness. His hands shook at his sides, and his face was deathly pale.

The King braced himself. "What has happened?"

"My brother Morcar and I heard that Tostig and the Norwegians had landed. We mustered a large army of our housecarls and the thanes and villagers of Mercia and Northumbria. Gathering at York, we marched along the river till we reached the village of Fulford Gate. There we found them waiting for us." Edwin spoke with great weariness.

"The battle began quickly, and at first we drove hard so that their right flank fell back. But then Harald Hardrada rallied his men around his Landwaster banner. He pressed forward upon us, and we lost what we had gained. He pushed us back into the fens, and the hand-to-hand fighting was like that of snarling dogs. The slaughter was so great that the Norwegians walked dry-shod through the marshes over the bodies of the fallen. There were heavy losses on both sides, and the wounded shrieked all around us. We scrambled out of the wetlands as best we could and retreated to York. There we re-formed our lines and fought again. But by that time the shire reeve and some of the other great men of York talked of surrender. Archbishop Ealdred counseled against it, and as for Morcar and me, we would rather die. But there were many who, during the lull in fighting, came forward to Hardrada in submission."

"How many?" Harold asked.

"I don't know. Hundreds, perhaps. They are vile traitors," Edwin said in a low voice. "The Norwegians gladly took hostages to ensure peace in the city. Then, because they had lost so many of their own men, Tostig and Harald Hardrada left the city and returned to their ships downriver from York. And now, I am told, they plan to march upon us again this morning to accept more hostages from York at the little town called Stamford Bridge. With York falling to the enemy, everything is lost."

Edwin, exhausted, ended his story and covered his face in his hands.

Harold knew the young Earl needed time to compose himself, and he did not want Edwin's men to see their lord so tired and discouraged. Edwin took his hands from his face as the King led him down the slope to the riverbank. When they climbed back up the embankment a few minutes later, Edwin stood taller, with his shoulders squared. The weariness had left his beardless face, and he looked his men in the eyes again.

Leaping onto a supply wagon so that his voice carried over the campground, Harold turned to Edwin's dejected men. "Your Earl, Edwin of Mercia, has defended his people with courage and strength. His battle-ax has spilled much Norwegian blood, and he has confounded his enemy. His fiery heart prompted him to take up arms against the dreaded Harald Hardrada, the greatest Viking warrior alive, one who fought at the bloody Battle of Stiklestad, who journeyed to Constantinople and served in the Varangian Guard under the Empress. He is the terror of Sicily and North Africa. He slew many near the Black Sea and then returned north to redden the earth of Denmark with the blood of men.

"Yet we will defeat him. He is no match for us. This is our land, and he shall not have it."

The men of Edwin's and Morcar's armies lay exhausted from the battle. Harold's men, too, had dropped to the ground, on the brink of sleep from their long march north.

Harold gazed with compassion across row after row of spent men, yet he knew that he could not give them the rest they craved. "If we are fleet," he said, raising his voice, "and act with cunning as our ancestors did, we will catch this viper coiled under his Landwaster banner."

The men slowly lifted their heads and listened.

"We must not sleep while this Norwegian fouls our English soil," Harold said in his rolling tenor voice. "There can be no rest till we have won victory over the foreigners. It is little more than two leagues to Stamford Bridge. Quickly now, before the blood of our brothers dries on their swords, let us be away."

The housecarls, shamed to have been resting while the King stood, climbed to their feet and refastened their armor. They slid on their helmets and strapped them under their chins. They slung their kite-shaped shields over their shoulders. The archers counted their arrows, while the foot soldiers quickly refilled their water bags at the riverbank. Forming a loose column, they followed the housecarls, who had already mounted up and led the ranks. King Harold, flanked by Edwin and Morcar, spurred Thunder onward.

Only a little more than two leagues away, the Norwegians strolled through their makeshift camp set up along the river Derwent. There the great fleet of three hundred ships lay anchored end to end like a huge, nightmarish serpent. Though it was still early morning, the sun warmed the camp quickly. The Norwegians were in high spirits, singing and outdoing each other with tales of their battle prowess. Their Fulford Gate victory was good reason to celebrate, for Tostig, the renegade English Earl, had promised them all choice land in his lost earldom of Northumbria.

More than half of Harald Hardrada's army had received orders to march to Stamford Bridge to accept more hostages from the city of York. Because it was so hot, most of the men left their coats of mail and heavy shields behind. What had they to fear? Had they not defeated the combined armies of England's northern earls? Was not King Harold Godwinson far away on the southern coast? And were they not led by the invincible Harald Hardrada? They were merely marching a few leagues to Stamford Bridge to accept hostages from the beaten English.

Tostig swung gracefully up into his new saddle, a gift from Harald Hardrada. With a satisfied smile, he said, "It is a fine day for gathering a few dozen Northumbrian hostages."

The Norwegian King, a giant of a man, grinned arrogantly. "It is not the first time I have gathered hostages, my friend."

"No, indced," Tostig said, flattering his new ally. "Your fame as a warrior exceeds that of all others. The name Hardrada is spoken with fear, and when your Landwaster banner is raised on the field of battle, your enemies cower like mewling children."

They allowed the horses to amble along down a beaten track that bordered thc river. Overhead in a bright blue sky a flock of starlings flew south. Shielding his eyes from the sun, Tostig peered up at the birds.

"It is too hot by far," Harald Hardrada commented, wiping his brow with his forearm.

Tostig did not hear his ally's complaint. He had begun his journey as an outlaw with only one thought in mind: to destroy his brother Harold and to seize again all that he had lost. He closed his eyes for a moment against the bright sun and recalled, without wishing to, a day many years ago, hot and breathless like today, which he had spent with Harold in mock battle honing his weapon skill. They were only boys then. When Tostig fainted from the stifling heat, Harold had hoisted him over his shoulder and carried him home by the back path so that their exacting father, Godwin, would not see him weak as a toddler.

Tostig shook himself from his reverie and put his sour thoughts into words. "Harold is not the man he once was. It is his fault that I lost my earldom, and I intend to have it back. It will not be long before I return to my Great Hall in York."

"You will have it, Tostig Red Hair," Hardrada said, and the great Norwegian smiled.

Tostig scanned the dirt lane before him. Already he could see the old wooden bridge leading across the Derwent River. Stamford Bridge was not far beyond. They would negotiate terms of surrender with the Northumbrians and accept their hostages—it would not be long. Already the vanguard of the army was crossing the narrow bridge.

Suddenly Tostig's attention shifted to a distant puff of dust. He lifted his nose like a hound to the scent. As the cloud of dust drew near, scarlet banners grew distinct. The glint of sun upon metal-rimmed shield and mail shirt pricked his eyes. He turned to the Norwegian King riding at his side.

"The English have rallied," Tostig said fearfully. "Let us retreat to Riccall for reinforcements and fetch our armor."

"No need to retreat," Hardrada answered. "It is only the remnants of a broken army."

"No, it is more than that," Tostig said. "You must call for

reinforcements." He had seen the Fighting Man banner. He knew who led that army, and it wrenched at his heart.

The Norwegian smiled at the Englishman's concern. "If it pleases you, my friend, I will send for reinforcements, but we will not retreat to our ships at Riccall. My Norwegians must join us as they can."

When they saw the size of the army before them, chaos broke out among the Norwegians. From where had it come? Had they not defeated the English only days earlier? Why had they so foolishly left their shirts of mail behind?

Quickly the men retreated from the bridge. Harald Hardrada and Tostig dismounted and stood ready for battle. It was with difficulty that the King of Norway urged his men to form a shield wall. "Where is your courage?" he bellowed.

A shout rose among the English as they spied their enemy. A score of riders among them broke forth and rode toward the Norwegians to make an offer of peace. They were led by a man with golden hair who raised his hand for his comrades to halt. His voice, a vibrant tenor, carried across the field. "Let us speak first," he called to Tostig. He and his black-haired squire rode forward alone until they were less than ten paces from where Tostig and Harald Hardrada stood.

Looking straight into Tostig's brown eyes, the spokesman asked pointedly, "Is Earl Tostig in your army?"

There followed a long silence as Tostig glared back. Finally he said, in a voice edged with steel, "I am Tostig."

The other man steadied his restless horse and said, "Your brother Harold gives you greeting, and this offer: you can have peace, and all of Northumbria for your own. A third of the kingdom rather than no agreement."

Tostig sneered and squinted out from under his long

black eyelashes. "It is a better choice than you gave me last winter. But what does King Harald Hardrada of Norway get for his trouble?"

The Englishman leaned forward in his saddle and spoke in a lower, harder voice, enunciating each word with cold, clear precision. "A burial place . . . seven feet of English ground. Or, because he is taller than most, as much again if he needs it."

Tostig shivered involuntarily but quickly regained his composure. The outlawed Earl looked up at the rider before him. "Go back," he snarled, "and tell the English to make ready for battle. It will never be said in Norway that I brought Harald Hardrada to England, and then left him to join his enemies."

The man with the golden hair drew a deep breath as if he would say more, but whatever it was he wished to say remained unspoken. Instead he raised his arm in a formal salute, gazing sadly at the man before him. Tostig slowly returned the salute. The rider wheeled his horse abruptly and spurred him back toward the English lines, his squire following behind at a gallop.

When they had gone, Harald Hardrada asked, "Who was that man who spoke so smoothly?"

Tostig's face, once so handsome and animated, hardened as he said, "That was my brother Harold Godwinson."

The burly Norwegian said curtly, "That I should have been told before. They came so near that Harold should never have gone back to tell of what he saw."

"True enough, it is a reckless thing he did, and we could have taken advantage from it," Tostig answered. "I saw he was going to offer me peace, and that I might be the death of him if I told you who he was. But I would rather let him be the death of me."

The Norwegian King, puzzled, studied Tostig's face but found no answer.

The battle began, and, like a wizard hurling thunderbolts, Harold Godwinson conjured an attack that made the very ground shake. He threw his housecarls, mounted on lathered horses and stern-faced behind their low-browed helmets, against the Norwegian shield wall. Three times the English horsemen charged, and each time the Norwegians staggered before the blow. As the cavalry retreated, Harold signaled his archers to nock their deadly iron-tipped arrows. With a hum of released string and a whine of flying feathers the arrows skimmed through the air, thick as hail. The Norwegians fell back, tripping over their own dead as Harold led his men into hand-to-hand combat. They raced forward and hurled their throwing spears and unsheathed their long swords. Those who favored the battle-ax marched onward, cutting a bloody path before them.

"Stout Norwegians! Sons of Vikings!" Harald Hardrada bellowed. "Stand your ground!" He fought in the thickest part of the battle. His rage kept even Harold's champion housecarls at bay, as a wounded bear keeps the hounds beyond striking distance. Even so, by midafternoon the Norwegian losses were many. Many a man died cursing his decision to leave his armor back with the ships.

The discipline of the English troops, who acted as one body under Harold's commands, proved superior to the individual courage of the Norwegians. The shield wall broke where Hardrada's warriors fell, and the English pressed their advantage. By late afternoon the tall, bearded adventurer who had fired his men with lust for foreign plunder fell. Harald Hardrada, who had survived so many battles that his men claimed he was immortal, sank to the ground with a spear thrust in his throat. Those near him, who had used his strength to bolster their own, fell soon afterward. The Landwaster banner dropped in a heap and was trampled under the surge of English feet.

But Tostig, with his hair turned to fire by the blazing sun, retrieved it and rallied the Norwegians. Once more the battle trumpets sounded and sword sought soft flesh. In the cloudless sky carrion birds circled, waiting their turn.

During a lull in the fighting, Harold sent an offering of peace to Tostig and to all who remained with him. But the former Earl of Northumbria, desperate now and battle-crazed, screamed, *"No! . . . No! . . . No!"* over and over again until his voice became a hoarse cry. The Norwegians took up the shout, and the battle renewed itself with an angry roar.

Though by custom squires did not fight in battle, Evyn remained near Harold throughout the day. He left only to retrieve weapons or to carry water to the wounded. Late in the day as he returned from one of these trips, he found Harold locked in combat with an opponent so evenly matched that it was difficult to guess the outcome. Harold's enemy fought with graceful agility and savage violence, his fury infusing his muscles with added strength. The Norwegian wore a tunic of blue silk, and bands of gold circled his arms. Then Evyn saw the hair. *It is no Norwegian,* he thought with a shudder.

Tostig leaped forward, grasping his sword in both hands. He slashed at Harold again and again. The King parried each blow with his iron-rimmed shield. Harold thrust with his own sword, but only to fend off the other warrior, not to harm him. Thrust and parry, the ring of Tostig's sword upon Harold's shield clanged through the air.

Evyn watched as he quickly made his way back to Harold. Time slowed, and the only sound to reach his ears was that horrible clang and thud, always the same. It grew clear to Evyn that even if the King could, he would not strike the fatal blow at his beloved brother. The sun beat down upon them mercilessly, and Evyn knew that Harold, burdened by his heavy armor, could not continue for long. Already the sweat dripped from his chin strap.

Evyn strode through the crushed, bloodstained grass. As the air around him echoed with the shrieks of the dying, he took up the sword of one who had fallen. It felt heavier than he remembered from his days in the practice field. Heavier and deadlier. When Harold staggered backward and fell under a sharp blow from Tostig's long sword, Evyn stepped between them. Recalling everything Hakon had taught him, he aimed surely and swiftly. But Tostig blocked it, and with a dancer's agility he easily sidestepped Evyn's next blow, too.

Shaking his sweat-dampened hair from his eyes, Tostig smiled maliciously. "When Harold cannot conquer he sends for his Shadow." The ruthless traitor beckoned to Evyn. "Come forth, Shadow, and fight a man of substance. He who is dumb must let his sword speak for him. Speak, Shadow," he cried, "or is your sword as dumb as you?"

Tostig charged, and Evyn barely dodged the sword point. The blood pounded in Evyn's ears, and his heart knocked against his chest. What had Hakon taught him? His brain whirled. Tostig was clearly his superior in skill and strength, but Evyn was not tired from a full day of combat as his opponent was. Neither wore armor or held a shield. It was a dangerous duel. Soon Evyn's arm ached from gripping the sword hilt, and sweat rolled into his eyes, blinding him. He knew that he must act quickly, but Tostig caught him off guard. With a hard and sudden blow he knocked the sword from Evyn's grasp and rushed upon him like a wild animal, all flying hair and bared teeth. Evyn hopped back lightly to avoid the next blow and automatically reached for the dagger at his belt. He stabbed Tostig low in the ribs with a hard upward thrust into his heart. At once a dark spot stained the blue silk of his tunic.

With a surprised look, Tostig dropped his sword, like a puppet whose string master has lost interest. He put his hand to his chest, and when he drew it away it was scarlet with blood. As Tostig's knees buckled, Harold swooped forward like a hawk from behind Evyn. He gathered his brother up and carried him to the English rear lines. There he cradled his brother in his arms and watched with pity as the blood drained from his body. They exchanged anguished whispers until Tostig's head drooped, and the King buried his own tearstained face in his brother's fiery hair.

1066

. . . and while they sat at the victory feast in York a weary messenger limped to Harold's side.

By the time the first stars shone in the purple sky over Stamford Bridge, the English claimed victory. They had slain Harald Hardrada, the Norwegian King, and chased the savage Vikings all the way back to their ships at Riccall. Tostig lay dead, too, and there was no one left to rally the Norwegians. So the invaders laid down their weapons and surrendered, throwing themselves upon the mercy of the English King.

As was his custom, Harold proved generous in victory. He took pity on Harald Hardrada's family, permitting the Norwegian's youthful son, Olaf, to rejoin his mother and his sisters at their refuge in Scotland, and return across the sea-road they had traveled. There were few companions to go with them. So great was the slaughter from the two battles that of the huge fleet of three hundred dragon ships that brought the Norwegians to England a mere twenty-four were needed to carry the survivors home again.

The day following the battle, Harold attended to all the details a warrior king must oversee. He had his men collect the weapons and armor of the enemy. A mountain of battle plunder rose higher and higher as the English stacked up chain mail shirts, helmets, shields, and war axes. He left commands that the wounded should have their injuries attended to and then be carried in wagons to the nearest monastery, where they might recover or die in peace. Returning to the field near the old wooden bridge, Harold said, "Now it is time to bury the dead of both armies."

"Leave the Norwegians for the ravens and wolves to feast upon," Edwin argued. "It is our custom. If the victory had been theirs, they would have left us for the ravens to eat," he added as he strode after Harold through the meadow littered with the bodies of fallen warriors. "Or worse, they might have taken our heads home on spikes as battle trophies."

"No, Edwin," the King answered after hearing him out. "We must put aside the old barbarian ways."

The giant Norwegian King was given the seven feet of English soil he had been promised. But when Harold came to Tostig's body, which had been laid in the King's own tent, he insisted that it be anointed with holy oil and dressed in a rich quilted tunic of forest green from the royal clothes chest. When that was done, Harold slid a circlet of beaten gold around Tostig's bright hair and pale brow. At dusk on the second day, they buried him in the sun-warmed earth of Northumbria as Archbishop Ealdred read the prayers for the dead. Soon the last shovelful of dirt fell upon Tostig's grave.

Seeing the stricken look on Harold's face, Ealdred spoke. "Though you grieve, and rightly so, there are still many reasons to give thanks. The blow to England came, and you repulsed it. You and your brother earls, Gyrth and Leofwine, survived the battle, which means that the south remains in secure and experienced hands. Edwin and Morcar, too, have lived and have proven their courage and their loyalty to you at the battles of Fulford Gate and Stamford Bridge. Winter approaches, and the seas grow rough. The Norman Duke will not launch his ships till spring. Let us celebrate in York. Your men are exhausted and need time to rest."

"Yes, you are right, as usual, Counselor. But I had so hoped it would not end this way," Harold said, glancing one last time at the fresh grave before he walked away to be alone in his pavilion.

During the following days, Evyn avoided Harold. He watched his master from a distance, where he would not be seen by Harold. After the battle, Evyn assisted the field surgeons in their work of washing and bandaging wounds. The English victories had cost them dearly, for the dead were beyond counting and the wounded numbered in the hundreds.

Evyn's thoughts accused him without ceasing, and he plunged himself into the work of healing to escape the voice in his head that whispered, *He hates you now.*

Once, when he looked through the open flap of the hospital tent and saw the King approaching, Evyn ducked out. Later, after the English army moved its temporary headquarters to York's Great Hall, Evyn ate and slept with the other squires. He did not take his usual place at Harold's shoulder at the High Table or at his chamber door at night. He could not bear to let the King see him. He slew Tostig to save Harold and did not regret his act. But what must Harold think? He must loathe him for slaying the brother he loved. Evyn was certain of it. Hour by hour, the boy's agony grew. He had wanted only to serve Harold, whom he had grown to love like a father. But in saving Harold's life Evyn felt that he had dealt a death blow of another kind to the King, one from which Harold would not recover. Evyn knew that his presence would be a constant reminder to Harold of Tostig's death.

What a cruel trick this is, he thought, jeering at himself. *At the moment when I conquer my own fear, when I act bravely, without thought for myself, I should destroy the only thing of worth to me—the King's goodwill. I thought I should be happy if I could just once act like one of the champions I used to tell of . . . I have gotten my wish, and it has brought only sadness. There is only one thing for me to do now.*

On the third morning after they moved to York, Evyn found the King walking with Archbishop Ealdred in the meadows. He watched as they strode together under a damp, overcast sky. Even at a distance he knew the King immediately as he walked along, barely favoring his leg. The scarlet cloak, which swung at his knees, dipped just a little lower each time Harold put weight on the old wound. He lifted his head for a moment as a curlew cried over the next field, but he did not see Evyn.

Evyn stopped. *It is too hard to face him.* Beyond the river Ouse, fields and pastures stretched as far as he could see. A few sheep cropped the grass and a lone kestrel circled in the sky above. Then he stopped and cursed himself—had he no courage left to do what he must? Despite his misgivings, Evyn forced himself to continue onward, and soon the Archbishop's deep voice grew audible.

Ealdred strode with his arms folded across his chest. He was taller than Harold by a head and wider through the shoulders. Speaking in a low rumble, he shared his wisdom with Harold, who kept pace with him along the path that an early morning rain had turned soft. He walked with his hands clasped behind his back, as a man does when he has much to ponder. Nodding now and then, he sometimes questioned his counselor, but more often he silently drank in the words of advice Ealdred offered him. He turned his head a bit, and Evyn saw him smile slightly at something Ealdred said.

Evyn took a deep breath as he drew near the King. Did he dare do this? Had he really made the right decision? Perhaps he should leave. It wasn't too late. But at that moment Harold glanced back and saw him. There was no turning around now.

Evyn drew out the note he had written and handed it to Harold. He knelt before his master, and the tall, wet grass brushed against his elbows. Harold read it in silence while Evyn remained on his knees, his head bowed. When Harold finished, he handed the note to Ealdred, who read it aloud:

"*Like a thief I have stolen your brother*
from you and for that I must be hateful
in your sight. Therefore, I beg leave to
be excused from your service.
My gratitude shall remain unwritten,
for it exceeds all the words I know.
Evyn of Carmarthen"

"It is strange, is it not," Harold said to Ealdred when he had finished reading, "that I should receive a message such as this from one I know not. I do not know *this* Evyn of Carmarthen," the King said, tapping the note, which Ealdred still held. He paused, fondly gazing down at the squire who knelt before him.

"I know an Evyn who is sometimes called Evyn Blackhair or Shadow. I know the Lady Ealdgyth Swan Neck calls the one who serves me best the King's Shadow. *This Evyn,*" he said, tapping the parchment in Ealdred's hand again, "claims he killed my brother. But I know none such as that. I do know one called Evyn who gave me my life a few days ago when my duty to my people faltered, when I could not bring myself to do what had to be done. I have come to know and love this Evyn over the past few years. He is one I would not part with for anything."

Evyn felt hot tears well up into his eyes, much to his shame.

"If it is true that he has taken my brother from me, then he must replace that brother with a worthy gift." He paused for a moment before speaking again. "There is one whom a man cherishes even more than a brother, and that is a son. If it pleases you, Archbishop, have it read from the cathedral this afternoon that the King takes a foster son, and that foster son is the one whom the people call the King's Shadow."

"It shall be done," Ealdred said, with a smile lighting his dark features.

Harold took the parchment from Ealdred's hand, tore it into pieces, and let the wind carry the fragments away. The timbre of his voice grew lighter now. "I do know that if this son of mine remains kneeling in the grass much longer, he will be too wet to be presentable in the cathedral this afternoon."

Evyn didn't know what to do. His head spun. *The King's foster son.* He had certainly never expected this. But Harold made it easy for him by drawing him gently to his feet and wrapping his arm around his shoulder.

That afternoon Evyn knelt next to the King on the stone flagging of York's steep-roofed cathedral. Ealdred, surrounded by acolytes and monks, chanted the victory prayers at the altar. The heavy aroma of incense filled Evyn's nostrils, and a warm, dreamy haze drifted across the cavernous cathedral. Finally, after saying the prayers of dismissal, Ealdred announced, "The King has taken a foster son. He is the one the Saxons call Shadow, the King's squire and clerk."

Evyn, who had grown accustomed to the stares of the Saxons over the years, felt the eyes of the people on him once again. He knew that they thought him odd. He had even heard the whispers of some who said a Druid witch from the Welsh hills had cursed him with silence. Mothers kept their little ones from coming too close. But tonight the whispers were different.

"The King's foster son . . ." they said with awe.

"He saved the King's life."

"It was he who slew the cursed outlaw Tostig."

It was late afternoon when Harold and Evyn burst out of the cathedral. With a whistle of wings the frightened pigeons fluttered up to their niches above the west doors. The King and his new son crossed the open square before York's Great Hall. As a great crowd surrounded them, Harold draped his arm around Evyn's shoulder and said, "Now comes the victory feast I promised." They entered the Hall and were seated, the smell of food wafting through the room. Joints of steaming venison were passed out, followed by joints of beef, ham, and mutton. Bowls of apples sat on the tables flanked by pitchers of mead and plates holding huge wedges of cheese. Baskets of fresh bread rested beside platters of small honey cakes. The Hall was crowded with tables and benches to accommodate the victors. Banners hung from the rafters, indicating the noble families of Mercia and Northumbria.

The King took his place at the High Table, and, for the first time, Evyn sat by his side. The music of harps rippled through the air, and the feasting began. For men who had been on the march, who had had nothing but stale bread and brackish water, who had faced death and lived, it was a feast to be spoken of in their old age to their children and grandchildren.

After each had eaten till he could eat no more, while there was still an hour of light left, Edwin took his leave, begging the permission of the King to return to Mercia now that the threat of invasion had passed. Morcar, at his brother's side as usual, also asked leave of his duties as host to ride to the Mercian border with Edwin. He promised to return the next afternoon. The King gave his blessing, and they departed with their thanes and housecarls.

The remaining men loosened their belts and rested their elbows upon the tables. The Northumbrian women sat by them, listening to the stories they told. Relieved of the burden they had carried all week, the men in the Hall grew joyful. When the conversation quieted, the King called out, "Let the storyteller come forward."

A man rose from a bench at the far end of the Hall, and, as he came forward, a housecarl he passed cried, "Tell us of Beowulf."

"Yes, Beowulf the Warrior King," another echoed.

"Let it be Beowulf's fight with the Fire Dragon."

The *storiawr* came to the High Table and stopped near the fire not far from Evyn.

"Shall it be Beowulf and the Fire Dragon, Sire?"

"Yes, it is a good story," Harold answered, "one that is fitting for the heroes in this Hall."

The *storiawr* stood with his back to the fire so that his blond hair appeared as a halo around his dark face. The logs shifted and a shower of sparks flew up behind him. A hush fell over the Hall and all faces, of warrior and woman, young and old, turned toward him. He spoke in the lilting cadence of the border Saxons of the Severn River valley, and there was fire in his voice:

> *"Then for the last time Beowulf spoke to his warriors,*
> *Greeting them man by man. 'Dearest comrades,*
> *I am ready now—let the dragon face me if he dare!*
> *You, my warriors, stand patient on the headlands*
> *and watch—this fight is none of yours.' "*

As he told the story, the servants quietly closed the window shutters against the chill evening air and lit the torches and lamps.

> " *'My courage surely shall kill and win the treasure,*
> *unless fate—*
> *Whose word is final, to whom in obedience*
> *unquestioned*
> *Even kings must bow—shall deal me death.' "*

Beowulf's story was an old one among the English, but to Evyn it was new, and he listened intently as the storyteller wove magic with words. The man was not tall like the other English. But with his hooked nose and his quick, birdlike movements, he gave the impression of a majestic bird of prey. He paused often for dramatic effect, and the sudden silences drew everyone's attention. This was the story of the death of a king.

Even kings must obey fate. And even kings must die. Evyn shivered as if a cold finger slid down his back. He looked around and saw Gyrth swirl the last dregs in his cup before gulping it down. The gentle and quiet Leofwine, whom Evyn had liked from the beginning, rested his chin in the palm of his hand. One of the hounds pushed his big head on Leofwine's knee, and Harold's youngest brother cupped his other hand around the dog's ear. He kept his eyes on the storyteller as if he, too, was hearing it for the first time. Then Evyn felt someone watching him. When he turned he saw the King looking at him solemnly.

Harold leaned over and spoke as one man does to another when he has precious words to share. "It pleases me that fate brought us together. I am proud to call you son."

Later, when vespers rang from the cathedral bell tower, many of Harold's housecarls put their dice away, rolled up in their scarlet cloaks, and fell asleep in the far corner of the Hall. Others remained wakeful, talking quietly among themselves. The usual boisterous carousing, which so often followed a great victory, was curiously absent. The men remained subdued and thankful for their good fortune. There would be no cruel boasting tonight. At the High Table, King Harold relaxed with his brothers Gyrth and Leofwine. He talked with them of Tostig with sorrow but not regret. Tostig had caused his own downfall, and though they missed him sorely, they had upheld their duty to protect the country. But often their thoughts drifted far back in time, to happier days when they had all gone hunting with hound or hawk, to the days when Tostig was young, before the bitterness entered his soul.

The trestle tables were taken apart and put away, and

one by one the thanes of York left with their wives and their children and their housecarls. The women of Morcar's household bade the King good night and withdrew to their upstairs quarters.

Ealdred's hooded eyes gleamed by the light of the fire. As he rose to take his leave, he promised thirty days of Masses for Tostig's soul. Harold gripped the Archbishop's hands gratefully in his own. "And offer, in my name, thanksgiving Masses, too, for the victory, and the cathedral school shall be enriched by the Norwegian coffers," Harold said.

Ealdred departed with the few monks who had joined him. As he left, he passed a guest newly arrived. Few took notice as the man slipped into the Great Hall. The housecarls continued to snore peacefully, while those talking quietly looked up for a moment and then resumed their conversations.

Thorketil limped in, his gait contorted by pain. He passed the sleeping housecarls and the small clusters of men and women. He hobbled under the dragon banner of Wessex and the banner of Northumbria. Slowly he dragged himself beneath the hanging lamps. The light caught his face, showing the dark circles under his eyes and the long, black eyebrows drawn together in a tortured grimace. When he reached the High Table where Harold sat, he stopped.

Harold looked up from his talk, and when he saw Thorketil's face, the warmth drained from his own, for though he treasured Thorketil's skills, he knew this spy rarely brought good news. "What information do you carry, friend?" Harold asked softly.

Thorketil collapsed at the King's feet. Evyn hurriedly jumped up from his place and attended him. His pulse was weak, and protruding bones showed that the man was half-starved. The palms of his hands oozed with sores where the reins had rubbed against them. He must have ridden hard and fast. His soft kidskin shoes were little more than bloody rags.

Evyn took a cup of warm mead and held it to the spy's lips. Thorketil sipped weakly and finally his eyes cleared.

"I rode from the south, my lord, from Hastings. I rode until my horse dropped from under me, and then I stole another and rode till that one dropped as well. After that I ran for as long as my heart held out." His voice barely rose above a hoarse whisper.

"I would gladly it be another carrying this tale," he said before fainting away again. While they waited for him to regain the little strength he had, Evyn bathed his face in warm water and filled a plate with bread and cheese for him.

But when he opened his eyes once more, Thorketil waved the food away. "Duke William of Normandy has landed near Hastings at the head of a vast army." He spoke quickly, as though fearful of fainting before he finished. "He has swollen his own Norman army with mercenary soldiers from Flanders and Brittany. He has gathered mounted knights, footmen, and archers. The Narrow Sea is clogged with more than seven hundred ships. They jam the harbor at Pevensey near Hastings. Such a fleet I have never before seen, and each ship was crowded with war-horses and stout warriors armed with sword and shield, ax and mace."

Thorketil filled his aching chest with air. "This is not all, my lord. In Normandy, William constructed a wooden castle in pieces to be assembled here on English soil. From this fort he rides forth each day with his men, burning every farm and homestead in his path. He claims he is the rightful heir and that you are a usurper. He says"—and here Thorketil faltered, for although he knew Harold to be a fair man, he knew not how the King would react to his next words—"he says you are an oath-breaker."

Gyrth jumped to his feet. "That bastard grandson of a tanner!" he yelled, spitting his words out with a vicious anger.

Harold, painfully recalling the oath he had been forced to take in Normandy, said, "Yes, he is a man without honor, but it is by his own choosing. It has nothing to do with his birth."

Harold turned to Leofwine and Gyrth. "We must send word to the hills of Mercia and to the broad, flat land of East Anglia, to the strongholds of the Jutes and to my people in green Wessex. Let the Britons of the Welsh country ride swiftly on their mountain ponies, and call the Northumbrians to come down from the moors and join us. Tell the riders to leave at first light with the message to meet in London. But for tonight," the King said with compassion, "say nothing."

Evyn gazed at the men throughout the Hall. They were still speaking quietly among themselves, a snatch of laughter here and there. Contentment warmed their faces, for they remained unaware of the spy's message.

"Since there is nothing more we can do now, say nothing. Let them rejoice tonight so that no thief can steal their gladness."

1066

Then Duke William sailed from Normandy
with a great fleet.

"I thought we had more time," Harold said in a low, angry voice to the group at the High Table. "I thought the Normans wouldn't land until next spring. In the past week the country has fought two pitched battles the likes of which haven't been seen in England in my lifetime. The north is wet with our blood. The men are so tired that they sleep on their feet."

Far away to the north the cry of a wolf floated upon the nighttime wind. It sounded over the meadows. It drifted over the walls of York and into the Great Hall. The hounds lifted their heads from their paws and listened.

"I thought we were safe until the end of winter. I thought we could rest and rebuild the fyrd and be ready come spring. But this news . . . this monster in Hastings who burns our people in their homes . . ." and his voice trailed off.

"When I accepted the crown, I dreamed of peace," Harold went on. "I wanted to build roads and bring more land under cultivation so that there would always be food for our people. I wanted to establish more monasteries and bring learning to my thanes. There are so few who can read. But in the short time that I have been King there has been nothing but combat and contention. I have spent all of my energy chasing Tostig and pushing the Norwegians out. This is what I have brought my people: they are ignorant and starving and drowning in battle blood."

The wolf howled again, and this time it was answered by another.

Gyrth, whose face was flushed from the mead, said, "My ax is still sharp. You will see me and the men of East Anglia riding south tomorrow."

"I too," Leofwine said, his long face very solemn. "You can count on London and the land of Kent."

As Gyrth and Leofwine went to their guest chambers, Harold gently shook Thorketil, who had fallen asleep. Evyn drew a bench up to the warmth of the fire. With the exhausted Thorketil propped up between them, Harold bade his spy to tell everything he knew, sparing no details.

"Last spring, after bringing you news of Tostig's alliance with Harald Hardrada, I took passage on a merchant ship sailing for Normandy." Thorketil paused to rub the sleep from his eyes. The long, black eyebrows arched over his knuckles. "When I reached Dives, I knew that the rumors of an invasion were not just the talk of idle sailors. Duke William was in the midst of building a fleet the size of which was nearly beyond counting. Seven hundred ships, my lord. I wouldn't have believed it if I hadn't seen it with my own eyes."

"All fighting ships?" Harold asked incredulously.

"Oh, not all fighting ships, no, many are transport ships, like the kind the ferrymen use on the Thames to carry horsemen and wagons back and forth. They are broad-decked boats to store goods and carry horses. They need a calm sea to navigate safely." Thorketil covered a yawn before he continued.

"William prowled the harbor nearly every day, overseeing the shipwrights. 'Hurry,' he said to the carpenters. By midsummer the Duke sent out a call for mercenaries, so I disguised myself as a wandering knight looking for service and was accepted into his army.

"Though the fleet was ready soon after and everything stored aboard, the weather was poor for a crossing—too much rain and wind from the north. Then, on the twelfth day of Holymonth the wind shifted. The fleet pulled up anchor and left Dives. But as soon as we reached the open sea, a sudden storm blew up from the south. The Duke's ships raced to the Norman city of Saint-Valéry for cover.

"For many days the weather was cold and wet, and the sky was dark with clouds. But then the wind turned, and the clouds broke apart. With rejoicing, the Normans set sail again."

While Thorketil told his story, Evyn figured back in his head. William had tried to cross the very week that Harold allowed the fyrd to leave for home and harvest. The evening at the Dover watchtower when the sun turned the water blood-red . . . that was the same evening the Normans were caught in the storm that sank many of Harold's own ships. While the Saxons buried their dead at Stamford Bridge, William anchored his ships in Pevensey's wide, sheltered harbor.

Thorketil took the cup from Evyn's hands and drank till it was empty. "But William's flagship, the *Mora*—now, that is a fighting longship," Thorketil said, placing the cup on the table. "I was able to sneak aboard as the fleet disembarked from Saint-Valéry. We lifted anchor in late afternoon when the winds grew favorable for a crossing, the rowers pulling us out into the sea. When dusk fell, William ordered the lantern raised on the masthead as a beacon for the other ships to follow. The *Mora* is a sleek, swift ship. With the wind in her sail, she skimmed over the water like a swallow, so that by dawn we found ourselves alone on the sea with neither land nor ship in sight. Some of the sailors grew anxious to be cut off from the rest of the fleet, but the Duke acted as if he were on a picnic and called for his breakfast. 'Bring me spiced honey wine,' he said." Evyn smiled a little when he heard how accurately Thorketil had caught Duke William's growl.

"My lord," Thorketil continued, as he leaned wearily on Evyn's shoulder, "his blustering paid off. Before he finished his meal, we spotted the sails of the rest of the fleet following our sea-path. We sailed on together and landed at Pevensey, where the ruins of the old Roman fort stand. As they pulled their longships up onto the pebbled beach, the noise was deafening. The shingle was so crowded that they had to take turns unloading the horses and armor and food wagons." Thorketil shook his head. "I have seen armies before, my lord, but never anything so bold as this."

"Now tell me," Harold said, "how many warriors? What is the number of horses?"

While Evyn took a bowl of water and gently washed the raw sores on Thorketil's hands, the spy searched his memory and gave Harold every scrap which might be useful.

"You serve me well, Thorketil," Harold said, slipping a ring from his own finger and giving it to his spy. "Go sleep now. You have earned your rest."

"Thank you, my lord," Thorketil said with quiet dignity.

Morcar's steward came from the kitchen and extinguished the lights till only a few pale lamps lit the Hall. He built up the fire. "Do you desire anything, Sire?" he asked.

When Harold shook his head, the man bowed and retired for the night. The King stretched his bad leg out and rubbed his knee. Evyn leaned forward to catch the warmth of the fire. The embers glowed red at the edges and a steady flame crackled and spit. The heavy smell of roasted meat lingered in the air.

"I had so hoped to be a good king," Harold said, as if in a trance. He shook himself. "You should get some sleep, Evyn."

Evyn did not move. He would not leave Harold's side. Though the King was surrounded by his brothers and housecarls, he seemed lonely. Thoughts of the future weighed heavily on his heart.

"You will keep me company?"

Evyn nodded.

"Good. I am glad of it."

They sat and stared at the fire, waiting for dawn to break.

"The men of Iceland would call us coal-biters," Harold mused.

Evyn turned to him, puzzled.

"It is a word they use for friends who sit close by the fire all night, telling each other stories or unburdening their hearts."

At dawn, Harold and his army saddled their horses and cantered out of York. He had told his men Thorketil's story. The Wessex men, hearing that their homes and families were in danger, rushed to pack their few things. Evyn stuffed some food in his bag and swung up onto the saddle. As he spurred his horse on—for Harold was determined to reach London as quickly as possible—his thoughts sped where he wished they would not go.

He was the King's foster son now. He must be at the King's side when Harold faced Duke William. He so feared that his heart would prove cowardly. Why did others have the gift of courage but not he? He had been so frightened of the sons of Gryffin. And his heart had raced like that of a sparrow caught in the hand when he first looked upon Harald Hardrada. He had never seen such a fearsome warrior. He knew why Edwin's hands shook. After he fought Tostig he had thought, for a few days, that he had conquered his fear, that he was courageous. But it quickly faded. He found himself anxiously biting his lip whenever he chanced to think upon William of Normandy.

Courage slips through your fingers like water.

Now he must face the treacherous Norman Duke, and there would be no masquerade of courtesy this time. Evyn remembered the heads thrust upon the spikes at the entrance to the Duke's city. He had seen his cruelty in battle, the homes burned and the men mutilated. He remembered the Duke's disdain even for his own men when Harold saved the Norman soldier from drowning. Thorketil had said, "The English fly from William. They hide in the cemeteries, less afraid of ghosts than they are of the Normans."

Harold often left his place at the front of the long line to ride slowly back along the road. He encouraged his soldiers, saying, "Let us hurry to the south. We will push the Normans back into the sea. We will push them out." He raised his sword in the air and shouted, "*Out!*"

Men up and down the long line repeated his cry: "*Out! Out! Out!*"

They stopped only once each day, when the sun was at

its highest. Fathers and sons shared what bread or salted meat they had brought. Some washed their feet in cool river water. Others collapsed in the grass, falling into an exhausted sleep.

At every crossroads, Harold posted riders to the nearest towns to alert the local thanes and shire reeves to send the militia. Every hour more men, some on horseback, some on foot, joined the long column as it wound its way south to London. After they passed through the Bruneswald forest, a rider from the south reached them. He carried tales of William's destruction.

"He ravages the land. He burns everything in his path, and he kills every Englishman he comes upon. Sussex is becoming a land of widows and orphans. The people weep in Hastings and all along the coast road. They beg your help."

Later that same day, after they had covered another three leagues, a second rider burst over the hill before them. "William has already erected a wooden castle near Hastings," the man said, amazed. "It was all shaped and framed and pierced to receive the pins. The Normans raised it in only a few hours' time and encircled it with a strong wall of timber and dug a ditch around it." This was the castle Thorketil had described, built in pieces in Normandy to be easily assembled after landing in England.

Harold spurred his horse even faster then.

On the fifth day of Winterfyllith, the weeks the Romans called October, as they drew near London, a small entourage galloped north to meet them. Harold raised his arm to halt the growing army following in his wake. He rode ahead alone.

It was she. The Lady Ealdgyth Swan Neck cantered her mare forth from a wooded area. She was framed by golden maple leaves and black branches and her auburn hair flowed unbound past her shoulders, as though she had saddled and ridden quickly without waiting for her woman to braid it. Spying Harold, she signaled her housecarls to stop as she, too, rode forward alone. It had been months since they had last seen each other.

Harold reached over and took her reins to steady her horse for her. The pinched expression that often covered the King's face now slipped away. He sat in his saddle speechless, as though he were a boy again, seeing her for the first time. She pulled a stray lock of hair from across her face where the wind had blown it. Her gaze wandered from the lines under his eyes, and the sharp planes of his cheekbones, down to his hands, worn by so many days of hard riding.

"You are tired, Sire," she said softly. "Come to Waltham with me and rest in your chamber. A king needs to gather his strength to lead his army."

"No, I must go on. I must stop the Duke of Normandy."

She smiled a little, for she knew he would answer her this way. "Take me with you, then," she said, determined to be by his side.

The man who commanded the armies of England was powerless to deny her. He raised her hand to his lips and kissed it.

"The witan awaits you in London," she said.

"How is the south?" Harold asked. His heart ached for his homeland.

The glow left her face as she answered. "The south is in flames."

While the King's small fleet of longships ferried the army from the north shore of the Thames to the south, Harold called a hurried meeting of the witan. When the King entered the chamber, a mob of troubled voices reached his ears.

"Thank God and all the saints! You are here, Sire."

"What is your counsel, friends?" Harold asked as he sat in the great chair at the head of the table.

"We can agree on nothing," one thane said angrily.

"Let us delay while we gather more of the fyrd," the shire reeve of London advised. "The army is incomplete. The men with you are exhausted. Many of them have fought two pitched battles back to back."

But Eadric, Harold's chief landholder in Dover, whose city lay in Duke William's path, countered. "Each day that we delay, William destroys more of the countryside. He's burned whole settlements. He slaughters the sheep and pigs and lets them rot in the fields. I have seen the black smoke, and I have smelled the stench of decay."

A man from the north said, "His own provisions will not last forever. Perhaps we should wait and let his army starve."

Eadric smashed his fist upon the table. "Why do we sit here talking while the coast lands cry for our rescue?"

Harold spoke. "William is only a man, and like all men he has much to fear. I will send an ambassador to him to tell him that I have won a great victory in the north over the dreaded Harald Hardrada and that my mercy has run out. Let the ambassador tell him to leave England immediately."

This was accepted by all. An ambassador, carrying a diplomat's flag, left within the hour escorted by heavily armed troops.

"Now we must wait," Harold said.

. . .

Five days later an arrogant Norman monk arrived in London with William's message.

"What does Duke William say?" Harold asked as the monk was escorted into the witan's chamber.

"Duke William says," the monk began haughtily, "that Harold's words are not those of a wise man. He says England is his by right of kinship to King Edward. He says, 'Have you forgotten the oath you swore to me? Do you not know you have committed perjury?' "

Harold turned white with anger. "It is by a crooked path that William claims the throne!" he shouted. "You are foolhardy to come here and repeat these words to my face. I should have your ears cut off." Harold strode forward. He came within inches of the messenger's face. It took all his self-control to refrain from laying hands on the man. "Return to your master. Tell him to sharpen his sword. By God's Holy Cross, may you say his funeral prayers!"

After that Harold set his mind on war. The time for ambassadors was over. He brushed those away who cautioned him to delay.

"We will wait no longer!" the King said.

1066

King Harold gathered together a great host, and came to oppose Duke William at the gray apple tree . . .

"What is this place called?" Harold asked the boyish scout by his side as he reined Thunder to a halt beneath the branches of a wide-spreading apple tree. It stood alone on a hilltop commanding a view of the countryside. Beside him Evyn reined his bay horse in, too, as did Hakon, who took the chance to pluck a ripe apple and bite into it. The English army stretched out along the road behind them. They had marched south for three days since leaving London. The lowering sun threw long, unnatural shadows from the men and horses.

"There is a little settlement called Senlac over the next hill, my lord," the scout answered.

"Senlac . . ." Harold repeated slowly in his golden voice so that the word sounded like poetry. "That is Sand Lake in the old tongue, is it not?"

"Yes, my lord. The people say there was a lake here once in their grandfathers' time. But it was shallow, and the marshes grew across it over the years. There are still marshes to the west and farther south," the boy said, pointing to the reeds growing in the distance. "If the Normans come this way from Hastings, the wetlands will slow their passage, for the roads are poor here and broken up by mud and marsh."

"We'll camp by this apple tree tonight," Harold said.

Shielding his eyes with his hand, Harold checked the position of the sun. It hung low and bright just above a grove of trees in the west. The King studied the horizon in every direction and seemed disappointed to see nothing more than the shimmering of the tall grass. He turned suddenly as the haunting cry of a curlew rose from the horsetail reeds, but there was no one there.

"I know he is near," he said quietly. "I can feel it."

As the orders were passed along and the men began to make camp, Harold rode ahead a little way with Evyn, Hakon, his brothers, and a few of his housecarls. The scout rode first, down the slope past the apple tree. They took a dirt lane and followed it for nearly a furlong till it reached the wider road to Hastings. There they found themselves on a ridge, which sloped away abruptly to the south.

"This is Senlac Ridge," the scout said.

The position commanded an excellent view to the south. It leveled off at its summit and sloped gently back to the apple tree. The field before them was rough, with little dips and hillocks.

"If William comes inland," Harold said, "he must take this road." He looked to each of his men. Gyrth nodded in agreement. Leofwine shook his hair from his eyes and peered down the empty road to Hastings. Hakon smiled knowingly. The King narrowed his eyes, and the sharp planes of his face seemed starker than before. The sun lit his skin so that it seemed fashioned from rough leather. Evyn had never seen him look so ruthless. There was silence among the war leaders, for each sensed Harold's thoughts.

"He will come up this road," Harold said grimly, "and find us waiting for him."

That night the moon rose late in the evening.

In the King's tent Harold said, "Evyn, walk among the men. Tell me what they say. I need to know what is in their hearts."

Evyn threw on his hooded cloak and ducked under the flap. Outside, he passed a circle of housecarls standing guard around the tent. He knew their hearts: they would never fail Harold. Battle was their lifeblood, and they would count it an honor to die for their King. It was the ordinary men who concerned Harold. They were tired, hungry, and footsore, and their wives and children were far away. Could they withstand another battle?

The autumn air was crisp, and the tangy scent of ripe apples lingered over the camp. The men gathered anxiously around their fires. They were glad to have left the thick forest of the Andredesweald behind them. They had marched the last day surrounded by huge oak and beech trees, often at a half trot, scattering herds of red deer before them. They had strained their backs pulling the supply wagons through the thickets and streams of the forest. Now, as they sat in tired groups, Evyn approached and warmed his hands before one of the fires.

"It is only two leagues to Hastings," one soldier said to the man next to him as he rubbed his blistered feet. "We'll find the Normans soon."

"Or they will find us," came the dour reply.

Another man spoke. "I, too, have a bad feeling on this one, friend. We should have waited for Earl Edwin to join us with his army."

"Yes, where are the northerners? By my count, fewer than five hundred joined along the way. We marched hard to help them at Stamford Bridge. But now that Tostig and Harald Hardrada are slain, they forget about us when we are in need of help. They sit around their hearth fires drinking warm ale while we sleep on the cold ground waiting for the Norman devils."

A man who had been silent said, "I would wager a month's pay that Earl Edwin is on his way."

"We'll all be dead before Edwin and Morcar get here," another interjected.

"Shut up and keep your cowardly thoughts to yourself," one of Harold's grizzled housecarls admonished. "Should we have waited in London while that Norman butcher ravages Wessex, the King's home?" He put down the bread he had been eating. "I trust Harold's judgment. I've been a housecarl with Godwin's family for sixteen years, back when the old man was still alive. It is true that his first son, Swein, was a nithing, a man without honor. And Tostig was little better. It was his greediness that is partly to blame for this danger we are in now. But in Harold we have a leader who is Beowulf's equal. He is a just man and knows the laws that have been handed down since King Alfred's time. His taxes are fair, and he has pity on the poor. His eloquence has kept the peace for us many times when other, more hotheaded, leaders would have dragged the country into war. He's brought prosperity to Wessex, and with time he'll do the same for the whole kingdom."

"If there is time," a voice shot through the crowd.

The housecarl threw the crust of his bread into the fire,

disgusted with his companions' doubt. "If any man can do it, Harold can. He is lifting the battle-ax for your sake. If the fight goes against us, and William conquers, can you see what England will become? The Normans will steal our land and turn us into a nation of slaves. Don't ask me to live like a thrall in my own country. If the worst comes, I would rather die in battle with Harold. That is the way of hearth troops. *Better a man should die than live a coward's life.*" The housecarl climbed to his feet and brushed past Evyn. With one last backward glance he said, "As for me, I'm going to find the blacksmith's grindstone and sharpen my ax."

The others fell silent. Some began to mend their mail shirts, reinforcing rings that had come loose. The archers checked and rechecked their bowstrings.

Evyn rubbed his hands before the fire and wandered away. Throughout the camp, men rolled up in their cloaks and tried to sleep. Many clutched their weapons in their hands. Some paced restlessly or sought out the priests to make their confession before the day of battle.

Evyn returned to the King's tent. "Who approaches?" one of Harold's housecarls challenged.

Evyn pushed his hood back and held his empty palms up to show he was weaponless.

"It is the King's Shadow," another housecarl said respectfully. "Let him pass."

Evyn pulled the flap open and entered the tent. A lantern on a small table cast a feeble light on the sleeping King. He was glad that Harold slept, for he knew how exhausted the King was. Evyn sat on the edge of his own cot, too restless to lie down. He prayed to God to give him courage, for it seemed certain that the dawn would bring battle. *Let me not disgrace my foster father.*

Harold turned in his sleep and groaned. Evyn got up and

covered the King with his cloak, which had fallen away. He sat by Harold's side and kept watch during the long night. Though he was tired, there was much to ponder. He had reached his sixteenth year last spring. He was more man than boy now, old enough to fight, yet he was afraid, and he hated himself for it. He did not see the glory in battle. Instead, he recalled his days at Aethelney Monastery and the cries of the wounded soldiers brought there. He remembered Stamford Bridge with horror. Evyn rested his head in his hands. He felt as though he had been skinned alive and all his nerves exposed. He was no warrior. *I am only a simple village lad, a voiceless storyteller, a poor clerk and servant.*

But fate had led him another way. He was the King's foster son, the King's Shadow. It was his duty to stand next to Harold and to serve him. Would he have the courage to do what he must?

The night wore on, and the third watch began before Evyn finally fell into a light sleep. When the whistle of the thrush marked the approach of dawn, Evyn woke immediately, his eyes burning from weariness. He stepped out from the tent and saw that the moon hung over the southern horizon where William and his army were expected to appear. One of the housecarls who had stood guard during the last watch saluted Evyn. "You'll have a chance to prove yourself today, lad. Stand tall. King Harold is generous in victory," he said, pointing to an arm ring of gold covering his wrist.

Evyn nodded. The man little knew the doubts in his heart.

A rustling sound came from within the tent. The King was awake. "Shadow," a voice called. Evyn turned as if hearing the name for the first time. The King's warm voice made everything sound like music. He went back into the tent and found Harold sitting on the edge of his cot.

"It is time to get ready," Harold said, running his fingers through his hair. Evyn fetched water and the King washed and shaved in silence. He combed his hair while Evyn laid out the heavy mail shirt and the helmet with the scarlet plume. As the King unpinned his cloak, he placed the heavy brooch in Evyn's hand. "This is for you, Evyn. It shames me to think I have not given you a gift before in token of the love I bear for you."

Evyn stared at the brooch. It filled his open palm. A large blood-red garnet sparkled in the center, with two smaller garnets on each side. The three gems lay nestled in a diamond-shaped setting. The outer edges of the diamond were laced with a wave of gold filigree studded with tiny yellow balls hardly larger than grains of sand. Beyond that were curls and spirals, some ending in tiny dragon heads, some in coiled tails. There was not another brooch like it in all of England.

Evyn had often seen it on Harold's shoulder, holding the heavy scarlet cloak in place. This was a gift worthy of a king, and Evyn felt embarrassed to hold it. He was keenly ashamed of his cowardly thoughts during the night.

"I have given you so little," Harold said.

Evyn looked up. How could Harold say such a thing? He had given him everything. He had made him his son.

Evyn's head pounded. He wanted to scream, *Only my freedom . . . only my life!* But he could only shake his head.

A scout suddenly lifted the tent flap. His eyes were wide. "The Norman army marches this way. They are one league hence, my lord. They will be upon us within the hour!"

Harold thanked the man calmly with his usual courtesy. "Call my brothers and the other war leaders and have them meet me at the command post by the apple tree."

Evyn quickly pinned the brooch inside his tunic, where it rested against his heart. There was no time now to try to explain anything. From the clothes chest he lifted out Harold's thick quilted tunic, the one with a tear in it where an arrow had pierced the King's armor long ago. Harold slipped it over his head, along with the hooded cope. Then came the heavy shirt of ring mail and the mail hood. Finally Harold buckled golden spurs around his ankles, for although the English would fight on foot, he, as was his custom, would ride Thunder in front of the men before the battle trumpets sounded.

"Quickly," the King said, gesturing for Evyn to hand him the heavy battle-ax and sword. "Now you."

Evyn hastily donned his own smaller shirt of mail and took the sword Hakon had taught him to use. He grabbed his helmet by the nosepiece and followed Harold outside.

The camp lay bathed in the pink light of dawn. Evyn peered across the rolling field. For as far as he could see, men stirred. Some stood and shook out their dew-dampened cloaks. Others buckled on their armor. The steady clank of metal against metal sounded, and a low murmuring filled the air as the scout's news spread throughout the camp.

A trestle table stood under the towering apple tree. The Lady Ealdgyth was there with her ladies, clasping her hands tightly together, and the look on her face made Evyn stop and allow the King to approach her alone. He drew her away gently by the arm.

"I wish you were safe in London," he said, gazing into her eyes.

"I want to be with you," she said, struggling to keep back the tears.

"If I die . . ."

Ealdgyth put her hand to his lips. "No, I don't want to hear it!" she cried.

Harold took a deep breath and clasped her slim white wrist in his own suntanned hand. "If I die," he repeated sternly, "go to King Dermot in Ireland. He will give you refuge." He stroked her hair and kissed her. He tenderly caressed the delicate skin above her cheekbone. Then he forced himself to turn away.

His brother earls, Gyrth and Leofwine, and his captains gathered around him now. Evyn unrolled a map of the area drawn the night before by a local man. He spread it out upon the table under the apple tree.

"From what the scouts say," Harold began, "we are evenly matched. There are eight thousand warriors in each army. Many of the Normans will fight on horseback. I have seen them in battle, and they are fierce. But we hold Senlac Ridge, and it is a strategic position. The high ground will give us the advantage. The field between us is rough; it will be difficult riding for their knights."

"The men are worn out," Leofwine said with a worried frown. "Many of them are armed only with clubs or farm tools. I fear this will be a long day for us."

"I would be a liar if I told you I think this will be an easy victory," Harold said. "It will take all our endurance to withstand what we are likely to face this day. But we have just beaten a mighty enemy in Harald Hardrada. Surely the Normans will have heard of it by now, and that stands in our favor.

"Gyrth," Harold said, turning to his brother, "we will make the war plan simple, since many of our men are farmers and shepherds and have no battle training. Take your housecarls and the men from East Anglia and form ranks along the western edge of the ridge. Leofwine, take your men of Kent and the Londoners to the east. Hakon and I will take the center with the Wessex men and my housecarls. We will build a shield wall so thick and so strong that even were the Normans as numerous as the sands of the shore, they could not break through. It will be a wall of warriors ten men deep. Put the housecarls and seasoned warriors in front. Tell the men not to break ranks. Our victory depends on the strength of the shield wall."

The King shifted his weight to his good leg and rolled up the map.

"We will let the Normans tire themselves with their assaults against the wall. We need only stand firm with our shields up. We must not pursue them in hand-to-hand combat. If we do, they will defeat us. But if our ranks are close, their horsemen will be unable to penetrate. It is when we give them openings that they can strike us down."

The King looked to his brothers and his war leaders, the men closest to his heart. "It is time to build a wall," he said.

1066

The King unfurled his banners at the summit of Senlac Ridge.

Like a mason with blocks of stone, Harold built a wall of men stronger than any he had made before. He commanded the men to line up on the crest of Senlac Ridge, and the wall began to take shape. It stretched the length of the ridge, so that if the man at one end stepped forward and peered down the line he would be unable to see the last man at the other end. Behind the shield wall, Harold set up his command post. There they thrust the Golden Dragon banner of Wessex into the ground. Harold's own gem-encrusted Fighting Man with its golden fringe fluttered in the breeze next to it.

When the wall was completed, Harold climbed onto Thunder's back and rode before his men. When he spoke, all eyes turned to him, and the murmuring in the ranks ceased.

"I've sharpened my battle-ax," he shouted, "and any Norman foolish enough to face me will not live to tell of it.

He will never brag about how he drove the English from their homes. It will not be said that Harold slept while his enemies burned English farms and villages . . . made our women widows and our children orphans. By God's Holy Cross, I will measure out justice today."

Harold steadied Thunder with a firm hand as the great black stallion pranced nervously. "The Normans fight for gold and with the hope of stealing our land. They'll slaughter our boys and sell our women and children in the slave markets. I fight to protect England—our land—and our families!" His eyes flashed under the rim of his helmet.

"Will you fight with me?" he bellowed.

A shout rose among the English that filled the sky. Thunder reared back on his hind legs, and Harold raised the sword he called Gyrngras.

"Good. We need only stand firm. Plant your feet, and let them come at us. They cannot break this wall," Harold said with pride as his arm swept the length of their formation.

His words are like fire in our hearts, Evyn thought. He stood in the center of the shield wall, surrounded by the tall, broad-shouldered housecarls of Harold's bodyguard.

A voice in front cried out, "Look—they come!"

Evyn peered around the arm of the man before him. Between the warriors, he could see down the slope and across the field. There, where the Hastings road emerged from a wooded area, the Norman banners snapped in the breeze as William's vanguard led the army onto the field. The Normans hesitated before proceeding into the open.

How must we look to them? Evyn wondered. In his mind's eye, he imagined Harold's army as the Normans must have seen it for the first time: a long, unbroken wall fronted by shield-bearing warriors armed with spear, sword, and battle-ax drawn up in such close formation that the rims of their kite-shaped shields touched. They would see a man wearing a scarlet-plumed helmet on a huge black stallion whose men cheered adoringly.

But the hesitation lasted only a moment. The great bulk of the Norman cavalry surged forward out of the woods, led by a giant of a man riding a sandy-colored horse.

Within minutes the Norman army assembled. Hakon, at the front of the shield wall, shouted to those in back who could not see the banners of the different battalions. "The Normans are taking the center position beyond our archers' arrow range. The men of Brittany are on their left, and the men of Flanders are on their right. They have horsemen, perhaps three thousand . . . no more than a thousand archers . . . and foot soldiers, four thousand to my guess."

Harold dismounted, and a camp boy led Thunder to the rear, for the King would fight on foot with his men. Harold took his place at the front of the wall, and Evyn saw with concern that he could no longer hide his limp. His plumed helmet made him an easy target for the Normans, but he refused to change it. "My men need to see me," he said when Hakon suggested it.

Across the wide field Norman battle trumpets blew. A single knight riding a white horse spurred his mount forth from the Norman lines. Like a reckless stableboy, he raced his horse back and forth before his own men. A cheer rose, and even Duke William, who rested heavily in his saddle, shouted his approval. The man continued to ride like a demon, barely clearing the front line of Norman soldiers. As he reined the animal to a sudden stop before the French and Flemish troops, great clods of earth flew up from his horse's hooves. Then, galloping back, he stopped dead-still before the Duke. When the cheers of approval quieted, he recited a war poem to urge the men on. His strong voice carried all the way across the open field. Though he spoke in Norman French, Evyn recalled the words from his time as hostage at Duke William's court.

"Charlemagne monte à cheval en colère,
Et tous ses soldats montent à cheval en colère et en chagrin."

Charlemagne rides in wrath,
And all his soldiers ride in wrath and sorrow.

The Normans were silent, spellbound by the warrior's words. Then the young knight took his lance and, riding into the open space between the armies, saluted the English very formally. As the men in the shield wall whispered to one another without taking their eyes from him, the warrior tossed the lance high into the air, as lightly as if it were a toy. Catching it by the blade, he looked up to the cheers of his men. With a dazzling smile, he repeated the feat two more times to prove it was no stroke of good luck. Then he galloped his horse dangerously close to the English lines, hurling his lance at the front ranks before racing back toward the Normans. It wounded one of the Wessex men, and there was murmuring and jostling around Evyn as the housecarls carried him to the rear. Evyn got a closer look at the Norman knight as he wheeled his pale horse and approached the open ground again. This time he drew his sword from its sheath. As with the lance, he threw the sword into the air, tossing it higher than Evyn had thought possible. The weapon climbed end over end as it soared heavenward. Miraculously, he caught it by the hilt as it fell to the earth.

"This is magic that he does," the men whispered. "He must be the Duke's wizard."

The mysterious knight grasped the sword and, like a man gone mad, charged the English again.

"He means to achieve glory for himself though it will cost him his life," Hakon said. "Look, he has not even troubled to don his helmet. My lord, give me leave to step from the shield wall. I wish to meet this warrior in combat."

"Yes," Harold said grimly.

Hakon stepped forward and flung his battle-ax at the charging Norman. It knocked the man from his saddle, and the English quickly surrounded him with upraised axes. The bile rose in Evyn's throat, and he struggled to act like a man. Though the knight had died honorably, and no doubt there would be songs for him among the Normans, there was nothing glorious in the bloody and mangled heap that Evyn saw as the housecarls quickly withdrew into the shield wall again.

The Norman archers, who had been waiting in the rear, now advanced to the front. Taking their stance, left foot forward, they nocked their arrows one by one all the way down the line. On command they drew their bowstrings back to their chests and took aim at the heart of the shield wall, releasing their arrows at a second command. The Saxons lowered their faces behind their shield rims as the arrows whirred through the air. Here and there the thud of an arrow hitting a shield sounded, but the morning breeze from the north caused most of the arrows to fall harmlessly in the field. By Evyn's count only eight or ten men fell and were carried to the rear. The shield wall was still strong.

William sounded the trumpet call for the foot soldiers. Charging across the field shouting, "*Dieu nous aide!,*" they advanced up the slope till shield crashed against shield. But they, too, were repulsed by the shield wall.

Harold had chosen wisely. His sturdy ridgetop defense

held. The Norman trumpets blew the piercing retreat call, and as the infantry fell back a Saxon shout followed them, *"Out! Out!"*

When the last of the Norman foot soldiers reached their lines, William hurled his terrible cavalry upon the English. As they charged over the rough ground, some of the horses stumbled, and their riders plunged heavily to the earth. But other horsemen raced forward and climbed Senlac Ridge. They crashed into the shield wall, but the English refused to break formation. The housecarls grabbed the reins of three or four unlucky soldiers, dragged the knights from their saddles, and killed them. Their frightened horses neighed pitifully and loped back to the Norman lines riderless.

At this retreat, however, some of the English broke away from the shield wall to pursue the fleeing Normans. Harold, supervising his left flank, did not see what happened at first, and when he did he shouted, "Back to your positions!" But it was too late. The Norman knights reined their horses around in a tight circle and turned upon the rash English, surrounding them and cutting them down. One by one the English who had left the safety of the ranks fell under Norman swords. Not one man returned to the shield wall.

Far away, across the field, William saw the error the English had committed, and commanded his knights to draw up in formation again. He rode from group to group, giving orders. Twice more in the space of an hour the Normans charged on horseback and then, as though wounded, they feigned retreat. The foolish English village boys fell for the trick. Not heeding the King's warning, they pursued the Normans, hoping to win glory in hand-to-hand combat or with the thought of taking a prized Norman helmet back home as a trophy. And as they did so, the shield wall began to crumble. The Norman knights wheeled their horses around, catching the Englishmen unprotected on open ground, and quickly cut them all down.

The sun was rising high overhead when Gyrth, angered by his men's disobedience, pushed his way through his bodyguard of housecarls to warn them.

"Shield wall!" he bellowed. "We are safe behind our shields. Do not break the shield wall. We must be our own fortress."

As he turned to face his men, a Norman spear caught him in the back. He pitched forward into the arms of his housecarls, the lifeblood pumping out of his back like a fountain, and his eyes rolled back in his head. His men carried him to the apple tree, where the Lady Ealdgyth Swan Neck closed his eyes and covered his body with the cloak she found in his tent.

"Tell the King his brother Gyrth is dead," she said sadly.

There was fury in Harold's eyes when he heard the news. During a lull in the fighting, he rode before his men again, exhorting them to courage and discipline.

"Stand firm . . . Do not break the shield wall!" he shouted to each section of the formation. "Nothing will defeat us if we keep the wall strong. Though I know it is in your hearts to rush into the battle, you must stand firm."

Although the English had often used the shield-wall tactic, they seldom kept to that defense for a daylong battle, as this encounter promised to be. It was not in their blood to stand still and shoulder the brunt of each blow as the Normans rode against them. But Harold knew that only by planting their feet would they carry the day. He had seen what William's cavalry could do when the riders had room to move freely among their enemies.

By afternoon the battle remained undecided. Many Englishmen had fallen, but more reserves came forward from the rear to fill the ranks. The bodies of countless Normans dotted the field, too. Evyn's legs ached from standing for six hours, and he saw that Harold's limp had worsened. Each time the King left his place to instruct or encourage his men, the sway in his step grew more pronounced.

The Norman riders charged again, and the ground shook with the thunder of hooves. William himself led his cavalry this time. "They're coming, lads. Brace yourselves," Hakon called to the men behind him.

Closer and closer they came, so close that Evyn could pick out the details of each rider: a spur, a chain-mail hood, a horse's bridle and the white of its eye. Suddenly a cry of excitement rose among the English. William's horse had stumbled and fallen to the ground, his legs snapping like twigs beneath him. The Duke of Normandy crashed to the earth and lay senseless for several moments. His knights lost their courage and wheeled their horses around in hasty retreat.

But William finally staggered to his feet and called to them in their language. "Look at me!" he cried, ripping his helmet from his head so they could see his face. "I am alive and will conquer. What madness has taken hold of you that you flee in this way? What path will lie open before your retreat?" Pointing to the English, he shouted, "Those whom you have it in your power to sacrifice like a herd of cattle drive you back and kill you. You abandon victory and undying glory and rush headlong to your own destruction and everlasting dishonor. By flight, not one of you will escape death."

Evyn understood his words and was glad that the others around him could not.

By midafternoon Senlac field ran with the blood of many

men. Scores of dead horses flattened its grass. The English ranks were far thinner now, and Harold drew the men closer together to keep the wall strong. Once more the Norman squadrons of cavalry dashed up the slope, then feigned a sloppy retreat to lure the English from their positions. The formidable shield wall broke open in spots, letting the Normans circle around and cut the English down, slashing with their bloody swords.

A messenger came from the command post with word that the gentle Leofwine had died. Harold left his place and limped to the rear. When he returned, Evyn saw a change on the King's face, and he knew that Harold had seen his brother's still body. They were all gone: the hot-headed Swein, the beguiling but dangerous Tostig, the warrior Gyrth, and now the quiet Leofwine.

Evyn went to the King's side, though there was nothing he could do to comfort him. Harold stood with his head bowed sorrowfully, unaware of his surroundings. His housecarls murmured uneasily. This was not the time to grieve—a king could not allow himself the luxury of sorrow.

He came to himself when the next shout went through the lines. The Normans were massing for another charge. Evyn instinctively lifted his shield as Hakon had taught him to during the summer. In the back of his mind he remembered those long drills. Over and over: "Shield up, weapon at the ready . . . Shield up, weapon at the ready." Evyn peered over the rim of his shield and watched the bold invaders charge. So many English had fallen that he was a front-line man now. His mouth grew parched and his stomach cramped as his old fears surfaced. It seemed to take forever for the Normans to reach them. *Why does time stand still?* Why was it he heard only the shrieks of the wounded and their desperate cries for water?

In the middle of the field a dying Norman soldier dragged himself in slow jerking motions to his own lines, leaving a bloody trail behind him. His own men rode around him without stopping. Oh, how Evyn wanted to flee, to close his eyes and be rid of this day. Then the miracle happened. The King called his name.

"Go to the Lady. You must take her from here, Evyn. My heart is heavy, and I would not have her see this."

Without a gesture or even a look, Evyn ran, grateful to be given a chance to live.

He reached the great apple tree with the dead and wounded sprawled all around it and found the Lady tending an injured housecarl. She tore strips of cloth from her own mantle to staunch the bleeding of the man's cut.

Through sign language and quickly scrawled words upon the ground, he made her understand that Harold desired them to flee. When she finally understood, the derisive expression on her face was unlike anything Evyn had expected to see. Her usually calm features twisted angrily. "No," she cried, "I will not leave. Though I am filled with fear, my place is with the King. I am the mother of his children. I will not leave."

With that, Evyn's heartbeat slowed, and her words echoed within his mind. *My place is with the King.*

Could the King's foster son leave the battlefield? Could he live with himself having done that? Though he was no soldier, he would stay and serve him, for it was his duty and his privilege. The urge to run faded away. Now he wanted to be by Harold's side—to fall at his feet if that was what fate decreed. Snatching his shield and sword, he dashed back to the front line, to the clash of sword against sword and the neighing of the frightened horses.

1066

The King fought against Duke William most resolutely with those men who wished to stand by him, and there was great slaughter on both sides.

The late afternoon sun slanted across the battlefield as Evyn returned to his post by Harold's side. It blinded him as he strode through the teeming mass of the shield wall. Evyn shouldered past the exhausted men, who by willpower had remained in their places for seven hours. Now they had reached the end of their strength. As the living wall shifted for him, Evyn caught sight of a scarlet-plumed helmet. He ran toward it, and the men to his left and right became a blur.

The corners of the King's mouth lifted in a mysterious smile when he saw that Evyn had returned. Evyn grinned. He felt foolish to feel so happy, but now he understood how the housecarls felt, their sense of loyalty and their pride in serving Harold.

"How fares the Lady?" Harold asked. In answer, Evyn nodded reassuringly and placed his fist over his heart, the sign for courage.

Before the King could speak again, the chaotic noise of battle resumed from a brief lull. The Norman cavalry charged, and the thunder of hooves filled Evyn's ears. A cloud of dust rose where the horses pounded the earth, and as they neared the English line, Evyn heard the jangle of bits and the steady rattle of ring mail. The sweat-streaked horses climbed the ridge, and Evyn lowered his shoulder into his shield. The Norman cavalry struck the shield wall like a hammer blow. Evyn staggered back, pushed by the weight of the front line, as Norman war-horses slammed into Englishmen. A cry pierced the air as a man fell under the trampling hooves of a horse. The frightened animal whinnied as another Saxon dragged its reins to the ground, and Evyn saw its front hooves pawing the air as the charger crashed on its back. The shield wall recoiled under the blow and recovered as the Normans retreated down the slope of Senlac Ridge.

Evyn drew a deep breath. A raven, the bird of death, called severely over his head and flew over the shield wall. *We shall not live through this day*, he thought.

"Our numbers are still evenly matched," Harold said to Hakon. In a louder voice filled with majesty he called to his men, "Push them back to Hastings and into the sea! *Out! Out!*" The men banged their shields and took up the shout, chanting, *"Out! Out! Out!"*

But as the Normans retreated to their own lines again, the English stopped banging their shields and rested, for they were weary. A wounded horse convulsed one last time and then lay still. Here and there across the field, Norman foot soldiers pulled the armor from dead men and gathered weapons to be used by others. Beyond that, among the great mass of Normans, Bretons, and Flemings, the trumpets sounded the call to re-form lines.

The sun slid behind the treeline. "We have barely an hour of daylight left," Harold said to Evyn. "If we can stand firm till dusk, the victory will be ours."

The last rays of the scarlet sun lit the King's skin, which was warm and golden and flushed with exertion. His hair, dark with sweat, curled out in damp strands from under his gilded helmet. The thick Saxon mustache edged with gray covered his close-lipped mouth. Though there were pouches from sleeplessness under his eyes, his expression was steady and resolved.

Everything depended on the next hour.

Harold pointed across the field where the Normans, tiny in the distance, swarmed like angry bees. "Victory is still within our grasp. But I am uneasy. It is in my mind to spare you."

Evyn shook his head vehemently. He had no desire to leave now. He wanted only to remain by Harold's side. The King's strength was ebbing. He would not insist that Evyn leave, for his heart was heavy, and he found the boy's comradeship comforting. "No, then? You will stay by my side?" He put his arm across Evyn's shoulder. "It makes my heart strong to have a son such as you here with me today."

That was the last he spoke to Evyn, for across the open space the Norman conference ended, and William, in one last attempt to carry the day, threw everything he had against the English shield wall. He had come too far and gambled too much to do anything less.

The Norman cavalry spearheaded the charge. "*Dieu nous aide!*" they bellowed as they spurred their mounts across the battlefield one more time. Behind them the infantrymen raised their swords or leveled their spears and marched forward in thick columns. Finally, coming up from the rear, the archers took their places, nocking their arrows as they planted their feet and aimed high into the darkening sky. At their commander's call, they released their bowstrings, and their arrows flew like rain before the wind.

The English were forced to raise their shields to cover their heads against the storm of arrows, but at that moment the first Norman horsemen climbed the summit of Senlac Ridge. They hacked down the men in the front ranks as the shower of arrows picked off the men deeper within the wall. Duke William had timed the attack perfectly.

Panic erupted within the English ranks as the men of the fyrd despaired and fled. The housecarls and those with strong hearts huddled in tight formation—too tight, for now there was no space to move. They stood shoulder to shoulder and chest to back, so that there was no room for the dead to fall. The slaughter that followed was terrible, and the flanks of the shield wall were swept away like a child's sand fortress.

But in the center the hearth troops stood firm. *Better to die than to live as a coward.* Evyn, too, planted his feet like a warrior. Harold's shoulder pressed against his, and Evyn felt the King's strength flow into him.

Seeing the rout that was taking place among the militia, Harold lowered his shield to shout to his men, "Take courage. Stand firm!"

It was then that the Norman arrow, aimed from afar with no particular mark in the archer's line of sight, struck the man fate had decided upon. The arrow pierced one of the King's eyes, and Harold staggered and fell. A Norman cavalryman broke through the last shreds of the hearth troops, and Evyn took an enemy sword between his ribs. His knees buckled, and he collapsed as though his legs had turned to water.

Evyn grabbed his side. It was warm and wet under the ring mail. He no longer heard the clamor of battle around him. He felt both confused and peaceful. *The sky grows dark*, he thought, calmly gazing into the vast expanse above him. The first stars glimmered faintly overhead. Then, for Evyn, the twilight deepened to inky blackness.

1066

King Harold was slain, and Leofwine, his brother, and Earl Gyrth, his brother, and many good men.

The sun sank below the horizon in the west, and the sky, which had flamed red, turned first to lavender and then to gray. The air became cold and damp like a stony death chamber. Ravens, which had circled the sky impatiently all day, began to alight here and there across the field as darkness fell.

Desperately, the housecarls continued to fight, surrounding their King with their shields facing out. Though Harold had fallen, they would not flee. As soldiers, they knew that the battle was lost and their fate sealed, but they preferred this to the shame of flight. The struggle raged on, with the Saxon housecarls holding the Normans at bay with their deadly battle-axes.

Within the protective circle of Saxon warriors, Evyn's eyes cleared, and he became aware of a terrible pain in his chest. By his side he heard the sound of a man struggling for air, and Evyn realized he'd fallen across the King. With the last of his strength, he rolled over so that Harold's final breaths could be taken freely. As he braced himself on one elbow, he saw with pity how the arrow had pierced Harold's right eye, while the left one gazed sightlessly toward heaven. Evyn reached over, though he thought he would faint again from the pain in his chest, and unfastened the chin strap of Harold's gilded helmet. How he longed to whisper, *Father, I am with you.* How he longed to show him some sign of his love. He took the King's hand. The warmth was gone from his fingertips. But then Evyn felt Harold's hand close upon his own firmly and affectionately. After a moment, the grip loosened, and the sound of the King's breathing ceased.

The invincible shield wall was gone. While the King lived, it had stood so firm that the Normans could not penetrate it. But as word spread of Harold's death, fearful men lost hope. The frantic cry rose and was repeated the length of the ridge: "Harold is dead! All is lost!"

In the growing darkness, the remaining English fled to the cover of the nearby woods, but the Norman mercenaries pursued them on horseback, cutting them down like wheat before the harvesters.

A man from Senlac Hamlet led some of the English from the field, striking out for the north. "This way, friends," he yelled, "follow me. It is our only chance." They raced past Harold's command post where the Golden Dragon of Wessex fluttered next to Harold's bejeweled Fighting Man banner, down the gentle slope, and then up again where the branches of the old apple tree waved. There the tents and pavilions of the great Saxon army stood empty. The women and camp boys clustered around the Lady, whose torn veil had fallen to her shoulders. She tried to console the frightened people as Norman horsemen charged through their midst. The Lady watched the English flee, and she knew that they had lost courage because their King was dead.

The man from Senlac shouted as he left the main track, "This way!" Striking out toward the right, he added, "We have one hope."

Before them, rising black and menacing through the gray twilight, stood the thick oak forest. They raced toward that shelter, where the Norman horses would be caught among the tangled branches and roots. But before they reached the trees, the man suddenly shouted, "Now! Get down now! There is a ravine just before the woods. The Normans will not see it in the dark."

The ruse worked. The pursuing cavalry spurred their mounts toward the tree line, unaware of the disaster before them. As the English hid in thickets at the edge of the ravine, Norman horses and riders crashed down onto the rocks below. Riders behind them, hearing the terrible commotion, tried to rein their horses to a halt but found they could not. Wave after wave of Normans plunged downward, and the screams of wounded horses and riders filled the air. In the confusion, many of the English made their escape.

Finally Duke William galloped up and called off the hunt for the retreating English. From the edge of the ravine he peered at the carnage below. "Come away from this evil ditch. Come back to the ridge," he growled to those who gathered by him. "I will lose no more men tonight."

Back at Senlac Ridge one last Saxon housecarl refused to retreat against the onslaught as both riders and foot soldiers swarmed up the hill like an unstoppable wave. Norman swords rang against the iron rim of a Saxon shield.

"By God's Holy Cross!"

Hakon, the King's captain, who had been Harold's right hand, still fought, shouting Harold's war cry and summoning all of his skill to ward off the flood of Normans that surged up the slope. He knew he would die, but he would also take many Normans to the place of death with him. Yet even Hakon could not fight all of the Normans at once. A last clash of steel upon steel sounded, followed by a thud as he fell to the ground mortally wounded.

"Ooohh."

Evyn heard a moan and realized that the sound came from his own throat. He felt himself being roughly tugged as the Normans dragged his armor from his body. They yanked off his helmet, and when he had been stripped of everything worth taking, they left him for dead.

Then a shout in Norman French broke the air. "The oath-breaker is here!"

The cry went up when the soldiers realized that they had found Harold's body. Four knights strode up to the spot and hacked at the King's body with their swords till it was barely recognizable. They jerked Harold's plumed helmet from his head and carried it to William.

The Normans showed no mercy to the wounded English. They quickly put to the sword those still living, and the groans of the Angles and Saxons, Mercians and Northumbrians were extinguished one by one like candles being blown out.

Duke William approached the ridge, clutching Harold's helmet and the Fighting Man standard, its jewels glistening by the light of Norman torches. When he reached the spot where Harold and the men of Wessex had stood, he said, "Erect my pavilion here. The victory is mine, and I will sleep where Harold died." His gruff voice betrayed no emotion.

Order slowly returned to Senlac Ridge, for the Normans

were renowned for their methodical ways. Within an hour campfires lit the ridge, and soldiers pitched their tents and tended their wounded. They counted their dead and put a circle of guards around the group of English women and camp boys who huddled beneath the apple tree.

Evyn felt himself being dragged a little way and dumped in a pile with the lifeless hearth troops. He opened his eyes fleetingly only to see the beautiful Fighting Man standard, stripped of its jewels, tossed into a Norman bonfire. Then he felt his head spinning again, and he lost consciousness.

Many hours later, when the light from the newly risen sun shone through his eyelids, he felt a soft and cool hand upon the side of his throat. Someone was checking for a pulse. He stirred, but found himself unable to open his eyes. A familiar voice whispered in his ear.

1066

The Normans had possession of the place of slaughter.

"Shadow, be still. Make no sound."

Where had he heard that voice before? It seemed to be inside his head as well as without. It was a woman's voice and it sounded familiar but different, too. It seemed to him that he remembered a voice like that which had been full of confidence and authority. The voice that spoke to him now trembled a little, as though the speaker was trying to overcome her fear.

Though he lay still, Evyn felt dizzy again. How he craved water. His mouth felt parched, and his lips were cracked and swollen.

Later more voices came. "If you wish Harold's body for burial, you must find it yourself, madam," the interpreter said after Duke William made his gruff announcement. The Normans laughed then, for Harold's mangled body had been tossed in a huge pile along with the bodies of his hearth troops.

The Lady Ealdgyth Swan Neck held her head up stiffly and went to the death place. With no one to help her, she dragged one broken warrior's body down after another.

"You'll never find it," someone taunted.

But the Lady knew what to look for—a man with golden hair and a jagged scar on the inside of his leg. Finally, when she found the body for which she searched, William dealt the cruelest blow of all.

Speaking through his interpreter, he said, "Thank you, madam. I would never have recognized the Earl of Wessex. He looks not as I remember him.

"I claim Harold's body. I will have neither shrine nor holy tomb built over his bones for the English to come to, as has happened elsewhere. I will be King now, and I will have no one praying to Harold's spirit."

All the color drained from the Lady's face. This was a sorrow too great to bear, and she stood in stricken silence. Suddenly she dropped to her knees and called out in a strangled voice, "I will give you his weight in gold if you will allow me to take his body away for burial!"

The great men of Normandy gathered around their victorious Duke: Odo, his half brother, who was Bishop of Bayeux; Robert of Mortain, his other half brother; William Fitzosbern, his counselor. When they understood her offer, they were inclined to accept it, but the Conqueror would not relent. He called to his men. "Take the body of the oath-breaker and put it under guard. I will not have it stolen."

The Lady threw herself at the Conqueror's feet and begged, "At least grant me the body of my foster son. He was little more than a boy, and his body poses no threat to you."

"Take it," he growled, pushing her away.

. . .

The journey that followed for the Lady Ealdgyth and a few members of her household was a sad one. They lifted Evyn up into one of the supply wagons and turned their faces toward the west, toward Aethelney, where the monks would give them sanctuary.

The jolting of the wagon nearly killed Evyn. His wound became infected, and he lingered near death. But somehow he clung to life, and when the ragged little group reached Aethelney two weeks later, Lewys, with his usual stubbornness, did everything he could to nurse Evyn back to health.

"He must live," he said as Brother Alfred shook his head over Evyn's torn body. Lewys refused to give up, though the days turned to weeks and Evyn showed no sign of improvement.

Finally, during the first week of the new year, Evyn awoke in the infirmary clear-headed. Brother Alfred put his hands together in a prayer of thanksgiving and sent a boy to find Lewys, who hurriedly rushed in, his robes flying behind him. He sat by Evyn's side and stayed the better part of the afternoon.

"Your soldiering days are over, friend," he said. "William has had himself crowned King in London. After the battle, which the Normans are calling the Battle of Hastings, William marched across the land, burning the countryside, till he reached London. There Edwin and Morcar, knowing they could not stand against William's might, grudgingly vowed to accept him as king. Archbishop Ealdred reluctantly anointed him in the hope of saving English lives."

Evyn's brows drew together in anger, and he tried to pull himself up, but Lewys eased his friend back down into the pillows. "They had no choice, Evyn," he said, his green cat's eyes serious. "There is no man left to take Harold's place."

Evyn motioned for the wax tablet lying on the nearby table. When Lewys handed it to him, he wrote, *Where is my Lady?*

"The Lady Ealdgyth has fled to Ireland," Lewys answered. "As the mother of the dead King's sons, she could not risk remaining in England. At the first sign of an uprising, William might take her and her sons as hostages."

Evyn sank into his cot. *At least the Lady is safe,* he thought.

"Oh, I almost forgot," Lewys said, fumbling with a drawstring pouch at his side. "We found this on you when they brought you in. It's a miracle the Norman scavengers missed it." He drew out the dragon brooch Harold had given Evyn. "Harold was a generous man, was he not?" he said.

Evyn took the brooch in his hand and shut his eyes tightly to keep the tears from sliding down his face. He nodded. *Yes, Harold was a generous man.* The winter sun set early, and Lewys left when the infirmary grew dark. Evyn rolled over inside his wolfskin cloak and slept a troubled sleep.

The weeks of Lent came, and slowly the days lengthened. Then Eostre approached. Evyn was able to walk about the infirmary now, but Brother Alfred refused to allow him to attend Mass in the drafty church. He was still too weak. One day when he dozed on his cot he overheard Brother Alfred say to Lewys, "He will never be strong again." It seemed to Evyn that the monk was right. His chest ached constantly, and whenever he tried to move faster than a walk he felt faint. But slowly he continued to improve, and by midsummer he was able to stroll through the monastery's orchard, his place of refuge since his first visit to Aethelney. As he sat on a bench under the trees, he closed his eyes to savor the fragrance of the apples. It was then that the words of the *storiawr* came to him:

It is fitting that a man
Should praise his dead master and lock him in his heart.

The words stirred him as they never had before. Though the "master" they spoke of was Beowulf, the Warrior King, Evyn knew that for him "master" meant Harold. It was fitting that Evyn should praise the dead King and lock him in his heart. Harold's reign had been so brief: he led a troubled kingdom for the space of but forty weeks, defending the land with his life as the last of the Saxon kings. Now that the Normans ruled, they did all they could to destroy Harold's achievements. Would Harold be forgotten? Or worse, would he be remembered with bitterness as the ill-fated man who died at Senlac Ridge? His brothers were dead, and Ealdgyth was gone. Only Evyn remained.

There is no other who knew Harold as I did. I was at Oxford when Tostig was exiled. I was at Westminster when Edward the Confessor died and Harold was elected to the throne. I fought at Stamford Bridge. I attended the war councils in London. I stood at the King's side at the battle they call Hastings.

Evyn knew then why fate had brought him here. All the events of the past pointed to it: his uncle's return; the brawl with Gryffin's sons; his days spent as a thrall; his education with Lewys; his years with the King. All of these prepared him for the task he set himself to do now.

Autumn came once again, and the leaves turned as scarlet as Harold's cloak. Evyn placed his pen on the table and watched the ink dry on the parchment. He turned and stared out the open window of the monastery scriptorium. Past the stockade walls, he could see the carefully tilled fields of barley spreading into the distance. A score of monks and novices bent to the task of harvesting, the setting sun drawing long shadows from their feet.

Evyn turned back to his work. He cupped his hand under his chin and remained motionless, lost in his thoughts.

He had been speechless for four years. Though he had been born a free man, he had been maimed like a thrall, made forever silent in a world where spoken poetry was the lifeblood of the people. That was his own cross to bear. Perhaps because he could not speak, God gave him the gift of writing well. Lewys often looked over Evyn's shoulder as he wrote. The monk would smile appreciatively and, pointing to a particular passage, would say, "This is very good."

Now Evyn chose to write it all down for the monastery Chronicle. It was a sad task dredging up the past, and he was loath to attend to it, but it was a task born of love. To Evyn it was a heartbreaking pleasure to write the name *Harold*, as if the carefully penned strokes of black ink could somehow conjure up the flesh and blood, the muscle and warm skin, and the powerful ringing voice of the King. He would bring Harold back to life for the English as best he could.

Evyn drew a deep breath, read over the words he had written, and continued, dipping the pen in the ink once more.

1063 *In this year Earl Harold of Wessex celebrated the summer solstice at the Lady Ealdgyth's estate near Exeter. With him were his brothers, Earl Gyrth of Anglia, Earl Leofwine of Kent, and Earl Tostig of Northumbria.*

At summer's end, Harold and Tostig fought against the rebels in North Wales, and many of the wounded were carried to Aethelney Monastery.

♦ ♦ ♦

1064 *In the early weeks of the new year, Harold gathered a force and rode into Carmarthen, where the upstart chieftain Gryffin harried the land. With swiftness and cunning, Harold surprised the enemy, and Gryffin and his sons were slain on the field of battle.*

In this same year, during naval maneuvers in the Narrow Sea, a mighty storm blew up, driving Earl Harold's ship off course. The Earl of Wessex and his men were shipwrecked near the coast of Flanders. That summer and autumn the English were detained by Duke William of Normandy.

♦ ♦ ♦

1065 *In this year, after the feast of Michaelmas, the Northumbrians united to outlaw Tostig, their Earl. They slew his housecarls, took his weapons, and carried off his gold and silver. They sent for Morcar, son of Earl Alfgar, and chose him to be their Earl. Morcar marched south with his men until he came to Northampton, where he was joined by his brother Edwin and the men from his earldom. There came Earl Harold to meet them, and they charged him with a mission to King Edward to request that they have Morcar as their Earl.*

Very soon thereafter a great council was held at Oxford, on the Festival of St. Simon and St. Jude; and

Earl Harold was present and tried to do all he could to bring them to an agreement, but was unsuccessful. Earl Tostig and his wife and all his supporters sailed south over the sea-road.

King Edward came to Westminster toward Christmas, and there had the abbey church consecrated which he himself had built to the glory of God, St. Peter, and all God's saints.

• • •

1066 *In this year King Edward passed away, and Earl Harold came to the throne and ruled for forty weeks and a day. But he was not to enjoy a tranquil reign while he ruled the kingdom.*

Evyn put the pen down again. He grew weary, and his side ached as it often did when cold, heavy clouds drew down upon the land. He would write again tomorrow, and the day after, and the day after that, until the entire tale was told. He had been blessed to serve a king, God's own anointed servant, the Fighting Man of Wessex. He was the King's foster son. He was the King's Shadow. It was his privilege to tell the King's story. He alone could do this, and he would do this for Harold and for Harold's people.

It was his fate.